SHELTER FROM THE STORM

Never did Nell think she would find herself in such close proximity to a common coachman—even one as uncommonly handsome and charming as Beauford. But a sudden torrential downpour had forced them together under a single umbrella, and it would have been unthinkably cruel, not to say rude, to ask him to step away though his lips were bare inches from hers.

Their eyes could not help but meet under such circumstances, and the look Beau gave her told Nell what was going to happen before it did. But she did not draw away, for she found she wanted it to happen, improper as it might be. His lips brushed hers, soft, warm and gentle. The kiss was plush as velvet, hot, and surprisingly dry in the midst of so much dampness . . . and Nell looked in vain, not for shelter from the storm raging around her but from the one brewing within . . . .

The Counterfeit Coachman

THE COUNTERFEIT COACHMAN

by

Elisabeth Fairchild

A SIGNET BOOK

SIGNET
Published by the Penguin Group
Penguin Books USA Inc., 375 Hudson Street,
New York, New York 10014, U.S.A.
Penguin Books Ltd, 27 Wrights Lane,
London W8 5TZ, England
Penguin Books Australia Ltd, Ringwood,
Victoria, Australia
Penguin Books Canada Ltd, 10 Alcorn Avenue,
Toronto, Ontario, Canada M4V 3B2
Penguin Books (N.Z.) Ltd, 182–190 Wairau Road,
Auckland 10, New Zealand

Penguin Books Ltd, Registered Offices:
Harmondsworth, Middlesex, England

First published by Signet,
an imprint of Dutton Signet,
a division of Penguin Books USA Inc.

First Printing, November, 1994
10 9 8 7 6 5 4 3 2 1

To Mum,
who started my journey to exciting
places and times, by way of books,
and to Dad,
who tells me I can accomplish anything
if I but set mind to it.

Prologue

A solemn fellow; a red- and blue-clad coachman for the Queen's Royal Mail, looked back at Lord Brampton Beauford when he peered into the mirror. The vision in frock coat and low-crowned, broad-brimmed hat, was disconcerting. The fifth Duke of Heste and master of Thorne did not recognize himself.

Did clothes really make the man, he wondered, that a nobleman might so easily lose all trace of his station? He sighed. The coachman sighed along with him. He had meant to shed grief along with his more accustomed clothing. But grief remained. Beau recognized the depth of it in the counterfeit coachman's shadowed eyes, drawn lips, and pensive regard. No costume could disguise his heartache.

The gloves were not right. Too new. The hat was not right, either. Or, was it perhaps his head? Beauford removed the weather-worn beaver and ruffled the fair, pomaded curls that his barber took such pains to coax into place. There, that was better. François would run shrieking for his comb, but Beau felt more adequately prepared for this brief escape from reality.

"Do I look the part?" he asked his valet, Gates.

"Like a regular knight of the whip. Don't you agree, sir?" Gates stepped back that Charley Tyrrwhit might see.

The duke's dapper friend stared at the counterfeit coachman in the mirror with something less than admiration firing his gaze. Beau found the look refreshing. There were too many frivolous, fawning admirers fighting for his favor since he had assumed his new title. Needle-sharp wit and unabashed sarcasm was what he had been in the way of needing. Charley always provided ample supply.

True to form, Tyrrwhit touched two fingers to his brow

in ironic salute. "You are kitted out, from head to toe, in unremarkable and unbecoming mediocrity."

Beauford took the verbal jab with unruffled composure. Mediocrity was exactly the effect he had set out to achieve. There was an undemanding levelness to mediocrity, a mind-numbing narrowness. Such a state was inordinately soothing to a man who had, of late, known nothing but extremes.

"You will not abandon this mad scheme?" Charley enquired.

"A-a-absolutely not!" Beau stammered. "I a-am fed up with always being depended upon to do what is quiet and respectable, pr-proper and pr-predictable. Life is too brief."

Charley nodded. As close to Beau as any family, he had to understand. Two days past had been the anniversary of the late Duke's death, and the rattling, great house called Thorne yet echoed with emptiness. The ghost of stale tobacco and a pomade no longer in use still haunted the place. The former duke's hunting trophies—disembodied heads of fox, stag, boar and wildcat, room after room of them, fangs bared, beady eyes staring down at one—could not fail to remind the new duke of his father's death. The old man had gone hunting death, foolishly goading a green horse into a flat out run over heavy ground, after a fox.

Beau felt that the boots he had to fill fit him no better than the hat now perched upon his head. He was not the neck-or-nothing rider, the brash, outspoken politician his father had been. His stammered eloquence would never hold the House of Lords spellbound. What kind of duke would he make? The concept overwhelmed him. And yet today he need not worry over such a question. Today he was nothing but a coachman, his greatest concern getting the Queen's Mail to Brighton on time. Beau's lips quirked upward in the extraordinarily attractive smile that his sisters claimed never failed to turn heads. The coachman in the mirror smiled back at him.

"Shall I enquire after the readiness of your vehicle, Mr. Tyrrwhit?"

When Charley nodded, Gates left them. Smoothing an imaginary wrinkle from the eye-catching yellow and blue kerseymere waistcoat that marked him as a member of the

Whip Club, Charley said, "I still can't understand why you refuse to wear Club colors. Folk along the post road are accustomed to seeing the fellows doing the London-to-Brighton run."

Beauford's smile faded. Despair dragged down his spirits. By what right did he stand here quibbling over hat and coat? What did it matter? They were all worm fodder in the end. As the new Duke of Heste, he should be seeing to the disposition of his properties and the well-being of his servants, not playacting coachman. And yet he clung to the idea of carrying off this temporary escape, as tightly as his father had clung to his hand as he lay dying.

"Spots and stripes seem a trifle much, a-a-after the sobriety of so many m-months in black. I should feel frivolous in the very rigging that a-a-always made Father blanch."

Charley glared at the hat on Beau's head. "Well, the old man would sit up in his coffin were he to see what's taken its place. Have you checked that hat for vermin?"

Beau laughed. No one but Charley would risk such a remark.

"Your managing baggage of a sister is at the bottom of this mad masquerade, isn't she?"

Beau feigned ignorance. "Beatrix?"

"Yes, I hear the interfering minx meant to present one of her school chums for your examination and approval."

Beau whirled on him. "However did you hear of that? We left town before even they had a-a-arrived."

"Did we?" Charley's eyebrow lifted. "Ludd! Bea will be livid."

Beauford sighed ruefully. "They're p-probably p-peeling her off the ceiling even now. She's been lauding the p-praises of her beautiful Miss Au-Aurora Quinby for m-months."

"Beautiful, is she? Were you not curious even to see what Beatrix considers beautiful in a woman?"

"A-a-absolutely not. My sister is m-miserable in her own m-marriage. Why should I trust her to play m-matchmaker for me?"

"But why flee the beautiful Aurora? You had only to meet her, not marry her. Who knows, you might have liked the beauty."

Beau regarded the worn toes of his borrowed boots.

"M-might have, but I find m-myself too cynical since Father's passing. I have the sudden feeling that a-any woman who is a-attracted to me is reeled in by the lure of title and fortune."

"Oh! There's the rub of inheriting." Charley's words were heavy with sarcasm. "Too many beautiful women falling at one's feet. I knew there had to be some drawback involved."

Beau shrugged. "Will this beauty, or a-a-any other female who flocks to me, willingly a-accept a poor stuttering fool simply because he has enough m-money to blunt her ears?"

Charley's lip curled with characteristic cynicism. "Do you seriously believe that any woman who suffers your company must do so merely because you have come into your title?"

Beau smiled. Tyrrwhit came as close to complimenting him as he was able. "Through m-my sisters, I've m-met a whole parade of females who suffer me for no other reason."

Charley extended an elegantly gray-gloved hand, palm up. "You could always hand over the problem. I should not turn my nose up at a fortune and title and a parade of prospective wives."

Laughter exploded from Beau's lips, slightly uncontrolled laughter. It felt good to laugh. There was release in it. He had not laughed like this since before his father's passing.

"Not willing to go that far, are you?" Charley deduced sarcastically. "Well, don't come crying to me when this Quinby creature turns her pretty nose up at you for so rudely snubbing her."

Chapter One

A high-perch phaeton stood dead in the middle of the fog-shrouded lane that led off the main post road to the White Hart Inn in Godstone. A gentleman sat on the high seat, his arm rising and falling as he brought his long whip cracking down across the backs of his team. The horses, flinching under the whip, would not go.

Clutching the straw hat that did not want to stay on her head, Nell heard the cracking of that whip over the rattle of the dogcart's wheels as her nine-year-old sister, Catherine, guided their pony into the lane, going fast, in a hurry to meet the post coach due within the quarter hour. The pony shied as the dim morning light revealed the looming bulk of the phaeton. The whip cracked again.

"Behind them, Aunt Ursula shrieked in dismay. "Look out!"

Nell exhibited no such display of nerves. "Steady, Cat."

Intent on keeping the pony, the cart, and its contents on the road without ramming the stopped vehicle, Catherine wasted no breath in responding. The only words that passed her clenched teeth were soothing ones, meant for the pony's ears, which swiveled back to listen. Safely, she navigated the dogcart to a standstill on the fog-shrouded shoulder of the road.

There, Nell could more clearly see and hear the driver, who continued to lash out at his team with both the tip of his whip and the equally wicked whip of his tongue.

"Make him stop, Nell!" Catherine insisted, outraged. "It is our dear old Tandy he is thrashing so heartlessly."

Nell was already out of the cart, a look of grim determination in possession of her jaw. She paid no heed to her aunt's imperative command: "Stop, Fanella! 'Tisn't safe."

Hitching up the long curricle cloak that shielded her skirts from road dust, she ran, a flurry of blue velvet. The recalcitrant bonnet flew off the knot of brown hair and into the lane. "Shame, Mr. Deets, shame!" she shouted. "Stop at once."

The florid, whip-wielding gentleman who sat so high above her did stop when she reached the animal's heads, not out of obedience to her cry, but because in his inebriated state he had succeeded in wrapping the lash of his whip around a low-hanging branch above his head. He tugged on the whip, showering dew.

"Out of my way, Mish Quinby," he insisted, weaving a bit on the high seat. "These horses are no longer yours, and I'll not coddle them when they trifle with me. They need to be taught a lesshon." Reasoning with the belligerent lack of good sense that comes with too much brandy, he gave the whip handle another terrific yank and was rewarded with a good slap in the face by a frond of wet leaves, and with a crashing blow to the forehead from the branch itself.

Deets's whip and wits momentarily incapacited, Nell ignored him. Dark eyes liquid with concern, she concentrated on the horses. Her lips pursed when the near-side bay flinched back from her, afraid of being struck as she lifted her hand to grasp his headstall.

"Easy there, Tandy. It's only Nell," she crooned, her anger growing as she examined a number of bleeding weals along the horse's sweat-slick neck. Why were fools like Deets granted the means to own creatures like Tandy?

"Stand down, Mr. Deets," she called up to the driver. "You're too foxed to be managing a team. Did you not examine the lines when the beasts refused to go? One of the reins had caught in the wheel!" Her voice was rife with anger, her color high, as she bent to untangle the frayed end of leather that she would have liked to use like a whip on the driver. "The horse did just as he ought in stopping—"

"How dare you presume to tell me how to drive?" Deets demanded, and as he did so, he rose, swaying, off the bench, only to fall back down again as the horses, the line now disengaged, stepped nervously forward in response to his shouting.

Nell paid him no mind. Catherine's high voice came

shrilly from behind the phaeton. "Nell! Carriage coming! Moving fast."

Jerked erect by the alarm, the freed bit of leather line still firmly clasped in her hand, Nell listened to the rumbling thunder of the approaching vehicle. She could feel the ground begin to vibrate beneath the soles of her high-laced shoes. Dust further obscured the soft, foggy outline of the hedgerow at the end of the lane. Above her, Deets foolishly stood up again, clutching tight to the sides of the phaeton, cursing her interference and the lack of cooperation from his horses.

Behind the phaeton, Aunt Ursula wailed, "Into the ditch, Catherine, else we shall be killed. 'Twill never stop in time."

Even as her brain sorted impressions, Nell acted on instinct. Time was short, and none of it to waste. Hiking up her skirts, she used the shaft tongue as mounting block and scrambled onto Tandy's broad back, as nimble as any postilion. The horses stepped forward. She leaned into the black mane, and chirruped, "Haw! Tandy, haw!"

The noise of the carriage entering the lane behind them, accompanied by the sudden frantic barking of a dog, spurred Tandy as much as Nell's voice did. Deets's phaeton lurched forward, bringing a startled whoop from Deets himself, who fell back against the squabs, feet windmilling. As a great cloud of choking dust rolled up over her, Nell could hear Aunt Ursula's wail of fear reach fever pitch. She closed her eyes, bit down on her lip, and waited for the crashing jolt, the splintering wood of the dogcart, the squeal of the pony.

Tandy broke into a jarring trot. The motion warmed Nell's legs, but her gloved fingers were cold and bloodless with the tension of waiting for certain disaster.

Disaster never came. There was no crash, no scream, no rending wood. Blinking in the dust that rolled over and past them, Nell became suddenly conscious of the steaming back of the horse between her thighs, dampening both her last good pair of silk stockings and the rumpled white skirt and petticoat that swaddled most inappropriately about her knees. Dirt soiled the only new item of clothing she wore, her recently spotless York tan gloves. Dust settled like a powdering of finely milled flour over everything. Her hat was gone, and her lovely hair, so carefully washed and coiffed for her trip to Brighton, was gray with dust and drooping in its pins. She sneezed. Her lips tasted of dirt. Sighing, for she knew what a scolding this stunt would earn her from Aunt Ursula's ready tongue, Nell bunched up the curricule cloak that had once been her sister Aurora's, and her own skirt and petticoats, in order to dismount from the shockingly unladylike straddled position she had adopted.

But in the great volume of cloth came an awful tearing sound. Part of her clothing had tangled itself in the traces. She could not jump down without risk of ripping something beyond mending and exposing all her limbs. Frantically, she tried to disengage herself.

Above her, on the seat of the phaeton, Deets had angrily righted himself. "What the devil are you doing on my horse?" he demanded with drunken curiosity.

Cat, eyes shining, came trotting around the side of the phaeton. "Saving your arse, Deets," she said indignantly.

"Cat! Watch your tongue," Nell insisted in a distracted manner as she continued to struggle with her cloak. It might be secondhand, but it was a pretty one for all that, and she had no desire to ruin it. She would not soon get another with such a wealth of black braid and lace. The Quinbys could in no way afford such luxury now that their father was gone and they had to survive on their mother's meager jointure.

"You should have seen it, Nell." Cat's eyes were gleaming. "They came within a hairsbreadth of climbing the back of the phaeton—four chestnut geldings, perfectly matched, and driven to within an inch of wrecking Deets's phaeton! The leaders reared up, ready to come crashing down, and as if God himself had reached out to push the wheels into motion, the phaeton moved just out of the way. It was an amazingly close-timed thing. Father would have been tickled to see such driving."

Nell jerked at her skirt, rending fabric again. "Father would not be tickled to see me displaying so much leg, Cat. Do help me free."

Cat laughed and stretched up on tiptoe to reach the tangle of traces. "You are hanging out a bit here, aren't you?" she said. Her glance flicked up over Nell's shoulder. "Deets is getting an eyeful. Aren't you, Mr. Deets?"

Deets laughed drunkenly.

Nell hated the sound of that laugh. She tugged at her petticoat, only to hear cloth tear again.

"Here, stop that. You're only making it worse."

Defeated, Nell threw an unhappy look over her shoulder in Deets's direction. He had stopped yelling to concentrate his open-mouthed attention on the amazing display of silk-stockinged ankle that was to be seen. Nell could be thankful that she had chosen to wear her best, undarned white stockings, with their fine yellow clocking at the ankle, but she was disgruntled to discover that Deets was not the only gentleman enjoying the unexpected delight of ogling them.

There were two greatcoated gentlemen just come out of the mist behind Deets, one of them with a black and white Shetland sheepdog at his heels, and when they caught sight of her situation, they stopped to take it in. The dog trotted into the ditch, sniffing enthusiastically.

The first gentleman was short and slight, with thinning hair and a chiseled nose. He wore the dapper white greatcoat, black spotted cravat, and Allan-brimmed hat that marked him for a member of the prestigious Whip Club, in which Cat, who had always wished herself born a boy, had more than once informed her sister she aspired to become a member. Eyebrows raised, a look of arrested interest about his half-open mouth, his gaze traveled with lingering appreciation over Nell's exposed limb.

She was insulted by the liberty of such a look, and turned a hostile glare on the second intruder, prepared to dislike them both. This gentleman's appearance was neither dashing nor prestigious, and she would have liked to take a comb to his tousled locks, yet Nell found something fascinating in him. His hat, coat, and boots all spoke of hard use, but his posture—and he was a tall, spare fellow—was graceful and proud. His hair was thick and lustrous, and his eyes, once met, were the most arresting feature she had ever encountered. A singular shade of clear aquamarine, they were so pale their color might be considered more of a liability than an asset, had there not lurked in their depths a vibrant hint of empathy, as if the man who looked out of them understood completely her moment of dire humiliation, and yet found room to be amused. There was something contagious about the candor in those pale blue eyes, something lively and knowing and likeable. The humor they shared with her drove all other thoughts from Fanella's head. For a moment time stood still. Forgotten was the predicament of straddling a horse with skirts up about one's knees, forgotten for that instant of eternity was the sadness and frustration of her father's death and the loss of house and circumstance. All was well with Nell as long as those pale blue eyes communed with hers. A window of truth and understanding had been encountered in a shuttered world. The power of a soul spoke to her through the peaceful blue. She abandoned herself to it.

Those pale blue eyes took in the condition of her skirts, and the reaction of both his companion and Deets, with darting glances and a final, more lengthy look to discover just what the victim herself thought of her predicament. The blue-eyed man smiled a slow, sweet, contagious smile, as if the two of them shared a funny secret. It was extraordinary how handsome an ordinary fellow might look when blessed with such a smile. Nell could not stop herself from dimpling in response. That surprised her. She was not much in the habit of smiling since her father's passing.

"May we offer a-a-assistance?" he asked, and Nell, as surprised by the faltering of his tongue as he was embarrassed, watched the stout column of his neck flush scarlet.

The question, for which he had removed his hat, received answer, in a bit of a garble, from both Cat and Deets.

Catherine sounded relieved. "As a matter of fact, help would be vastly appreciated. This mess is out of my reach."

Deets was bellowing with belligerent bad humor. "Get the gel off of my horshe, if you will, gentlemen." He leaned out of his phaeton to peer intently at the greatcoated figure who offered assistance. "Four-in-hand are you, then?"

Nell could see the two men understood Deets's condition in an instant. They exchanged a meaningful look.

"I shall never let you live down the embarrassment of that hat, Beau, if we miss the mail," the dapper gentleman said enigmatically as he pulled an elegantly embossed watch from the pocket of his waistcoat. "We shall be hearing the yard of tin in less than ten minutes. Will you see to the ladies, while I assure myself that no one means to come tearing into the lane? I have no desire to risk wrecking the phaeton again this morning."

The blue-eyed man smiled.

Nell's breath was stolen away by that smile. Beau meant beautiful in French, and for this smile alone one might justify the name. And yet when the smile faded, there remained an air of unprepossessing gentility, a quietness of thought and speech and manner, that made this man handsome in a way that was based more on the collective whole of him than on any one feature.

His expression underwent a change in the instant his gaze took in the fact that her skirt was hitched much higher between the horses than on the side where he had already had the privilege of examining her ankle. Eyelashes, thick and golden brown, starred out around his aquamarine eyes as they rose to hers. A wave of ruddy color washed his neck and face.

Her cheeks burned with what she was sure must be equal hue. "Mr . . . ?" She paused, watching him, waiting for his name.

He did not drop his eyes to stare, either at her stocking-covered knee, or the shocking bit of flesh and garter-tape that peeped ever so slightly from beneath the froth of petticoat. She appreciated his restraint, and yet could not help but feel that he was fully conscious of the exposed state of her leg, for his pale eyes seemed to grow larger and warmer, and regarded her face with such unguarded admiration that she had to look away.

"I am Beau-ford," he said, very slowly.

Nell's mouth felt suddenly quite dry. She was both mortified and wickedly exhilarated by the awe with which his eyes met hers.

"I shall require your overcoat, Mr. Ferd," she said in as quelling a manner as she could muster.

The Duke of Heste was enjoying his disguise immensely. His adventure was begun, and it appeared, rather ironically, that he had run head-on into the very elements of life he fled. To begin with a brush with death, in his flight from the mourning of it, seemed strangely appropriate. There was something poetic, too, in being placed in the role of rescuer of a damsel in distress, despite the fact that this female looked quite capable of rescuing herself. She had about her the look of Joan of Arc, straddled as she was across the stout back of the carriage horse. She needed but a lance and armor.

Beau relished this young woman's cool, detached attitude regarding her predicament. He relished, too, what he could see of her leg. This was the leg of a young lady unafraid of jumping astride a horse, unafraid of facing down a drunken fool, unafraid and unabashed when three men stood staring at her indiscretion. There was something very remarkable about such a young lady—and about such a shapely leg.

He looked up in the instant that thought crossed his mind to discover her huge, black-lashed eyes contemplating him, judging his interest in her. There was a sense within him that she understood the very thoughts that crossed his consciousness.

Beau stripped off his secondhand greatcoat and handed it over. She covered herself and granted him a little smile, as if he had been judged worthy of favor in restoring her dignity. It pleased him that he had managed to generate admiration in the eyes of this beautiful young stranger.

"You are very kind, Mr. Ferd," she said.

He could not bring himself to explain that she misinterpreted both his motivation in helping her, and the pronunciation of his name. He could not bring himself to say anything at all. Lord Beauford could only stare, and wonder if Charley was right about the strength of his opinion against women.

"She's caught up back there." The freckled young miss who stood beside the team pointed. "Shall I hold your hat?"

Self-consciously removing the secondhand hat, Beau handed it over. Wondering why he had been granted such a breathtaking privilege, he reached up under the blue cloak to fumble with the wads of muslin beneath.

With a gasp, the young woman on the horse whirled to see what he was doing as his hands stirred the fabric of both dress and petticoat. The heat of her agitated breathing lifted the hair on his forehead. The delicate odor of violets reached out to tickle his nose.

Beauford's gloves made him clumsy. They grazed against some part of her anatomy as he searched for the snare. She yelped and exhaled heavily, her breath smelling of tea and cinnamon. Embarrassed, for he had no idea what part of her he had so inadvertently encountered, he stepped back from the nest of fabric into which he had delved and stripped the gloves from his hands. Dropping them into the hat that the girl called Cat held so patiently for him, he reached back up under the curricle cloak. His palms were sweating, and the heat of the horse's back matched the heat he felt rush into his face and lower extremities. He was required to lean very close to the agitated rise and fall of the young lady's chest in order to reach the spot where the petticoat was caught. With his cheek brushing the soft velvet of her coat, his hips lost in the tumbled wealth of her skirts, he closed his eyes, pulse pounding in his ears.

Beau could tell that she was affected as profoundly as he by the captive embrace in which they both unwittingly participated. She was so close, he could hear her every breath. The intimacy of witnessing such a fragile sound was very stirring.

"It's a good thing you jumped up here—"

"Otherwise you should never have had an opportunity to fiddle about under my skirt," she said waspishly, clearly outdone with her obligation to his assistance.

"Otherwise," he corrected her calmly, "I might have killed you. I should never have forgiven myself that." He paused.

The words sank home. The erratic rise and fall of her breast diminished.

"Also, two of the best lead horses in a-a-all of England would have been injured, perhaps m-m-mortally. My companion, Mr. Tyrrwhit, should never have forgiven me that. They a-are his p-pride and joy." He listened intently, curious to hear if she judged ill of him for his stumbling tongue. She seemed more concerned with what he said than with how he said it.

"That would have been a dreadful waste," she agreed. "Cat tells me they are magnificent animals."

Beau was listening intently to the ebb and flow of her breathing. "A frightful waste," he agreed. He leaned back to look up at her. He was not referring to Charley's chestnuts.

She was beautiful, he thought. Not in a conventional way, but in a far more vibrant manner than the current conventions dictated. Her ancestry looked to hark back to Romans come long ago to Britain to build roads and walls, baths and cities. Her nose, prominent but regal, spoke of such bloodlines, as did the lack of a proper British paleness in the tone of her complexion. Her eyes, too, large and brown and liquid, framed by long black lashes and dark, finely shaped brows, reminded him of the brushwork of an Italian master. Her chin was firm and cleft. Her long, heavy brown hair, uncut or curled at the temple, as was popular these days, was smoothed back on either side of her face, from two perfectly symmetrical widow's peaks, in the style of a Madonna. He could see that when brushed out of the wealthy knot in which it remained fairly contained at the nape of her neck, it would hang thick and course and healthy, with little of the tendency to fly away like most fine, truly English hair. He longed to release the hair from its constraints, longed to test its weight and texture with his hands.

He realized he was staring at her. Dropping his gaze, he held up the frayed bit of petticoat that had been caught on the harness. "It's ripped, but not beyond mending."

"I am free?" she enquired hopefully.

He nodded, and withdrawing his hands from their happy task of rummaging about in the swelter of her garments, stepped back to help her dismount.

Her color was high. "Thank you, Mr. Ferd."

He reached for his hat. "You a-a-are welcome, Miss . . . ?"

It was the little girl returning hat and gloves to him who answered, "Quinby, sir. I'm Catherine, but you can call me Cat. Everyone does. That's my sister, Nell."

"Qu-Quinby?" Beau dropped one of his gloves, so great was his surprise. How very odd! In fleeing one Miss Quinby, he had run smack into two more.

"Yes. Have we met?" Nell regarded him in a probing manner, as if indeed she recognized something in him.

"Met? No. I could not have forgotten that," he said, with such unwavering conviction that the words had impact.

Her eyes changed. Lashes fluttering a little, the black centers of her eyes swelled, until he seemed to swim in them. He stood there, one glove on, one glove off, entranced by the rare pleasure of looking up into the wonders of such a lovely face from such proximity.

As he did so, the plump partridge of a woman who had at first been shrieking at them from the ditch, and then had fainted away when it looked as if the two vehicles were about to collide, came tottering around the side of the phaeton, with the bonnet on her head knocked askew and the one clutched in her hands mangled almost beyond recognition.

"Fanella," she was crying. "Catherine, what's happened to Fanella? Her hat has been squashed flat. Please tell me she has not met with a similar fate."

"I'm quite safe, Auntie Ursula, unlike my poor hat."

Nell—she was Nell to him now—placed the warm weight of both her hands quite unexpectedly on Beau's shoulders and looked down into his eyes very gravely.

"Will you help me down, Mr. Ferd?"

Heart singing, for he was more than happy to assist, Beauford lifted both his hands to span the warmth of Nell Quinby's narrow waist. Pulling her toward him with the pressure of one hand, he reached out with the other to guide the falling fabric as she swung—fairly gracefully, for all the wadding of material she had to drag with her—across the horse's rump and into his arms. His hands, one gloved, the other still blessedly bare, made sure her skirt fell free. Lord Beauford had the strangest sensation of drowning as the scent of violets and the wickedly arousing weight of her legs, along with his greatcoat and her cloak, skirt, and petticoat, washed over his waist, his thigh, and his own braced leg, in a knee-weakening wave of muslin and velvet.

She hit the ground before him unevenly and tipped forward on her toes into the ready prop of his chest, quite crushing the majority of the nosegay that cheerily decorated his lapel.

Ignoring the loss of the flowers, Beau steadied her with both hands. For one strangely irrational moment, with the

heat of her pressed into his breathless chest, and the soft-
ness of her arm beneath the palm of his hand, he fought a
disinclination to let her go.

She was taller than the average. The dusty crown of her
head was just above the level of his chin. If he leaned forward he could press his lips to her forehead.

"Thank you, Mr. Ferd," she said, before he could act on
the impulse. He took a half-step backward. The forehead
that he had considered bussing wrinkled with concern. Her
huge brown eyes lifted to his, full of sad contrition.

"Your flowers. I'm sorry, I've mashed them."

Before he could think of telling her she might happily
mash his flowers anytime if it were to be done with such
deliciously close contact between her person and his, she
had stepped away, to shake out her rumpled cloak and
skirts. Beau could not take his eyes off of her as she performed the simple task.

She seemed to sense he stood staring at her, and turned
her head to regard him, a shy, wise, observant quality in the
look. The new Duke of Heste felt as if Miss Fanella Quinby
found something both engaging and bothersome in his continued regard.

It was Charley Tyrrwhit's decision that those who meant
to catch the mail should make haste to do so in his carriage,
while he saw to driving Mr. Deets safely home. Little
Catherine Quinby offered to show him the way in the dogcart.

"You would do so much for the fool?" Beau asked
Charley.

"I do so for you, fool." Charley directed a suggestive nod
in Nell Quinby's direction. "Unless I mistake the looks the
two of you were exchanging, you must not miss that
coach!" He threw a contemptuous glance in Deets's direction. "With any luck, this obnoxious sot will tumble out on
his way home." His eyes narrowed. "If he does, I shall
leave him under a hedgerow to sleep it off."

Beau grinned. "A-A-And no more than he deserves."

"Right, then." Charley took up the reins. "I shall see to it
that your trunk comes down with me, but I've no idea

where your dog has gotten himself off to, and no intention of worrying my head over him."

Beau grinned and whistled up his dog as he took pleasure in handing both Miss Nell Quinby and her Aunt Ursula up the steps of Charley's smart new four-horse equipage.

Miss Quinby, her gaze concentrated on the course she must navigate in order to obtain the heights of the bench, firmly grasped Beau's hand and made her way up with agile grace. Her eyes strayed from their course for a flickering instant, to look back at him whenever he whistled piercingly for his dog, and when she discovered that he seemed to be waiting for just such a glance, her eyes sparkled with naive curiosity.

The warm promise of Nell's swift look was frozen by the chilling look of hauteur Beau received from Ursula Dunn's severely compressed lips as she too accepted his hand in mounting to her seat. The thinning mouth was meant to remind him that he was merely a coachman, and therefore quite impertinent to be exchanging glances with a young lady.

"I understand we have you to thank for seeing to it that there was no damage to our lives or property?" Nell's aunt said with more severity than such a remark would seem to require.

Eyebrows raised, Beau nodded.

"Well, I thank you, Mr. Ferd," she said, regally extending her hand. "But I must insist that you avoid making that piercing noise. I suffer from the headache."

Before he could correct the continued abuse of his name, she rattled on magnanimously, firmly putting him in his place, "If you should ever find yourself in need of a coaching position, and you are not a man prone to drinking, smoking, gambling, or whistling overmuch, you must apply to my husband, Mr. Bartholomew Dunn of Ipswich, or myself, Mrs. Ursula Dunn of both Ipswich and Brighton, where I go to take the seawater cure at the recommendation of my physician."

With a polite nod, Beau settled himself on the driver's bench, and with a gesture to Gates, who stood at the horses' heads and would jump up behind, shook out the reins. The chestnuts threw themselves willingly into the harness, and yet they had no more than begun to move when a sound reached them. An unmistakable sound, it brought up all heads, and Ursula Dunn uttered, in the tone of one who has just heard her own death knell, "The mail!"

It was indeed the mail, or to be more precise, the yard of tin horn that every postboy carried as a means of announcing the coach's approach at each tollbooth, so that the turnpike gate might be open and waiting for them to sweep through unheeded.

The duke gave the chestnuts a touch of the whip. Meeting or missing the mail, it was going to be a close call.

Chapter Two

W e shall never make it in time!" Ursula fretted.

"I have every confidence in Mr. Ferd," Nell contradicted her calmly. It was difficult, at times, to believe Ursula was indeed her father's sister. Father had been the eternal optimist. Ursula was quite the opposite.

Even now, Aunt Ursula could not be relieved of her concerns. "Where shall we obtain a bonnet to shade your complexion in the wilds of Surrey?" she moaned. "The changes are too quick to allow time for shopping, and no more than villages until we reach Lewes, which is useless, for it is half an hour out of Brighton itself."

"It does not matter, Auntie. We have booked inside passage," Nell said blithely, well knowing what havoc the sun would wreak upon her already slightly olive complexion should she go an entire day exposed to its rays. She would, as her mother always complained, ruin all chance of finding herself a husband if she insisted on ruining her complexion. And yet today it did not seem to matter, for today Nell had seen herself reflected in the pale blue eyes of a young man who found her beautiful.

She felt transformed, as if as long as Mr. Ferd beheld her, she were become as attractive as her sister Aurora— and Aurora was a beauty who turned heads wherever she went. Nell had seen this appreciative look before in gentlemen's eyes, but never for herself. It had never occurred to her that someone might one day regard her in such a way, for while she was not at all homely, she had not the divine, pink-cheeked, golden fairness that Aurora possessed, and when the two sisters were seen side by side, as they had so often been throughout their young lives, it was to Aurora that all eyes were immediately drawn.

Father had been good about telling all of his daughters they were pretty. But, Fanella had never really trusted in his objectivity. Odd that it took the opinion of a stranger to inspire that trust.

Nell knew now why Aurora fussed so much with the color and cut of her dresses and the selection of reticules and ribbons and bonnets. It was most pleasant to be so admired. The look she kept encountering in Mr. Ferd's eyes made her feel as if their owner were regarding a work of art in her, to be studied with interest whenever opportunity allowed. It mattered not that he was but a coachman who could not speak without stuttering. He found her fascinating. That was what mattered.

Nell forced herself to stop thinking in this nonsensical manner, and turned in the seat to wave farewell to Catherine, who had the pony, with its now-empty dogcart, rattling along at a smart trot in their wake. Cat grinned and rolled her eyes, but she did not take her attention from her driving. The responsibility of leading a member of the Whip Club through the country lane appeared to weigh heavy on her mind.

Before Nell faced front again, the black and white dog she had seen earlier at Mr. Ferd's heels shot out of the trees along the road beside the dogcart. In a sudden, bounding burst of speed, the dog passed through the dust that the pony raised and charged straight for them, barking, as if it mean to grapple with the very wheels of the phaeton.

"Mr. Ferd," she said. "Your dog!"

The coachman threw a look over his shoulder and reined in the chestnuts ever so slightly as he shouted, "Up, Bandit!"

Aunt Ursula covered up her ears. "Drive on man, drive on. We shall never meet the mail if we stop."

Mr. Ferd directed an amused look her way.

It proved unnecessary to stop. Even as they slowed, a ball of black and white fur vaulted into the carriage, and as if accustomed to such gymnastic behavior, Mr. Ferd immediately urged the team on again.

Aunt Ursula let out a little exclamation of fearful surprise.

The dog, grinning as only a thoroughly happy dog can,

ignored her screech, and snaked beneath the bench upon which she perched, to plant himself, panting furiously, between his master's knees. He was, Nell thought, a slightly ragged specimen. Not at all a gentleman's dog, he was of a breed that was preferred by shepherds for their intelligence and good working habits. His eyes were bright, his coat thick and attractively marked but dulled with dust from the road. One of the ears, so alertly pricked for any word from his master's voice, was missing a notch, as if it had been bitten through.

"Does he bite?" Ursula regarded the beast with approbation.

"Bite?" The coachman's pale blue eyes were twinkling. "Not unless you want him to, ma'am."

"Is he called Bandit then, for his black eyepatches?" Nell asked, in an effort to interrupt what she was sure would be her aunt's insistence that they put the dog down off the coach again, regardless of delay. She was pleased to see the sign for the White Hart Inn through the trees ahead of them. They might just catch up to the mail after all.

"He is called Bandit because he is in the habit of holding up my coach," the coachman said without trace of his stutter, which surprised Nell, for as he spoke, they were trundling through the Elizabethan gate to the White Hart, at a speed that took her breath away for fear they should catch a wheel in one of the gateposts.

The mail stood waiting for them, in shining red and black glory. In a flurry of movement around the back boot, bags of mail were loaded and unloaded as the team of four horses were led out of their traces. A fresh team stood waiting to be led in. Passengers leaned down from the roof and out of the windows of the coach, as baskets and trays loaded with bread and cheese were distributed, along with flasks of ale and jugs of water.

"See to the horses," Beau Ferd addressed the servant, Gates, as he jumped down to help Nell and her aunt to alight.

He held onto Nell's hand a moment longer than was strictly necessary when she stood firmly upon the ground. "We have had an a-a-adventure this morning, have we not?"

Nell felt as if she fell for a moment into the laughing depths of a pair of disturbingly pale blue eyes. "We have that," she breathed, and disengaged her hand from the heat of his.

As it turned out, the morning's adventure was not yet over.

Beau found his seat readily enough. He had but to call out to the man who sat the foremost bench of the coach. "I'm Beauford. You're expecting me."

"Oiy! If you be Charley's friend," the coachman agreed. "Figured that had to be you when I saw the way the gingers was set to through the gatepost back there," he laughed. "Jump up beside me, lad, and we'll see the prads down to Brighton at a spanking pace."

"I shall just see the ladies comfortably seated." Beau politely tipped his secondhand hat.

The coachman nodded. "Make it quick. I'll not let the mail come late for no man, nor no lady either."

Nell Quinby and her aunt were booked for inside passage, where comfort was generally assured, for no more than four were allowed. But when the coach door was opened it became quite clear that no more than three would ever manage to squeeze themselves into this particular mail coach.

The enormous bombazine-draped woman who took up all of one seat was asleep, her expensive velvet hat tilted down over her eyes, so that two of the feathers that graced its magnificent crown fluttered back and forth with the regularity of a pendulum, in rhythm with the light snores that whistled through her nose.

The woman who occupied the second seat, while still wearing the weight that came with the bearing of the new baby that rested in a basket on the seat beside her, looked quite small by comparison. Her eyes rounded with growing concern when it was made clear to her that two additional women had booked inside passage and stood waiting to crowd in with her.

Beau could not resist a smile when he heard the peal of laughter that escaped Nell Quinby's lips, but he did not stand about waiting to see where the argument would lead when Nell's aunt insisted that this was no laughing matter, for where in the world were they supposed to squeeze themselves?

"Never waste time bemoaning what one has no control over," his father had always admonished. "There is bound to be some aspect of any situation one can affect, if need be."

"I shall be quite ill before we've gone a mile if I am forced to ride upstairs," Ursula Dunn complained. "And you've no hat, Fanella, so I cannot ask you to sit outside."

Beau knew he could be of more assistance than in trying to make room where there was none to be had. Directing an encouraging smile Nell's way, he ducked under the low beam of the door that led to the taproom of the White Hart Inn.

"I shall ride up top," he heard Nell offer sensibly, as his eyes adjusted to the dim interior.

He called in an authoritative manner for the innkeeper's wife. A short, heavyset woman came running.

"Have you a-a-a Sunday b-b-bonnet?" he asked breathlessly.

Her eyes popped and she looked him up and down with disbelief, as if she faced a madman. A bright-eyed lass, who looked to be the woman's daughter, seemed to take in the meaning of his urgent request in an instant. "Has one of the lady passengers lost hers then, sir?"

"Yes." He rewarded her understanding with the flash of a coin and gracious smile that had her beaming back at him. "A pound for the best hat you have to offer."

She took the coin. "I've no bonnets worth all of a quid, sir, but half a minute, and I shall run and fetch my best."

Beau, who could see through the low doorway that the postboy, resplendent in his scarlet coat and tall hat, had taken up his yard of tin to sound out their leaving, called after the girl, "Toss it from the window. The coach would leave without me, otherwise."

The horn sounded.

Beau ducked swiftly out the door and scrambled to his place beside the coachman, even as the wheels began to move. Almost on a level with them, one of the windows of

the inn flew open and the girl leaned out, waving a straw
bonnet.

"Sir, catch, sir!"

Snatching up the bonnet at it sailed out of the window,
Lord Brampton Beauford, seventh Duke of Heste, gra-
ciously presented it to Fanella Quinby.

With a look of astonished appreciation, Nell promptly
placed the bonnet on her head and tied the pink ribbon beneath her chin. "I shall see you knighted, Mr. Ferd," she
said gratefully. "Thrice in one day have you rescued a
damsel in distress."

Nell was touched by the consideration she received. A
gentleman gave her his place on the bench behind the driver's, where the swaying of the coach would not be so uncomfortable as at the hind end of the roof, and gallant Mr.
Ferd had cleverly seen to the last-minute delivery of a bonnet. She began to think that she would never to able to
repay this young man's repeated kindnesses, and that bothered her. She did not like to remain beholden to anyone,
most especially handsome young men with dancing blue
eyes.

An opportunity for restitution presented itself when
something behind them in the road caught the attention of
most of the topside passengers, as well as the postboy and
guard, who perched on the very hindmost bench of the
coach, above the back boot, gun in hand.

"Stupid creature," the guard said to the postboy. "Looks
as if he means to follow us."

"Shoot at him," the postboy recommended. "That will
turn him away."

The guard lifted his blunderbuss to his shoulder, ready to
oblige.

Nell craned her neck to see what it was the men meant to
shoot. A flash of black and white fur caught her eye.
"Stop!" she shrieked. "That's Bandit!"

The blunderbuss jerked up, discharging quite harmlessly
into the air, but the explosion of shot, coupled with the
words "Stop" and "Bandit," unsettled all of the passengers.
Even the baby and the enormous woman inside the coach
immediately voiced their distress, the one by bawling at the

top of its lungs, the other by rattling off a stream of invective that grew in volume to compensate for the full-scale howl that the baby eventually attained.

Mr. Ferd, who had been handed the ribbons, slowed the team, all the while fending off the original driver, who urged him to "Whip 'em along, man! We can outrun any highwayman in England with four fresh rare 'uns 'tween the shafts."

"I am sure we can," he agreed calmly. "But, a-a-as I've no wish to outrun this particular Bandit, we shall spare the horses the whip. Gates!" He called to his man.

"Yes, sir," Gates murmured with an agreeable grin, and as the coach slowed and Beau Ferd called out firmly, "Up, Bandit, up, boy!" Gates stretched out over the side of the coachtop, caught hold of the leaping dog by the scruff of his thickly furred neck as, nails scrabbling on canvas, it valiantly attempted to board.

"See, the scamp holds us up again." Beau leaned back to share his amusement with Nell. The sparkle in his pale blue eyes was an unexpected intimacy.

However, before she could so much as nod, Gates called out, "Got 'im, your grace," and Mr. Ferd leaned forward to touch up the team.

Chapter Three

The dog, Bandit, eyed Nell from beneath his master's seat from the moment he settled there. To be sure, he kept his ear cocked in the direction whence he might hear the coachman's voice or whistle, but his great tawny orbs stared at her with that hopeful look most dogs fasten on someone they think might offer them attention, affection, and a scratch behind the ear.

Nell had a fondness for animals. It was rooted in a deep, spiritual reverence for life, a reverence intensified by the unexpected death of her father. Death pointed up the tenuous gift that life was. To Nell, animals represented the very essence of that gift. They offered labor, food, clothing, transport, and companionship to man. They were living, breathing, thinking creatures possessed of a spark just as vital, in its essence, as that within man. Life. It was precious and all too brief. It should not be wasted.

Animals sensed her affinity for them. Mr. Ferd's dog was no exception. It was Bandit, and not the bleak and treeless course through the gentle hills of the North downs, that received the majority of Nell's attention. She scratched the battered ears and stroked the eager nose and wondered what had taken such a toll on the animal at her knee.

Mr. Ferd leaned back. "I must warn you that Bandit steals hearts as frequently as he holds up coaches."

In leaning back, the earlobe of the young man whom Gates had addressed as "your grace" was, for an instant, very close to Nell's nose. There was something disconcerting about being in such proximity to a stranger's ear. Nell could smell the clean, masculine tang of sweated neck. Her lashes swept downward, shutting out for an instant the distraction of eyesight. She longed to lean closer, to breathe deep. Mr. Ferd was not a smoker or drinker. There was no taint of the horrid weed about him, no reek of the tap either. There was instead a pleasant, manly odor that was uniquely his own.

Nell opened her eyes with a sigh. The movement of her breath across his ear visibly affected Mr. Ferd. He sat forward swiftly, as if pushed by a hand, and a flush of red color stained his neck and swept up into his face, into the very tip of the ear on which her breath had played.

Nell's eyes rounded. There was something very exhilarating in having caused such a reaction, no matter how unwittingly.

"I shall do my best not to allow this fellow to seduce me with his very speaking eyes." She patted Bandit on the head, her voice hovering on the edge of laughter.

The original driver, the graying gentleman who sat beside Mr. Ferd, turned in his seat. "This is the Weald," he said to all of the topside passengers, indicating the land about them. "It were once a great oak forest that stretched as far as a man can see and beyond. One hundred and twenty miles it went. The Romans, when they marched through, called it Anderida, for so awe-inspiring was the sight of the woods that it required a name all to itself." His voice flattened. "What were once a wall of trees is fallen to the woodsman's axe, and the charcoal maker's fire—felled to stoke the furnaces of the Sussex iron foundries. There's pockets left. You'll see some of old Anderida in Ashdown Forest once we've stopped for horses in East Grinstead. You'll see there what all this once was, before progress"— he used the term derisively—"changed the face of things."

As he spoke, his huge hands gesturing in highly worn and work-stained gloves, Nell noticed how very different those gloves were from Mr. Ferd's. The more she looked from the one set of hands to the other, the odder she found their differences. These were coachman's gloves, these stiffened things, dark with use and weather, molded to their owner's hands. The stitches were rubbed through, the seams loose between every finger that held a leather line. These were unmistakably the gloves of a man who drove a coach on a daily basis.

Mr. Ferd's gloves, by contrast—the very gloves that had touched upon the bareness of flesh beneath her skirts, looked completely out of place. They were fairly clean, unusual in an item of clothing that was used daily in the proximity of dusty, sweaty horseflesh. The leather was of a thinner, softer, more supple variety. The gloves seemed strangely at odds with the rest of Mr. Ferd's attire. All else spoke of thrift and long use.

Nell wondered if she made too much of a simple thing. The hands within the gloves behaved like coachman's hands. They handled the lines with comfortable finesse. Mr. Ferd seemed to sense her interest. He turned to look her way. Feeling prettier and more feminine and more interesting merely by having met such a look, Nell promptly forgot all about gloves and fell to contemplating just what it was in a pair of pale blue eyes that could make her feel so warm and quavery inside.

At East Grinstead, a lively market town, the passengers were informed they had time enough to stretch their legs and relieve bruised and jostled kidneys as the horses were changed. Nell was the first to step down. She went in search of the innkeeper's wife, rather than its facilities, to obtain permission to pluck a handful of pinks from the garden.

Returning to the coach to mount the steps to her seat, she was met by her Aunt Ursula, who was only then disengaging herself from the interior of the coach. Without really understanding her own inclination to be secretive about the flowers, Nell hid them behind her back.

"I do not know how I shall survive this trip, my dear," her aunt confided wearily. "For while I am not chewing dust, as I'm sure you must do topside, I am smashed in beside the baby basket, with nothing to look at between a dirty window and that snoring gargantuan. And while I was most relieved when the baby's mother offered up her breast in order to quiet the infant's cries, I could not feel altogether comfortable for a stranger to so expose herself. I do hope you are having a better time of it, my dear."

Indeed, Nell was having a better time of it, for the weather was fine, the dust not too choking, she was not feeling at all downcast over her father's demise, and through the eyes of an intriguing coachman she had been made to feel beautiful. Hoping that she might slip past her aunt without the flowers being noticed or questioned, she said bracingly, "Three changes to come, and we shall have you happily home again, Auntie. It is so very kind of you to have me down to the seaside for a fortnight, when it was Aurora you originally meant to have back with you."

Ursula gave her head a little shake. "But of course. How were we to know that she was to be offered a Season in London, and an introduction to the new Duke of Heste and his set?"

"Lady Cowper is exceedingly kind to Rora."

"Well, I have every hope your sister will catch herself a good match with such sponsorship," Ursula said. "She has got all the looks in the family, that girl, and worth her weight in gold if she should only put them to good use."

"If anyone can marry well, it will be Aurora," Nell said with unruffled certainty.

"And perhaps you, too, my dear. All of the Prince of Wales's set does come down to Brighton on occasion. You may meet someone who will do well by you."

Nell laughed, "I have not come husband hunting, Auntie, but only to keep you company while Uncle is away, and to forget for a while Papa's passing and our fallen circumstances. I trust in Aurora's beauty to save our bacon, for I've neither intention nor inclination to marry into money. There is some comfort in not being born with all the looks of the family, you see, for then one is not expected to sacrifice oneself up on the altar of matrimony on everyone else's financial behalf to some well-heeled young man who requires a wife for no other reason than to get him an heir, or some dour old pinchpenny in need of a housekeeper."

"Shush, Fanella! It is unnatural in you to say such things. Your parents had not such a marriage."

Fanella laughed. "Well, I am a most unnatural creature, Auntie. Has not my mother told you so? I've little appreciation for marriage at this moment. Father loved my mother, but because she did not see fit to produce him with an heir, his property is willed away from her and we are as good as thrown into the street like unnecessary baggage, by my

Uncle Andrew, who has been unkind enough to insist that we vacate before poor Father was even grown cold. What is the sense in forsaking love for money if the money is so easily snatched away from a widow?"

"But, Fanella, a man's real property must remain in the family line. It is the law. Your mother retained all of her personal property, and a jointure. You are not in danger of Dun Territory."

"Such a law is a contradiction in terms, for what are a man's wife and daughters if not family? Mother has sold off all of the furniture, the horses, the carriage, and her jewelry, and even with all that gone she speaks of needing more money, with three daughters to support and a new household to set up. So Aurora must find herself a wealthy husband to save us from the predicament one is placed in when a woman survives her husband. Is it not ludicrous?" She gestured emphatically with her posy.

Ursula gasped, and shook her head with vigor. "Fanella! You are far too young to entertain such cynical thoughts." She blinked at the bouquet. "Do you mean to choke those flowers? They will only wilt if you continue to abuse them in such a manner."

Nell frowned at the flowers. "Oh! How stupid of me. These are for our coachman. To replace the ones I flattened."

Ursula frowned and looked about her to be sure they were not overheard. She even thought to look up, for they stood next to the door to the coach, and started when she discovered two bright eyes fixed on her with great interest. They were of the canine variety. She flapped a hand in Bandit's direction and went on with what she meant to say.

"I do not recommend such an action, Fanella. It will not do for a young lady of your class to mix with a mere coachman. The young man will be getting ideas in his head if you offer up favors."

"Nonsense!" Fanella said stoutly, even though such a thought had crossed her sensible mind. She argued to convince herself as much as her aunt. "He was kind enough to procure me this bonnet, which must have cost him dearly on a coachman's salary. A handful of flowers is merely a gesture of similar kindness. Besides, I am no longer certain what class it is that I belong to, for while Father was knighted, his title will not be carried on to any of his daughters. We no longer have land, so I cannot say that I am a member of the gentry, and Mother insists that we are neither smart enough to qualify as intelligentsia, nor trade-wise enough to be classed as bourgeoisie, so just what is it that I am these days but a poor relative that has been foisted onto you, dear Auntie, I do not know."

"What nonsense, Fanella! You have been foisted on no one. You are a well-educated young lady of good family. I daresay you may do as well as your sister in finding a husband." She looked pointedly at the flowers. "You may certainly set your sights higher than a coachman."

Nell dipped her nose down to smell the flowers. "I might like to marry a coachman, were he a kind and gentle man who loved me as well as his horses," she teased, with a mischievous smile.

Ursula Dunn allowed her forbidding expression to unbend. "You are your father's child, my dear. I will not scold you for such, but think on this, if you will. It is just as easy to fall in love with a duke as a dustman. Far easier, I should imagine."

Ursula took herself off to stretch her legs.

Nell mounted the steps that led to the top of the carriage, thoughts of her father's recent death weighing down her spirits. It was death that had so harshly pointed out to her the vagaries of being born female in Great Britain, a creature whose fate was determined almost entirely by men. In giving oneself into marriage, a woman gave herself up completely—her rights, her name, her dowry, even her children was she powerless to control under the current law. There was something akin to the relationship between man and beast, as between man and wife. A woman, she thought, could but hope for a just and gentle keeper in a husband who outlived her. She was frowning with such thoughts when her head came up over the rim of the coach-top.

There, alone on the foremost seat of the carriage, nibbling on a bit of bread and cheese, with Bandit waiting expectantly for a handout, sat none other than the young coachman she and her aunt had just spoken of so freely. Nell almost lost her footing.

A smile lurked about Mr. Ferd's provocative lips and mischief sparkled in the clear depths of his eyes. Nell's cheeks burned with humiliation. He was certain to have overheard them! She hesitated, ashamed, wondering if it would be better to return to the ground awaiting the return of her aunt than to continue up the steps to face the young man's opinion of what he might have heard.

"May I offer you my hand?" He stood, and leaned down over the steps, gloved hand extended.

Nell decided that it would be churlish in her to refuse. "If you please," she said.

With steady clasp he firmly brought her up beside him. She found herself blinking, both from the brightness of the sun and from the keenness of the look he bent on her. Mr. Ferd's pale gaze seemed capable of cutting through to the heart of her. Nell felt exposed. Her gaze fell.

"I am sorry for what you may have heard." Self-consciously, she held forth the flowers she had brought for his buttonhole. "These are for you. I hope you will not think me too forward in offering you replacement for those I have crushed."

"To the contrary, Miss Quinby. There is something rather more b-b-backward that f-f-forward in your offering."

She frowned. Did he mean to insult her? "Backward?"

His eyes were sparkling. He smiled very sweetly. "Yes, I have never had the p-p-pleasure of a young lady offering me a p-p-posy. The situation is generally reversed."

Her heart turned over. No man had ever before looked at her in the manner that he did. She smiled. "I have never had cause to offer a gentleman flowers before. I suppose it is both backward and forward in me."

He laughed and shook his head. In taking the posy from her hand he managed to turn her knees to water. "Not a-a-at all, Miss Quinby. Your gesture is p-p-precisely right."

Deftly, he removed the smashed flowers from his buttonhole. Their stems were encased in a small water vial. The vial was not unexpected, but the cut glass and silver it was made of was. Nell would not have thought that a coachman could afford such a luxury. She wondered if he might be of as gentle a birth as she, and fallen on equally hard times. She regretted again his having overheard her conversation with her aunt.

He tucked the fresh pinks carefully into the vial.

"My posy is yours for the crushing once a-a-again, Miss Quinby. They are a-a-a far better r-r-re . . ."

He sighed, as if disgusted with his inability to speak without stuttering, and something fluttered in Nell's chest. She did not want this kind young man with the speaking blue eyes to feel bad about his stutter, any more than she wished him to feel inferior to her because of his position in life. She liked him too much.

"A far better what?" she pressed gently.

Again, he blessed her with the magic of his smile. "Replacement," he said slowly, and she could tell by the shift in his gaze from her face to her hat that he meant to belittle his own kindness to her.

"I feel very fortunate that it was only a bonnet that was crushed this morning." Both her look and her answer were quite direct, and he seemed to see or hear something that widened the heart-stopping smile.

"We are f-fortunate indeed," he agreed.

There was no time for more, for the rest of the passengers were climbing aboard. Nell felt a sort of relief that such was the case. She had begun to wonder if her aunt was not perhaps right about encouraging conversation with a coachman, no matter how kind. She had never felt so warm and exhilarated in conversation with any other gentleman of her acquaintance. As she took her seat, and the passengers prepared to get under way again, Fanella found herself wondering how easy it was to fall in love, duke or dustman.

Chapter Four

The passengers settled in their seats. With a thoughtful expression, Mr. Ferd began to whistle. Nell was struck by the wayward impression that it looked as if he meant to kiss the flowers she had given him, so similar was the pursing of his lips in whistling to that other oral pursuit. The tune, so cheerfully rendered, was vaguely familiar to her. She tried to place it as the postboy took up his horn to hurry the laggards, but had not managed to put name to it even as the horses fell into a trot.

Nell found something vastly disappointing both in her inability to recognize the tune and in no longer being in a position to regard the expression of her new acquaintance. Not that Mr. Ferd's was an unattractive back. It was broad and tautly muscled. Cloth capes, stretching provocatively from left shoulder to right, telegraphed every move. His wind-tousled hair was attractive as well, both in cut and color beneath the low-brimmed hat, but Nell, having once been introduced to the more speaking aspect of a pair of pale blue eyes, found herself anxious to face again what she considered his better side. She found the turnings of Mr. Ferd's agile mind far more intriguing than the curling tendrils of hair at the nape of his neck.

She knew she could not, with any decency, begin conversation with him herself, and while there was some contentment to be found in examining the strength of his jawline, and the ingenious way in which nature had seen fit to attach pink-tipped ears to the sides of his well-shaped head, Nell could not help but wish that he might bless her with another of his complimentary blue-eyed looks.

Fortunately, a gentleman passenger who sat behind Nell pointed to the attractive sandstone edifice, constructed in the Jacobean style, that they were passing. "What is that building there?" he asked.

"That's Sackville, sir," said the older coachman. He spat a stream of snuff from the wad that bulged in his cheek. "It's for them that's gone tuppy or has not got two megs to rub together."

"What's that he says?" the gentleman's wife asked of no one in particular, clearly confused by the cant.

Mr. Ferd turned toward them. Nell found the shape of his lips utterly fascinating as he stopped whistling and lightly passed the tip of his tongue over them.

"It's an a-a-alms house," he explained. "Built by the Earl of Dorset in 1619. It was originally meant to house his r-r-retired r-r-retainers." He threw back his head as if reined in by his own tongue, and a shadow seemed to darken the pale blue of his eyes, before he surged manfully on. "But I understand the earl's charity has been extended to a-a-all those in the village who a-a-are maimed or penniless."

An awkward silence fell. This exhibition of the young coachman's speech impediment, hitherto unrealized by the vast majority of the passengers, rendered them all speechless.

Herself struck dumb by Mr. Ferd's surprisingly detailed knowledge of a long-dead earl's largess, Nell was bothered by the silence. It stretched too long not to be noticed, and Mr. Ferd's fascinating eartips appeared to flush deeper rose as a result.

Gently, she filled the silence. "The earl was a kind and charitable man."

"Kind indeed," the gentleman who had first enquired about Sackville murmured.

"Kindness is an excellent quality to cultivate," Mr. Ferd said softly, turning to look at her with an expression in the cool depths of his eyes that convinced her he was not unmoved by her intervention.

Nell was touched by a thrill of pleasure. She found she could not take her eyes from the back of Mr. Ferd's weatherbeaten hat as the coach rumbled across the Medway River bridge and into the strangely desolate remains of Ashdown Forest. Had she just been thanked for her own charity? She could no more be certain of it then she could be certain of what it was the curious coachman began to whistle again. The name of the tune still eluded her.

It was not until they crested a small hill that led into the village of Forest Row, when the postboy took up his yard of tin to echo a bit of the whistled melody in bugling tones, that Nell finally remembered from whence the music came. It was a refrain from a Beethoven serenade that their coachman had all of this time been whistling with kiss-pursed lips, while his companion on the driver's bench spat snuff between the horse's hooves in time to the music.

The notes from the horn died away. Mr. Ferd twisted in his seat to shout back at the postboy with a pleased look, "You're quick to pick up a tune."

Nell knew it was neither ladylike nor polite to turn and stare, but she could not resist twisting to look at the postboy as he grabbed up the heavy canvas mailbags. He was grinning.

"I've always got me ear out for a new lick. That tootle works right smart on me yard of tin, don't you think, sir?"

"Capitally so," Mr. Ferd agreed, returning his attention to the team as they swung into the yard of a posting house and the postboy rose to his knees with the timing of familiarity, to fling one of the stout mailbags off the roof, near a woman in an apron who stood waving. Before they had left her behind, the postboy was wielding a long-poled crook, with which he snagged up the waiting bag of outbound mail.

"There's more, if you'd care to hear it," the coachman shouted as the bag was stowed.

"Aye, sir, whistle away," returned the postboy.

Nell straightened her position in order that she might once again regard the intriguing coachman who was familiar enough with a contemporary composer that he might whistle his tunes for half the morning. There was something strange and wonderful in listening to a coachman and a postboy for Her Majesty's Royal Mail, as between them they made the great forest once known as Anderida ring with the music of Beethoven.

It was in Chailey, with its ancient church and its pretty windmill high upon the breezy common, that the music stopped. The horses were to be changed out again. Two departing passengers were the only ones to leap down, for the change was a swift one.

In the short, flurried pause, Brampton Beauford allowed himself the luxury of turning about completely on his bench, his gloved hand stretching down under the seat to stroke Bandit, who lay, tail thumping, beneath. The dog was not the primary reason for his movement. Beauford had a great desire to look once again upon the fair face of Miss Fanella Quinby, whose words had given him cause to consider in a different light the financial difficulties females faced with regard to marriage.

She looked quite fetching in the pink muslin-lined bonnet he had procured for the protection of her complexion. The color suited. It matched the roses that bloomed on each cheekbone. What drew his attention irresistibly back to her was not so much her pretty face as it was the turnings of this young woman's mind and the expression that played about her engaging mouth. She regarded him with amused and uncensored approval. Such tolerance struck Lord Beauford quite profoundly. He was not at all used to receiving direct or admiring glances from attractive young females once his stutter was discovered. Pained sympathy, blank glassiness, or fearfully shuttered looks usually settled over feminine features when his speech impediment made itself known.

The pained ones usually tried to finish his sentences for him, or at the very least, they played a humiliating sort of guessing game with him as they tried to predict what word it was he meant to utter. The blank and fearful ones quickly ended all conversation that they might escape to more articulate company.

To be sure, his sisters, Anne and Beatrix, did not behave so, but they had grown up beside him, and beyond a fixed need in both of them to mother him more than he cared for, it appeared they had accustomed themselves to his halting speech. Miss Quinby seemed unfazed by his handicap, capable of looking beyond it to what it was that he was saying. He could tell by her calm, unhurried manner that she felt quite comfortable waiting for his tongue to catch up with his thoughts. He read no censure, no offended withdrawal, no unwanted pity in her steady gaze. He could, in fact, at times read a curious sort of admiration there, and such a look was enough to make his blood sing while the hair lifted quite perceptibly along the nape of his neck.

"Do you do well enough u-u-up there, Miss Quinby?" he asked.

"Well enough?" she said in a chiding manner. The expression in her huge brown eyes was one of open curiosity, as though in him she found a puzzle that needed solving. "Why, Mr. Ferd, 'twould be churlish in me to complain, for through your kindness I've not only a new bonnet to shade my face, a breeze to cool my brow, and fine scenery to entice my eyes, but unless I do mistake, the strains of a Beethoven serenade to please my ears."

These last few words were uttered with elevated brows and a mildly challenging tone. "I would not have thought a coachman so musically informed," she prodded, when he made no immediate effort to satisfy her curiosity.

"I'm glad my whistling does not offend," he said. "I have met up with some females who do not care for it overmuch."

"Are you referring to my aunt?" she demanded in the comfortable, joshing manner of an old friend or beloved relative.

His lips curved upward in the irresistible smile. Relieved that there was no time for more, he swung halfway around on his bench again, only to hear Miss Quinby's voice following him as he took up the reins.

"I have not decided, Mr. Ferd, if you are a gentleman coachdriver, sir, or a coaching gentleman," she said, as if she saw right through his disguise.

Mr. Hoby, the old coachman, leaned back to quip with a knowing laugh, " 'Tis a fine line divides the two, love."

She laughed suggestively. "A line drawn in coin and birthright, a line that men on either side might wish to straddle."

It was in the climb past Mount Harry, where Henry the Third was beaten in the battle of Lewes in 1264 by the barons who rallied under Simon de Montfort, that the mail overtook a fellow traveler whose actions so incensed Beauford that he very nearly abandoned his masquerade.

A tall, wasp-waisted young smart was seated on the bench of an eye-catching curricle drawn by two sleek liver bays, their tails fashionably docked and their heads reared back with the bearing rein that had so recently come into vogue. The flashy equipage, for all its dash, could not seem to make it over the crest of the hill, which was very steep.

Beauford eased the mail past, his wheels within hair-raising inches of the stalled vehicle with its blowing bays, but even as the driver on the seat beside him was chortling, "Well done; now we shall show him our heels," the disguised Duke of Heste was pulling the team to a halt at the crest of the incline and throwing on the brake.

"Hold them," he ordered, with all the authority his station afforded him, tossing the reins to their rightful owner. Before the older man could object, he had slipped down the side of the coach and onto the road, where he sprinted back to confront the red-faced driver of the curricle.

"Set the brake, man, a-a-and help me off with these confounded b-b-bearing reins," Beau insisted in a voice that had all of the passengers on the roof turning to see what their coachman was about, to be challenging a gentleman in such a tone. The passengers inside let down the windows with a snap. Even the sleepy fat woman craned her neck to watch.

"Who are you, to be telling me what to do?" the fop angrily asked.

Beau lowered his voice. The man's pride stood between them. " 'Tis the damned bearing rein, sir, that's keeping your team from carrying you easily o-o-over. You must release the a-a-animals' heads on a hill as steep as this."

The young man set the brake, as if compelled, but he was not about to back down. "I shall take my lash to you if you lay a hand on my horses, you stuttering imbecile," he threatened.

Beau froze in front of the team, his eyes icy, but before he could tell the man exactly who he was, and just what he thought of such an abuse of horseflesh, a sweet, feminine voice called from the coach.

"Halloo, sir. You are not from London, are you?"

The driver, as distracted as Beau, turned his florid face toward Nell, who leaned out from the coach in a most feminine pose, batting her eyelashes and smiling. Beau blinked in disbelief. There was something so changed in Nell's countenance, so simpering and coy, that he hardly recognized her.

Ursula Dunn twisted her head to look up from inside the coach. "Fanella? Is that you?" Her voice wavered. "You must leave this to the gentlemen, dear."

Fanella ignored her aunt's advice. "You are wondering how I knew that, aren't you?" she chortled.

Beau winced. He had judged her to be above such wheedling ways, and yet she went on salving the fop's ego with her treacley tone. "I can see that you are well informed in matters of fashion," she cooed. "Your equipage is comparable to the finest in London."

The driver, his high color fading, lifted both his chin and his hat. "How did you know then, that I came not from London?" There was something as wincingly honeyed in his manner as in that of the young lady.

A heated disgust rose in Beau's chest. He had believed that Miss Quinby was above such coyness. To find his judgment of her so flawed, trebled the disgust with which he listened to her fawn on another man.

Nell dipped her attractive head to one side. Her teasing manner seemed to melt the anger from the fop's expression while increasing the rate at which Beau's offended bosom rose and fell. "I knew it instantly when you refused to listen to our coachman. In London, amongst all the young men who aspire to be whip-hands, there is none whose advice is held in higher esteem than that of a four-in-hand coachman."

Beau blinked in amazement. It would appear she meant to champion his cause in a rather roundabout fashion.

She went on talking, with the look about her of a cat that has just swallowed a canary, without the bird ever ceasing to sing. "Why, do you know that there are any number of dashing young noblemen who vie—who do in fact pay good money—for a seat beside such a coachman as ours."

She looked directly at Beau as she spoke, and there was a dawning recognition in the look, as if she realized that he was, in fact, an example of what she described. Her smile made them coconspirators. "There is no substitute for the advice of an expert, you know. I am quite sure our Mr. Ferd is in the right of it in advising you to release your horses' heads. Will you not give him the benefit of the doubt?"

"I cannot disappoint a lady," the driver said with a cloying exhibition of teeth and gums. The smile faded. Eyes narrowed, he glared down at Beau, who still stood in the way of his team, arms akimbo. "Take them down, man, as the lady says." The fop flapped a hand, as if the Duke of Heste were no more than his personal lackey.

A vein worked in Beau's temple. He felt like grinding his teeth. It was, in many ways, difficult to stand in the shoes of a coachman. And yet he had gotten what he wanted, so he reined in his tongue and loosed the first horse's head.

"There," he heard Nell say with satisfaction to the cretin he would have gladly harnessed into the bearing rein and driven up the hill. "You can see, already the poor animal breathes easier."

The poor animal was blowing like a steaming kettle. How could she remain so civil? And yet, as she went on, he realized she too had gotten what she wanted, and now the silly fop sat and listened with a vapid grin while she lectured him.

"Fashion and nature are sometimes at direct odds, sir. It is up to an intelligent person like yourself to determine which is which. I realize that it is all the rage to dock tails and raise a horse's head, but ask any true horseman and he will tell you that you have cut years off the working life of any animal along with his tail in removing the fly swatter God so judiciously allotted him. The bearing rein is an instrument of torture. It will ruin the wind of even the soundest animal by forcing an unnatural carriage. I have heard that the Earl of Portland and the Duke of Heste, both of them horsemen of repute, will have nothing to do with bearing reins."

Dumbfounded to discover that Miss Quinby was informed of his pet peeve in equestrian fashion, the Duke of Heste stood back from the freed team and regarded the young lady with renewed respect.

"Give them a chirrup, sir," he said, taking his hat obsequiously between his hands, "and see if they don't walk on a-a-a bit easier without the nasty choker."

The driver, with a look of haughty contempt for the hatless duke, bade his team walk on and was clearly surprised to find that his flashy bays could now easily transport his vehicle over the crest of the hill.

Beau returned to the post coach.

"You've a way with horses, miss," the only other female passenger who rode the roof was saying to Fanella.

"And with men," the counterfeit coachman murmured wryly.

Nell smiled self-consciously. "Horses have a way with me. As for the men . . ." She watched Beau climb the side of the coach. "It is my sister who has a way with them." She threw back her head and, smiling archly, batted her eyelashes in example. "I have learned to mimic her talent when the occasion suits me."

"Ah, so we've a pretender on board then, have we?" Hoby chuckled, with a sly wink and an equally sly nudge to Beauford's ribs. "The Duke of Heste would have been proud to see the clever way in which you managed to take down those poor blowing prad's heads. Wouldn't he, lad?" Again, his elbow found purchase in Beau's ribs.

"Quite so," Beau agreed, before he was further bruised. "Do you pretend to be your sister very often, Miss Quinby?"

She smiled provocatively. "Do you not, now and again, pretend to be something or someone you are not, Mr. Ferd?"

Beauford grinned despite another prod in the ribs, and turned away from the equally probing wisdom of her look. "There is something most invigorating a-a-about a masquerade," he admitted.

Chapter Five

A thousand years of history had left their mark on Lewes, where the mail made its last change of horses. The town was beautiful, Nell decided. But everything was beautiful to her now, seen through the rosy glow of satisfaction she was feeling as a direct result of having eased the pain and suffering of two dumb creatures who could not speak for themselves. And this man, this wonderful, thoughtful, heroic young man upon whose shoulders the sun beat down before her very eyes, was especially beautiful to her in this moment—so beautiful, in fact, that she had to stop looking at him and concentrate instead on the town of Lewes, else her eyes begin to water with the shine of him.

The town was situated on a hilly spot, its streets jumbled higglety-pigglety. The Downs rose up behind the town, the River Ouse ran through it, and while the coastline was not yet to be seen, its effect on the local architecture was evident in the distinctive wood and plaster houses, tile-hung from the eaves to head height in protection against the evils of coastal weather. Lewes had a prospering, well-to-do look about it. Shops lined the road and new building was in progress, but the past was not to be denied, for there was the ruin of a Norman castle to be explored, had one the time.

The mail allowed no such time. There was a schedule to keep, and the change of horses stood waiting for them. And yet Nell was not surprised when her beautiful Mr. Ferd took advantage of the few minutes it took to make that change to turn completely about in his seat so that he might ask her, with a piercing, blue-eyed look, "How is it that you know so much a-a-about horses, Miss Quinby?"

She shrugged. "I suppose it is on account of my love, sir, for a carthorse named Boots."

"Boots?"

"Yes. He was the largest and the most beautiful honey-brown creature I have ever encountered, with an unforgettable face—the face of a creature both mythic and bewitching to a child of five. It was divided, you see, unevenly down the middle by a wide white blaze that ran like a great splash of milk onto one cheek. Add to this the intrigue of Boots's amazing eyes. One was large and liquid and as brown as a chocolate drop, while the other, in its field of white, was pale sky blue. There were any number of the country folk who feared him for this same inequity in his coloring, but there was no need for fear. I fell in love with him at first glance. A sweeter, more gentle creature never walked the earth."

It was odd, Nell thought, how well she got along with this stranger. She felt as if she might talk to him about anything and have him understand. Such accord was sweet and rare and as comfortable as old shoes.

"And because of Boots your father then educated you in equestrian ways?"

"Yes. Myself, and all of my sisters, for even Aurora could not be afraid of Boots."

The horses were ready. Mr. Ferd chirruped to them and the coach got under way once more. "A-A-And what became of Boots?" he asked without turning, as the coach made its way into the narrow street.

Nell frowned. How changed was her life become! "I am sorry to say Boots was sold along with all of the rest of the stable when my father passed away this last November." Her voice thickened with emotion. A sour taste twisted her lips. It was disgraceful, she knew, to feel anger toward the dead, but she could not completely subdue a flickering of just that dreadful emotion whenever her family's financial situation was touched upon. Father had led them all to believe they would be comfortable for life, that money would never be a concern.

His death had proven otherwise. The loss of house and furniture had not concerned her, but that they had been forced to sell all of the horses had cut her to the quick. She had felt somehow betrayed.

Beau Ferd had been reverently silent for a moment. "I am sorry to r-remind you of your father's passing. My own father died r-r-recently." He spoke gingerly, as if the words did not belong in his mouth. "Such a loss tends to turn one's entire life upside down, does it not?"

Nell could not but agree. She tried to smile. "I had it all mapped out in my mind, down what road my life would travel. With Father's death, it is as if all the territories on that map had their boundaries redrawn." She blinked quickly, holding back tears. "The road is strange to me now."

He settled his disconcerting blue eyes on her face but a moment, with an understanding that touched her deep within her wounded heart. Then he smiled his irresistibly contagious smile. "There is adventure in untraveled roads," he said gently.

"Yes," she agreed, smile fading as sadness rose up to meet her again. "And death is perhaps the last and greatest adventure of them all."

There was a salt smell in the air, a thick, nose-biting tang that made Beau think of tears, all along this last leg of their journey. Miss Quinby distanced herself from him as the salt smell thickened. The closer they drew to Brighton, the further she seemed to pull away from him, as if in anticipation of their inevitable separation. Beau knew that their relationship, as it now stood, must soon end, but he had to admit he regarded this young woman, whom he had only met for the first time this morning, as someone he would like to know much better. He wondered if she were inclined to regard him in a similar light. He hoped so.

The fresh team made up for lost time and carried them swiftly from Lewes. West they went, through Falmer, a village of flint, brick, and timber, standing at the head of two valleys, the one leading to Brighton and the other back to Lewes. The breeze picked up as the sea was exposed to their view, and there was a feeling of anticipation that had all of the passengers restless in their seats as they drew ever closer to their final destination. The restlessness affected the horses, who knew this road rather well, and Beau had his hands full managing the team until he pulled them to a final halt in the busy coachyard of the Castle Inn in Brighton.

The yard of the inn, built like all of the houses in Brighton, with its back to the ocean, whirled with a breeze that kicked up dust and tugged at coattails and hat brims with alarming fervor. That the breeze should cause the ladies greater discomfort than the gentlemen became quite clear to Beau when Nell and the other woman who rode the roof of the mail faced the ticklish dilemma of climbing down from their perch. It was clearly difficult to navigate the iron rungs that carried one to the ground without losing modesty to billowing skirts, or having one's bonnet lost to the caprices of the wind.

Beau leapt nimbly down. Nell moved rather more deliberately. Resolutely clutching at her bonnet, she turned her back on the dispersing passengers below as her Aunt Ursula, who stood looking up, called, "Fanella, my dear. Your skirts, love. Do be careful with this naughty wind."

Her remark captured the eyes and attention of every male within hailing distance. The wind was cheekily lifting Miss Quinby's skirts. Her blue cloak was small help in maintaining a demure facade. It allowed her skirts just the freedom required to display the yellow clocking on her white-ribbed stockings for the second time that day.

Nell was aware of her dilemma. Her right hand, which should have remained tightly fixed to the railing that aided in her descent, kept reaching down from the brim of her bonnet to bat at the wayward skirts, and her bonnet turned first this way and then that as she tried to see both where she was going and what the wind did with her attire.

Lord Beauford's attention fixed itself, as did every other man's, on the provocative display. His gaze was irresistibly drawn to the dangling hazard of Nell's petticoat, that only this morning he had freed from the harness of a carriage horse.

She was about to catch her heel! He leapt forward.

As he reached her, arms outstretched, his premonition of imminent danger was fulfilled. Nell caught her heel on the dangling linen. With a cry of surprise, her high-topped white kid shoe flailed in a mad attempt to find purchase, while one gloved hand slid dangerously down the railing.

Beau threw himself against the wind-teased sway of her skirt. His arms wrapped around her most familiarly, reaching for the iron railing, pressing her between the unyielding forward thrust of his chest and the coach. She let loose an abrupt sigh, the very breath knocked from her lungs.

The smell of violets and the thunder of his own agitated heartbeat filled Beau's head as sweetly as Nell filled his arms. There was something loverlike in the brief clasping moment in which he held her fast. She sagged into the curve of his body in her relief, the soft pillowing of her buttocks planted firmly on the hard supporting surface of his chest.

"A-a-are you a-a-all right, Miss Quinby?" he enquired gently, the words thick as porridge. His cheek fit into the sweet curve of her lower back. He closed his eyes a moment, to savor the fact that though she fell it was into his arms. Miss Quinby was firm and warm and stiff with fear beneath the layers of cloth he had wrapped his arms about.

Grasping the calfskin of her boot, he unhooked the errant petticoat and placed her foot firmly on the rung where it belonged. With regret he released her and stood back.

"Are you a-a-all right, now?"

She stood quite motionless, body pressed hard against the side of the coach, breathing heavily. Her knuckles were white against the railing. With a deep, shuddering breath, as if to gather herself together, she said in a very small voice. "Will you be so kind as to assist me, Mr. Ferd? I find myself quite immobilized by fear."

Beauford returned with alacrity to her side. "The torn petticoat is what tripped you up, Miss Quinby. Shall I hold it out of the way?"

"Please do." Her voice sounded so small that Beau wished to take her in his arms and comfort her like a frightened child. He had been convinced she was strong and independent and unshakable. Her vulnerability rattled him. He took up the edge of her skirt and the damaged petticoat in his left hand, while the right reached up to steady the warmth of her waist.

"I've got you."

She moved stiffly, carefully. He kept the torn petticoat out of her way until she had set foot on the ground.

She startled him then by clutching at the lapels of his coat, saying in a voice that knew not whether to laugh or cry, "I have mashed your posy yet again, sir."

She then turned into the arms of her Aunt Ursula, who had been waiting with pent-in breath for her niece to touch ground. As she was led away he heard her say, in a voice that tugged at his heart, "I have never been so terrified of falling, Auntie. It has quite taken my breath away."

"There, there, dear." Ursula soothed, assuming the role that Beau would have loved to have taken, in clasping the young woman to her matronly bosom and patting the sweet curve of her back.

Nell sat unsteadily on a bench outside the door to the inn, her mind a rattled mixture of relief and arousal as her body reminded her in a multitude of ways that it was Mr. Ferd who had saved her from breaks, sprains, and bruises, that it was on Mr. Ferd's broad chest she had seemed almost to sit when he threw himself against her to stop her fall. One instant she had been assailed by the frightening sensation of tumbling to the ground, and in the next she had met with the equally dizzying sensation of being clasped tightly in the stout arms of a young man she had spent the greater part of the day admiring. There had risen within her a strange panic. She had, in one mad moment, thought to fight the very arms that saved her, to push them away, for the warm intimacy of their clasp was almost as big a threat to her equilibrium as the interrupted tumble. She had not been so foolish, of course. Even as she had stiffened against the intimacy of his hold, she had to admit that of all the men who might have stopped her fall, she was heartily glad it was Mr. Ferd.

She shut her eyes and tried to slow her breathing, but there was no hope of success in this endeavor, for no sooner had she done so than a deep voice she could not help but recognize said, "I have taken the liberty of be-speaking a-a-a cup of tea for you, Miss Quinby. Is there a-a-any other way in which I might be of a-a-assistance?"

Something soft brushed against Nell's leg. Her eyes popped open. Bandit had come to offer comfort as well.

"You dear, sweet man," Ursula gushed, fumbling about in her reticule. "You have been the epitome of kindness, and here I have gone off without so much as tipping you."

Nell looked up from Bandit's scarred face with the feeling that she was being watched. Mr. Ferd was staring at her, his pale blue eyes brimming with concern. He smiled at her, and for a moment, as her aunt counted out a crown and sixpence in tip, Nell allowed her gaze to remain locked on his. As the moments ticked past without her withdrawal from such visual contact, a warm vibrance was born in the depths of Mr. Ferd's eyes. The blossoming of that look forced Nell to drop her gaze.

She could not, however, refrain from glancing up again, throughout her aunt's vociferously worded awarding of the generous tip, and the delivery of the cup of tea that had been requested by Mr. Ferd for her enjoyment, to see if he still watched her. Each time the blue eyes locked on hers, with a glow warming their depths that made her heart unruly in its tempo.

"You must, I insist, Mr. Ferd," her aunt was saying, somewhere in the background of her mind, which seemed capable of focusing on nothing outside of a pair of blue eyes. "You must come to my husband if ever you are in need of work, for I should very much like to return the favor of assistance, should you find yourself in need."

It was in response to this remark that Mr. Ferd looked away at last.

"I a-a-am touched by your generosity, madam," he said with a bow. "I shall keep your kind offer in mind." He turned once again to Nell, and it was with a sad sort of dismay that she realized he took leave of her.

"Miss Fanella Quinby. Enjoy your stay in Brighton."

"Mr. Ferd!" Her hand flew out to stay him.

Amusement flickered in the penetrating blue gaze. "Miss Quinby?" His eyebrows rose.

Her hand sank. "I must thank you. You would seem to have rescued my very life twice in this one day."

The light in his eyes, the earnest admiration she could not quite believe herself worthy of, kindled in the pale blue depths again. "My pleasure," he said. "Would that I might do so a-a-again."

She forced herself to smile. "I shall never again hear Beethoven without remembering you, sir."

The slow, sweet, enchanting smile warmed his lips. "Then I must wish your days m-m-music filled, Miss Quinby."

Nell knew there was no staying him a second time, but as he and Bandit left, she could not stop herself from smiling. He was whistling Beethoven's Entrada as he walked away.

Chapter Six

"We must see if we cannot find you a husband while you are here," Ursula announced to Nell the next morning over breakfast, with the self-confident bravado of a woman who is content with her lot and would see all the young women of her extended family in a similarly bliss-filled state.

Nell plucked up the secondhand bonnet she had been given by a kind young coachman whom she could not banish from her thoughts, and said with a roguish grin, "Perhaps we shall find one on the beach today, Auntie."

"Never there!" Ursula exclaimed, taking her niece's jest quite literally to heart.

Nell tied the pink ribbon beneath her chin, and found herself yearning, not for the first time since her arrival in Brighton, for the company of her siblings, either one of whom would have appreciated the humor of her remark. Why, even the coachman who had endowed her with this hat, and he a perfect stranger to her, had immediately caught on to her witticisms. He would most assuredly have blessed her with one of his very contagious smiles had he been listening. Not Aunt Ursula. Nell's aunt was not prone to jestful or satirical speech, and all such expression in her company, no matter how witty, was as wasted as a whisper in a deaf woman's ear. It was disappointing, for now more than ever before in her life, Nell longed for laughter, that she might put aside tearful thoughts, regrets, and recriminations.

"There are no eligible gentlemen to be found on the beach, my dear," Ursula went on. "At this time of year, before the prince and his court have made their appearance, the seaside can boast few gentlemen worthy of interest. It is only decrepit old men who have come to take the salt-water cure who loiter idly about. I do hope you shall not be too bored. There are, of course, some ill-mannered young smarts who sit along the Steine with spyglasses for the purpose of ogling the bathers. They can certainly not be considered suitable companionship."

Nell smiled, and hoping to avoid either of her Aunt Ursula's favorites topics—the salt-water cure and the finding of a husband for Nell—said, "I will enjoy this opportunity to spend time with you, Auntie, in the warmth and peace of the seaside. Should we not find me a husband, I am confident we shall encounter some wealthy old woman in need of a companion."

Ursula sighed as she pulled on her gloves. "Are you on about the idea of working for a living again, my dear? I will not hear it, you know! Tonight we shall go in search of young people at the Assembly held weekly at the Old Ship. There are sure to be one or two young men attending who might interest you."

"I am sure there will be dozens," Nell offered agreeably.

Her aunt gasped. "Dozens, Fanella, really! You must learn to be more discriminating."

Nell laughed and took up her aunt's arm with a reassuring squeeze. "Do not fret. Men whom I find interesting, and men whom I might wish to marry, are not at all one and the same."

Charley Tyrrwhit took the spyglass that nestled beneath his arm and, stretching it full length, tested its powers as he and Beau set out across the Steine toward the beach. Beau knew that of all the things to see and do in Brighton, it was beach gazing that Charley enjoyed the most.

They were not alone in the pursuit. Spyglasses, opera glasses, and monocles reflected the bright light of the sun all along the highest ridge of the beach, like brilliants in a necklet. If asked, the numerous gentlemen (and not so numerous ladies) who participated in the gazing would have professed keen interest in the ships crossing the Channel, but it was in actuality the bathers who drew so much focused attention.

"Well, Beau." Charley sounded distracted as he selected

a large rock to sit upon. "Is masquerading as someone one is not as stimulating as one might imagine?"

"That would depend on one's imagination," Beau replied evasively. Sinking onto another large stone, he closed his eyes, listened to the sounds of the sea, and tried not to think about the aching void in his heart, and the many responsibilities that awaited his attention. The sun baked warm on his nose.

Charley seemed capable of reading minds. "When do you mean to cast off this disguise and return to London?"

"End of the week, I suppose," Beau said languidly. "I have already sent word to my solicitor as to my whereabouts should some emergency arise."

"I do not intend to leave so soon,'" Charley said lazily. "I mean to be here when Priney and the rest of his crew come down. I shall languish here at least a fortnight, drinking, hunting, and examining the wildlife on the beach. Have a look," he laughed. "Those atrociously unbecoming flannel bathing smocks are rather more interesting when wetted."

Beau stretched out his own rented spyglass and focused on the beach just as the door opened on a red bathing box and the stalwart, if water-soaked, dipper who hovered on the stairway helped its occupant down the wet steps. The woman looked as if she were more prepared to tuck into a feather mattress than the sea, clad as she was in her high-necked, long-sleeved bathing wrapper.

Charley inhaled noisily, the sound a sign of his delight, and followed with a low whistle. "Seawater cures all ills. Look there! That flimsy bit of wrapping becomes absolutely diaphanous when wet! Most appealing when the form beneath is worth viewing. It is as if one were privileged to witness a flock of sea nymphs rising up out of the depths."

"Or a school of whales," Beau murmured as he collapsed his spyglass. He was not consumed with delight in watching shivering seabathers embarrass themselves by standing sodden and for all intents and purposes unveiled to their fellow man, in the rolling waves.

Bandit, who had been snoozing at their feet, sat up suddenly, ears pricked. A high-pitched whine slipped from his throat.

Charley, gaze drawn from his spyglass, glanced down at the dog, and then followed the direction of the animal's nose, to see what attracted its fixed attention.

"Jove!" he said mildly, "Is that not your long-limbed horse leaper from Godstone heading down to the water just now?"

Beau brought his spyglass whipping out to full length and pressed it to his eye. There below, picking a path between the nets that had been set to dry along the rocky beach, stepped Fanella Quinby, dressed all in white save for the wide rose-colored sash at her waist, which matched the rose-colored lining on the old-fashioned straw bonnet that he was pleasantly surprised to recognize as the one he had bought her. She was further protected from the harsh rays of the sun today by an attractively frilled white parasol, from whose center post a number of thin rose-colored ribbons fluttered. She was preceded by her aunt.

"Yes, it is she," he concurred, "but you a-a-are in for a disappointment if you think to catch a glimpse of the young lady's charms today."

Charley chuckled suggestively. "No whale there, eh?"

"It is the a-a-aunt who takes the water cure," Beau said with benign certainty.

"Drat! I should not at all mind seeing the wetting of that one. Did you get a chance to chat her up on your way down from Godstone?"

"Miss Quinby is a high-minded young lady, Charley, and while I did not 'chat her up' a-a-as you have so vulgarly put it, we did have occasion to speak. You do her a-a-a disservice to speak so lightly of her person."

Charley laughed again. "Do I? One might almost discern a possessive note in your voice, my friend. Any female foolish or free-spirited enough to display her charms down there in the suds is fair game for every masculine eye trained in her direction." He waved his hand at the crest of the beachhead where sunlight glinted off an array of spyglasses, telescopes, opera glasses, and monocles. "If you did not take advantage, and chat her up, perhaps I shall have to do so myself." He squinted into his glass again and crowed, "Oh, ho! We shall see her wetted yet. It would appear auntie has requested her lovely niece's company."

Beau leaned into his telescope, experiencing a confused mixture of breathless anticipation and alarm.

Ursula Dunn stood poised at the top of the set of steps leading into a bright blue bathing box, a flannel bathing smock clutched in one hand, while with the other hand she desperately motioned for her niece to join her. One could almost make out the individual words in the steady stream of entreaty.

Looking coolly obstinate as she stood shaking her bonneted head and twirling the parasol in her agitation, Nell did not appear inclined to go.

The dipper who manned the bathing box, a stout, sunbrowned woman with tightly fleshed limbs and several layers of dripping cloth twisted about her barrel-like figure, entered into the discussion by offering another of the undistinguished flannel smocks to Nell and wagging both her tongue and her finger, first toward the beach, where a line of people waited for the bathing boxes that had not been booked ahead of time, and then at Ursula Dunn, who stood uncertainly on the bathing-box steps.

"Go on, be a good niece. Go with auntie," Charley encouraged from behind his glass.

Beau frowned at him, but then regretted having removed his attention from his own glass, for Charley let loose a whoop.

"That's the spirit! Have a go!"

By the time Beau refocused on the little tableau, Nell Quinby had collapsed her parasol, accepted the bathing garment, and mounted the steps.

"Ah, what I wouldn't give to be rolling out to sea in that box," Charley breathed, allowing his glass to fall.

"Oh, button it," Beau snapped angrily, his outburst giving rise to both his dog's ears and his best friend's eyebrows.

"I say, that's how the wind blows, does it? I'd no idea you were so taken with her. What happened to you on the drive down, anyway? No need to be close mouthed."

"Nothing happened," Beau said tersely, his gaze locked on the slow progress of the horse-drawn box as it trundled into the foaming surf, but he could hear the unwarranted irritation in his own voice as he said, "I cannot imagine why anyone would willingly immerse themselves in that briny drink without explicit direction from a physician. Not only does one come up smelling of salt and fish, but you can see they've been unloading coal along the pier. The sea is positively black with the stuff in places."

Charley laughed. "Testy, aren't we? And awfully quick to change the subject over this 'nothing' that happened. Have they stopped . . ."—he chuckled and fit glass to eye once again—". . . or do you mind me getting a good gander at the gel?"

"How can I object," Beau said irritably, "when every man-jack along the entire coastline is privy to the scene?"

"You're a brick, old man," Charley said, squinting at the bathing box, which had indeed come to a halt with the surf knee-deep on the horse. "Ah, the door opens," he breathed. "Who shall come first, age or beauty?"

Beau sucked in his breath. Encased in one of the ill-fitting and unflattering smocks, Nell peeped out. Assisted by the dipper, she moved carefully down the wet steps, to sink, gasping at the cold, thigh deep into the water. The dipper indicated that Nell would no longer feel the cold if she would only immerse herself, and she gave a lively and splashy demonstration of how to hold one's breath and nose, the more comfortably to go under.

"There we go." Charley kept up the running repartee. "All the way under, my dear. Ugh, there goes the hair like a dark mass of seaweed. Now, bob on up again, and let us have a look at you."

But Nell, once under, stayed under, at least up to her neck. She seemed to realize that she risked exposure in standing. She splashed about quite contentedly, while her aunt came uncertainly onto the steps, bashfully dipped her toes into a wave, and swiftly jerked them out again.

The dipper seemed unable to coax the older woman into taking to the water, but Nell cajoled and pleaded and playfully splashed water until her aunt agreed to release her grip on the bathing box door and began to come down with the dipper's assistance.

"Help her in, love," Charley crooned, "The old gel might slip without your shoulder to lean on."

As if Charley somehow directed the Fates, Ursula Dunn did come close to slipping, and up shot Miss Quinby out of the water, like a glistening nymph swum up from the depths to lend the gleaming wet support of one thinly clad shoulder to her aunt.

Beau caught his breath. Fanella Quinby was a water-bound sylph, a Venus, a Siren come to life. The outline of her body—breast, waist, and hip—was curvaceous, water-bejewelled perfection against the glittering backdrop of the sea.

"Good God!" Charley breathed. In the same instant that he spoke, a shout was raised from the combined throats of half a dozen officers who lounged along the Steine, also watching her. This accolade was echoed by a little whoop from an old gentleman to their left, who had, open-mouthed, allowed his peering glass to slip out of his eye socket and onto the rocks.

Oblivious to the stir, Charley said, "What an unexpected gem!"

Nell released her aunt and slipped back down into the obscurity of the dark water.

Beau, who had been holding his breath all this time, let it out in a deep, gusty sigh, and lowered his glass with shaking fingers. He knew that body. His hands held the memory of those curves. "A remarkable young woman, Miss Quinby," he said reverently, and there was something heartfelt in his tone that drew his friend's attention.

"Quinby? Not the same Quinby your sister was dragging about London?"

"No," Beau said absentmindedly, feeling dazed. "That was her sister, Aurora, the beauty of the family."

"The beauty! Good God, Beau, she must be something head and shoulders above the ordinary! Perhaps Beatrix is right and you should allow yourself the pleasure of being introduced."

Beau shook his head. "If I'm to further my a-a-acquaintance with any Quinby, 'twill be this one."

"What!" Charley sat up straight in a hurry. "Damn it,

man! What happened on the mail down from Godstone?
You must tell me."

Beau flicked his friend a sideways glance. "I should
think that were obvious, Charley. The coachman became
in-infatuated with one of his passengers."

Nell stepped down out of the bathing box, reclothed, re-
freshed, and reminded of a gentleman who occupied her
thoughts all too frequently of late, as she tied the simple
bonnet over her damply trailing hair. She really must make
an effort to forget Mr. Ferd. Chances were, they would
never cross paths again. And, it was probably best that they
didn't. It would not please her family in the least should she
become infatuated with a common coachman, no matter
that he was not in any way common in her estimation.

It was as she sorted through such thoughts that she spotted Boots, the piebald horse she had spent so much time de-
scribing to Mr. Ferd. Still the mild, wide-shouldered,
broad-backed beast of her memory, with shaggy mane and
shaggier tail, Boots had become bony and thin, a horse so
aged in the space of so little time, that Nell found it difficult to believe that he was indeed the same beast. The far-
rier who had purchased their carthorse had assured her that
her old friend would go to someone with light labor needs.
Nell did not concur with the idea that as sole bearer of a
heavy bathing box, which must be dragged out over the
shale time and again throughout the day, Boots had been
honestly done by.

She did not stop to think that she made a spectacle of
herself. She just ran, in a rather headlong fashion, considering the rocky condition of the beach, calling, "Boots,
Boots, old lad. What have they done to you?"

Behind her, Ursula picked her way more carefully, urg-
ing her, "Slow down Fanella, or you shall most certainly
break your neck."

His brown eye milky with cataracts, Boots could not see
Fanella well, but he recognized her voice and veered away
from the straight path he had been picking into the shore.
His waywardness earned him an oath and a crack of the
whip across his haunches.

"Do not whip him on my account," Nell cried.

The driver did not argue, only sat open mouthed as Nell flung her arms around his horse's neck, as the old nag came to a decisive stop some ten yards shy of where he was supposed to. The driver may have been unable to think of anything to say or do, but this was not so for the dipper, come down from her perch on the steps. "What's the meaning of this?" she demanded, and as she could clearly see for herself why the horse had stopped, she strode up to Fanella just as Ursula Dunn huffed onto the scene.

"Leave off, girlie," the dipper said stoutly to Nell, her muscular hands planted on swaddled hips. "The nag's yet to drag the wagon a ways, and I've customers waiting."

"Oh my, yes, what is the meaning of this, Fanella?" Ursula croaked.

Nell looked up at the dipper so fiercely that the woman fell back a step. "Only look at this poor animal's hooves," she insisted. "They are horribly split. He cannot see well enough to navigate these rocks."

"Hazard of the business, missy," the dipper insisted. "And the business is none of yours."

"But he was once our horse," Nell said, tears springing to her eyes as she stroked the tangled forelock. "And a grand brute he was. What do you feed him to make his ribs show so?"

Ursula caught hold of Nell's arm. "Come away, my dear. He's no longer yours to worry over."

The woman who had occupied the bathing box, a great, frazzle-haired thing with a pasty complexion gone red from too much exposure to the sun, came mincing around from the end of the wagon. "Why are we stopped? Do you mean me to walk the rest of the way across these bruising stones?"

The dipper continued to glare at Nell. "We'll be delivering you the rest of the route, madame, if you will just nip back into the box. We've had a short delay because this young lady once knew our horse, but she'll be stepping out of the way now, won't you, dearie?"

"Oh, yes," Ursula agreed. "We're just going, aren't we Fanella?" She plucked at Nell's sleeve.

Nell ignored her. "Will you sell the horse?" she asked desperately.

The dipper, annoyed by the interruption in her trade, frowned, obviously unmoved by the suggestion. There was an obstinate tilt to her chin that seemed to indicate her unwillingness to so much as discuss the possibility, but the driver found his tongue at last.

"How much will you gi' for 'im?"

Nell's mind raced. She had only her pin money to call her own, and not much of that. Anger, guilt and a sense of powerlessness assailed Nell. The anger was directed toward her father, the guilt rose from the ineffectual strength of that anger. She could not dismiss the feeling that there must be some means within her grasp to rectify this dreadful situation.

"Fanella, I forbid you to buy the horse back," Ursula said firmly, her lips compressed. "Your mother sold off the horses because she has not the money to feed the brutes, and I defy you to saddle me with a nag such as this one when you know how particular your uncle is concerning his cattle. Let this discussion end right here, love. Give the old fellow a pat on the nose and let us be off."

Never before had Nell so keenly felt the change in her fortune. Tears welled up in her eyes, but she did as he aunt bade, for she saw no other option open to her. The tears spilled over when Boots, his bleary eyes following her, refused for a moment to go on up the beach, despite two flicks of the whip. He just stood there, his dear old head turned in her direction. Nell, her heart broken, fell against her aunt's shoulders sobbing, "Dear Auntie Ursula, do but lend me a bit of money so that I might make life right again for my old friend."

Ursula was not an unfeeling woman. Her own eyes swam to see Nell carry on so over the broken-down old animal, but she did not relent. Gently she led Nell through the curious crowd along the Steine, crooning whatever soothing words she could think of and looking about for their carriage, for the jobbed-out coachman had promised to meet them there.

It was as they walked along thus that, with a tumult of barking, a black and white dog jumped down off the walkway above the beach and bounded toward them, his tail a white flag above his back.

"Oh, my!" Ursula cried, freezing in place, as if terrified that they were in danger of being attacked.

Nell sank down to meet the advance of the dog, crying joyfully through her tears, "Bandit! Is it you? I would have thought you halfway down the London-to-Brighton road right now." As the gleeful animal wriggled in ecstatic contentment under her petting, she lifted her tear-stained face to look whence the dog had flown. Tear-blurred eyes locked for a moment on pale blue, as if drawn by a magnet. He was here! What did it mean? Surely a coachman should be off driving his coach. Nell was embarrassed that of all men, this one should stand staring at her in this painfully unhappy moment. She knew she looked a dreadful sight, with tears in her eyes and her hair all wet and bedraggled and falling out from beneath the silly secondhand hat he had given her.

Weakly, she fluttered her limp handkerchief in subdued acknowledgement of having recognized Mr. Ferd. Then, sure that her swollen face and tear-reddened eyes were not a proper greeting for an acquaintance, she ducked her head down, and, giving Bandit one last heartfelt rub, raised her parasol like a shield and obediently followed her aunt to the waiting carriage. She had only one backward glance, and that one for Boots as he made his laborious way out to sea with yet another bather loaded in his box.

Beauford frowned as the carriage Miss Quinby occupied took off at a smart pace, drawn by an attractive pair of mismatched horses that drew Charley Tyrrwhit's eyes like a magnet. Bandit came, tongue lolling and tail wagging, back to them.

"What was that all about?" Charley wondered.

"Boots," Beau said thoughtfully as he squinted out at the bathing box drawn by the most pitiful nag on the beach.

"Boots? But it was the horse she was making a fuss over, not her feet."

"Where has Gates gotten himself off to?" Beau wondered, looking about.

Gates, who made an unobtrusive point of remaining within earshot, trotted up with an anxious expression. "Yes, your grace? May I be of some service?"

Beau took out his purse. "I should like you to see about buying a horse for me."

Charley's gaze still followed the carriage that contained Miss Quinby. "The gray? You saw him too, then, did you? Excellent conformation. I was just thinking to myself that he might be just what Barrymore is looking for. Looks right at fifteen and a half hands, does he not?"

Beau, his brow knitting with confusion as to what on earth his friend was rattling on about, concentrated his pale gaze first on Gates's eager countenance and then on the red bathing box drawn by one sad old piebald.

"I should like you to e-e-enquire a-a-after that piebald down there. Do you see him?"

As Charley whirled, open-mouthed, to regard him, Gates looked curiously at the horse, and then, blinking in disbelief, back at his master.

"The old nag, sir? The one pulling the red box?" he enquired carefully.

"Yes, Gates. The very one." Beau nodded, regarding the confused man with a trace of amusement. He knew he had a reputation for bang-up goers, barrel-chested gingers with sound wind and good legs. This poor creature did not at all fall into the realm of what Gates thought might catch his master's eye. "If the animal has one blue eye and one brown, and a blaze like a splash of milk spilling down one side of his nose, then you must buy him for me. Take this." He held out a handful of coins. "I trust you will strike a hard bargain."

Gates, forehead wrinkled, took the coins and tucked them carefully away in an inside pocket of his coat. "I'll do my best, sir. And where would you have me sending the animal once he's yours, your grace?"

Charley leaned forward to hear the answer, curiosity written plain on his face.

Beau narrowed his eyes, for until that instant he had given the matter little thought, other than that he would like to somehow alleviate the suffering he had witnessed in Miss Quinby's troubled expression. He himself had absolutely no use for such creature. His eyes widened as an idea came to him.

"Arrange to have him transported, in easy stages, to my

sister A-A-Anne's establishment, will you? Her children are of a-a-an age to begin climbing about on just such a docile beast. I shall compose a letter to a-a-accompany the horse."

Gates blinked again, for he would have thought a nice fat pony more to his master's—and surely more to Lady El-liott's—liking. But it was not his job to question, so he merely touched his cap and trotted off on his errand.

Charley Tyrrwhit had no such compunction against questioning his friend's mad behavior. "Are you gone all about in the head, Beau?" he insisted.

"Not a-a-at all," Beau said with a smile. "It is merely that I care for . . ."—he paused, unwilling to expose, so soon, his feelings—". . . horses. That old fellow is of an age to be knee-deep in clover, switching flies beneath an a-a-apple tree, don't you think?"

"I think you've gone soft in the head. Do you mean to empty every knacker's yard in all of Great Britain's empire into your sister's back paddock? Lord Elliot may object."

Beau grinned, for Anne and Edward were sure to be popeyed with amazement when the horse arrived on their doorstep. "Just this one old nag, Charley. Indulge me in this, won't you? I think Anne will."

Charley smiled sardonically. "You really must tell me more about the trip down from Godstone, old chap."

Beau smiled enigmatically. "You were saying something about a gray for Barrymore?"

Chapter Seven

The gray, it was decided, bore looking into.

That very afternoon, Beau and Charley set about discovering just where it was that Mrs. Ursula Dunn resided in Brighton. This was not a difficult undertaking, for any person one needed to locate was easily found by going directly to Donaldson's circulating library, where a registry of visitors and their addresses was kept quite meticulously up to date for the master of ceremonies, Mr. Wade, who presided over all the entertainments that were arranged. One did not receive invitations to said arrangements if one were not listed in the registry.

The very next morning, the two gentlemen, with Bandit at heel, hunted up the address. The door was opened to them by none other than Miss Fanella Quinby. She looked a trifle wan. Her mouth carried with it a sadness that touched the ache in his own heart, but her eyes lit up with astonishment and pleasure at seeing who knocked.

"Good day to you, Miss Quinby," Beau said. "I a-am happy to see you in better spirits than yesterday."

She blushed, the hint of sadness still tugging her lower lip. "Thank you."

She was dressed to go out. The rose ribbons on the old-fashioned bonnet Beau had given her were tied saucily to one side of her chin, and a trio of fresh pinks had been thrust through the band that wrapped its crown. Beau was oddly pleased that she seemed to take such delight in wearing the thing. It never occurred to him that her straitened circumstances might preclude the purchase of a new bonnet.

His sister Beatrix, had she been there, could have guessed as much. She would have pronounced Miss

Quinby's entire outfit hopelessly behind the times. Even Charley later remarked that her rig was not quite up to snuff, but Beau noticed only that she had carefully chosen from her wardrobe an entire outfit in colors that would suit the secondhand bonnet. Her simple, full-front, square-necked muslin chemise boasted no ruffles or flounces, and bore none of the deep Egyptian-style borders that were become so popular in London this season. But it had a pretty band of gathered muslin at neck and hem, and the material was fine enough to be worn with great effect over a slip the color of crushed strawberries. The sash, high on her waist, brought attention to the bonnet on her head, for it was of straw-colored velour. The overall effect was quite flattering to Miss Quinby's dark hair and eyes, and while few would be foolish enough to think a fashionable modiste dressed the young lady, most would agree she had exceptional taste and could update an old gown with panache.

Beau's heart warmed at the sight of her, for when her dark brown eyes met his, a charming flush of pink washed into the young lady's cheeks, in the exact same shade as the lining of her hat. She seemed less sad as a result of their arrival. For the briefest of moments he considered telling her what had become of Boots.

"Is that the coachman, come at last?" Ursula Dunn demanded tartly from somewhere beyond the door before Miss Quinby could so much as say Hello. "Whatever kept him?"

Charley looked at Beau, one eyebrow archly raised.

Fanella chuckled, the trace of melancholy vanishing from her demeanor. "It is a coachman, Auntie, but not the one we were expecting."

"Whatever do you mean?" Ursula poked her lace-capped head around the door.

Beau and Charley tipped their hats in unison.

Dismayed, Ursula let the smile chase away her frown. "Why, hallo! Are you in need of a position so soon, Mr. Ferd?"

"Mr. Ferd?" Charley mouthed in surprise.

"I do hope you will say yes," Ursula rattled on, oblivious to the exchange, "for while my husband has sent down my own vehicle and horses, we are jobbing out drivers, and a thoroughly unsatisfactory arrangement it has proved to be. This is the third time in as many days that we have been kept waiting."

"Won't you come in, gentlemen?" Fanella asked, standing back from the door.

Beau directed a warning look at Charley, but his friend seemed to know exactly what was required of him, for he said with mocking politeness. "Mr. Ferd," and indicated that Beau should enter before him.

"Come," said Nell as she led the way. "It will be best if we adjourn to the front sitting room so that we might watch for the arrival of our real coachman." She pronounced the word "real" with unnecessary emphasis and directed an amused if rather searching look at Beau.

"But, Fanella, do you mean to insult Mr. Ferd?" Ursula objected as she directed the gentlemen where to sit. "Is he in some fashion unreal?"

Miss Quinby flushed a darker shade of rose at this mild set-down. There was a trace of obstinacy in the set of her jaw. Her eyes sparkled mischievously. "I believe Mr. Ferd does but masquerade at being a coachman, Auntie." She directed a piercing look at Beau.

"Tut, tut, my dear," Ursula twittered. "Would you call the man a liar?"

His eyes locked on Nell's, Beau was struck by the realization that to call him liar would be no more than fair. In that fleeting instant, while Ursula Dunn's words hung in the air, waiting an answer, the new Duke of Heste was tempted to tell all. He was lying to these people, representing himself to them as something he most certainly was not. Fanella Quinby was clever to have realized as much. It was not fair, or right, or honorable in him to continue his deception, and Brampton Beauford prided himself in living a fair, right, and honorable life. And yet, in pausing to contemplate his inevitable return to the weighty responsibilities that were now his and his alone, and the prospect of Beatrix's matchmaking ways, in which Aurora Quinby was only one of a long parade of potential partners, his honor wavered. The truth, in this instant, would bring certain change in his budding relationship with Fanella Quinby. He would spend the rest of his life wondering "*What if?*" What if it were possible to win this clever and kind young woman's love and respect without her knowledge of his wealth or title? What if he told her the truth in this moment and alienated her forever? Surely the knowledge he stood to gain in his deception was worth this harmless stretching of the truth.

He chose to remain silent. He chose to perpetuate his little white lie.

Charley came to his rescue, deflecting Nell's challenge to his honor. "Our Beau's the real MacKay when it comes to coaching, Miss Quinby," he said with unblinking nonchalance. "There are only one or two I can think of who handle the ribbons better, and Beau has a most discerning eye for horseflesh. Which is why we bother you today. We could not help but observe the splendid pair of horses that your hired coachman drove up to the beach yesterday."

That was all it took. The moment of truth was past.

"My horses?" Ursula Dunn preened. "I am very flattered that you should notice them at all, for I am sadly conscious of the fact they do not match in color. But my husband was quite pleased with their purchase when he presented them to me for my last birthday, and he assured me they were prime creatures."

"Your husband is an excellent judge of horseflesh, Mrs. Dunn. Do you think I might convince you to part with one of the two, madame? It is the gray that interests me."

"Oh!" Ursula's eyes took on an inordinately startled look. "Such a thought had never occurred to me."

"I would appreciate your giving the matter serious consideration," Charley pressed. "I have a friend who drives only grays, you see, and he is most particularly desirous of obtaining one more animal to complete a set of four that might be considered mirror images of your own creature. Should the animal satisfy his tastes as much as I think it might, he would reward you well for the trouble it may cause, in searching for a mate to your bay."

"Oh, my!" Ursula faltered, her hand flying to her throat. She cast a drowning look at her niece. "What do you think, Fanella? You know far more about horses than I."

"I think we should write a letter to Uncle Bartholomew explaining that there has been a generous offer for the gray that he was clever enough to find for you, that entails the finding of a perfect match for the bay." She looked consideringly at Charley. "Perhaps we might tell him that two very knowledgeable gentlemen have offered to search out a match for you."

Her statement would appear to contain a question.

Charley nodded acquiescence.

Nell allowed herself a small, pleased nod in return. "We shall thus see if Uncle Bartholomew's feelings will be hurt too much by such a transaction. His reply should come back to us before the end of the week."

Ursula's head bobbed. "Oh, wouldn't that be lovely? I would like to have a matched pair."

Charley's lips twitched. "That's settled, then." He stood up to take his leave. "You have been most kind in receiving us."

Miss Quinby stood as well. "It is good-bye then, until we have further word on the gray or the bay. Unless, of course, we manage to convince Mr. Ferd to stay on as our 'real' coachman." She directed another challenging glance at Beau.

"Small chance of that," Charley said with a chuckle. "Mr. . . ah, Ferd has a full plate awaiting his attention back in London, haven't you, Mr. Ferd?"

Miss Quinby's knowing eyes spoke of disappointment. Not surprise—she did not seem at all surprised to discover he was on the verge of departing. But there was undeniably disappointment in her demeanor.

Beau realized as he looked at her that he could not return to his duties as duke until he had an answer to the great *what if* with regard to Nell Quinby. "How long would you require this coachman?" he found himself asking, before it sank into his mind that he was inclined to take the position. He must have his answer. Could this young woman truly care for him without knowing who he was or how much he was now worth?

"How long?" she repeated.

Charley was gawking at him in amazement.

"Yes, how long? You see, if you are willing to a-a-accept temporary help, I should be happy to serve a-a-as coachman for the few weeks remaining before the Season starts."

"You would?" Nell and Charley asked simultaneously. In the same instant they did so, the front door knocker thundered insistently.

"What in heaven's name . . ." Ursula started up from her chair.

Outside, Bandit began to bark.

Nell ran to the window. "Oh, my! It is the hired coachman, who appears to dislike dogs."

"However can you know such a thing, Fanella?" Ursula asked.

Nell laughed. "There is no mistaking his opinion in the matter. He is scaling the wall to the back garden in order to avoid Bandit."

"Oh, dear," Ursula exclaimed. "Something must be done! He will damage the espalliered pear trees."

Charley managed to keep a straight face. "Come, Beau, we must rescue the pears."

"Oh, yes, please do," Ursula agreed. "And if you are entirely serious about this offer of being our temporary coachman, Mr. Ferd, you may tell the gentleman on the wall that his services are no longer required."

As Beau closed the door to the sitting room behind them, Charley sank against the paneling, shaken by irrepressible amusement. Between stifled snorts, he demanded, "What the devil are you about, Beau? You cannot be serious about becoming private coachman to this woman."

"Oh, but I am."

Charley's humor subsided. "Is this a lark, or are you smitten with the girl, that you have become so foolish?"

"Completely and irrevocably smitten." Beau hooked an arm through Charley's that they might proceed to the door. "Can you blame me? For the first time in my life, I have e-e-encountered a young woman who is drawn to me, Charley, despite my stammering, without reference to money or title. Is it not wonderful?"

Charley shook him off. "She is drawn to you out of curiosity. She knows you are more than a mere coachman, and must solve the puzzle. It's no more than that."

Beau frowned. "Think you so?"

"Of course. Women love a mystery. Why not simply trot

on up to the gel and tell her she has solved it? It can only work to your advantage that you are a wealthy and titled nobleman, rather than a penniless coachman."

Beau opened the front door. "What shall I tell her? That I a-a-am a lying scamp masquerading a-a-as a coachman, who now wishes to call on her?"

Charley waved his hands airily. "Tell her that she is very clever to have found you out. Women understand a young man's larks. Just see if she don't."

Beau frowned in the sudden sunlight. " 'Twould change things."

"Change! Why of course 'twould change things. For the better, I'll be bound."

Beau's frown deepened. He headed for a section of the garden wall at the base of which Bandit sat chewing on a shoe. "I am not so sure, Chaz. You forget Miss Quinby's sister, Au-Au-Au—"

"Aurora. The snubbed beauty! I do not forget." Charley chuckled as the implications hit him. Beau could not tell if it was his predicament, or the pair of feet dangling over the wall, one shoe on, one shoe off, that so amused his friend until he said wryly. "Sisters fighting over you. Tsk, tsk. Your own included. You have set foot in a mare's nest."

It was after Charley had departed, with Beau's instruction to enlist Gates's services in the search for a bay to replace the gray, that Nell was asked by her aunt if she would mind showing Mr. Ferd the way to the mews, where the horses were kept and the curricle housed.

Nell did so readily enough, but as she led Beau into the garden her eyes settled on him time and again. Was there something crucial she had missed in regarding him? She had been so certain that this man was merely playing a part that it unsettled her confidence in her own judgement to discover herself completely off the mark.

"Have I smut on my forehead, Miss Quinby?"

"What?" She started. He was scrutinizing her with those compelling blue eyes as intently as she had been scrutinizing him. It was most disconcerting. "Was I staring?"

He nodded. "Yes. And while I have no objection to your looking at me a-a-as often a-a-as you should care to, you disturb me a-a-a little at this moment, for you seem to regard me with suspicion."

She stopped at the gate that led out of the garden to the mews, and turning her back against it, allowed her feelings to vent themselves. "I do regard you with suspicion, Mr. Ferd."

The fine golden brown eyebrows rose. "How so?"

She frowned. "Because, sir, no sooner do I think that I have figured out the source of your eccentricities than you go and upset my reasoning."

"However have I managed to do so much, a-a-all unknowing?"

She had a sudden desire to avoid answering him. Opening the gate, she suggested he follow her into the mews.

He followed, the silence between them thick, as he waited for an answer. Nell introduced him to Toby the groom, who sauntered by, grain bucket in hand.

Toby said he would be thrilled to lead Beau about and explain the arrangement of things, as Miss Quinby requested. "I'll be no more'n an oiyblink," he assured them, ruffling the thick hair on Bandit's chest. "Just as soon as I gets Highjinx water bucket filled, I'll show you about." When he left them alone again, Bandit followed at his heels.

Before Nell could saunter off as well, as she was very much inclined to do, Beau reminded her, "You were in the midst of explaining to me my way of 'upsetting your reasoning', as I recall, Miss Quinby."

She sighed. She would not get away without telling him. "I must admit, I am quite amazed that you have agreed to drive my aunt and myself about town, Mr. Ferd, if only for a fortnight. You see, I had decided that you were not a coachman at all, but rather a well-heeled young nobleman who pays for the pleasure of instruction from a professional boxman."

The pale blue eyes regarded her with interest. "I see. And the ec-eccentricities you mentioned?" he asked softly, "What might those en-en-entail?"

Nell smiled ruefully. This was terribly embarrassing. He would think her a snob. "Nothing obvious or offensive, I assure you, but first, there is your speech . . ."

He frowned.

She recognized his frown for what it was. He thought she meant to criticize his stutter. How had she gotten herself into this tangle? She rushed on. "Your vernacular and vocabulary do not ring true to what I am accustomed to hearing out of the stables."

He smiled one of his slow, captivating smiles. "What else?"

Encouraged, she ticked the items off her fingers. "Your friendship with Mr. Tyrrwhit is unexpected, the quality of your gloves and posy holder seem to be beyond the means of a coachman, as would your knowledge of the peerage and your appreciation of Beethoven." It still made sense to her that he was no ordinary coachman.

One of his eyebrows twitched. "But it would seen I have somehow m-m-managed to convince you that I am not a gentleman after a-all, despite so much compelling evidence to the contrary?"

Nell dimpled. She was glad he did not seem to have taken offense. "Yes, you have Mr. Ferd, for while a gentleman might disguise himself to ride the mail, I cannot think of any reason why he would continue such a deception in accepting the position of private coachman to my Aunt Ursula."

The enchanting curve of his lips increased. The blue eyes held as much amusement as his smile. "Not even one?" he pressed, pale blue eyes probing hers with such purpose that she began to think he meant to imply that she was involved in his decision.

Nell's eyes widened under the appreciative onslaught of his gaze, and then doubt as swiftly narrowed them. This young man, duke or dustman, coachman or king, was teasing her, and she must put an end to the liberty he took in looking at her in such a disconcerting manner. Her lips parted to speak and yet she could not seem to articulate the thoughts that passed through her head. Did she really want him to cease looking at her so?

"Cannot a coachman possess friends, Miss Quinby, and fine gloves, a-a-and an a-a-appreciation for music?"

Nell flinched, pained that he did indeed judge her a snob. "Of course. That and more, I'm sure. I do apologize for attempting to pigeonhole you. It was wrong in me. I'll leave you to Toby now." She nodded formally. The man was an engima, a cypher, a contradiction to all the rules that seemed to govern the separation of the classes. And as her own class was now in question, she found the smoky boundaries of his manners, mores, and interests eminently intriguing. "I hope you will be content with only two horses to drive. It will seem rather tame, I'm sure, after having four at hand."

"Not a-a-at all, Miss Quinby."

"Mr. Ferd?"

Again the slow smile transformed his features. "Yes, miss?"

She felt awkward in asking him to perform as ordinary coachman, having just explained her conviction that he was anything but an ordinary coachman. "I realize that this is short notice, but do you think the horses might be ready and brought round within a half hour's time? My aunt did most particularly wish to purchase a fan before this evening's Assembly."

Politely—almost regally—he bowed his head. "Yes, miss. As you say, in a half hour's time."

With one last searching look, for doubts still riddled Nell's confidence in his veracity, she nodded and left him.

Chapter Eight

Toby's tour revealed a small but neat stable that did but lack a certain level of spit and polish to satisfy the duke's discerning eye. It began in the tackroom and ended at the top of the steep, narrow flight of stairs that led to the room Beau was to call his own.

"This 'un's yours," the groom said as proudly as if he presented the wonders of the palace at Versailles. He opened the door. "It's a wee bit larger than me own flop, down at the end."

The room smelled as richly of hay and horses and leather as the stalls below. It was deep but not very wide, big enough to hold no more than a narrow cot, a washstand with plain pitcher and bowl, and a crate that served as both cupboard and chair. There was a shelf above the bed with a lamp perched on it, and three pegs behind the door for the hanging of clothes.

"Nice, aye? It's had a fresh coat of paint no more than a year ago." Toby cheerfully slapped the backside of the door.

Beau was touched. That so little could so well please was something foreign to him. Struck by how fortunate he was to have been born with a silver spoon in his mouth, he scrutinized his narrow domain. The linens might have been fresh at about the same time as the paint. He tested the bed. The ticking was sadly flat. Odd how one never really appreciated what one had until it was no longer available. Beau had never appreciated his father so much as in the months following his death. What would the old man have had to say about this cork-brained escapade his heir involved himself in? If history ran true, his father had kicked his own heels fairly high in the days of his youth.

Beauford crossed to the window. The dusty, fly-blown pane looked out over the back garden. Miss Quinby had stopped to pick some flowers there. The sight of her made his pulse quicken. She looked like a watercolor come to life, distorted as she was by the wavery unwashed glass. Like a watercolor, there was something elusive and unattainable in the image of her. The glass, like his willfully lowered station, separated them. He could see, but he could not touch. He shook such defeatist thoughts aside.

"The room will do quite nicely, I think," he said.

Beau returned to the promise of his window that evening as the sun went down. The day had turned out to be a bit of a disappointment. He had been unable to exchange a single word with Miss Quinby since morning. To be sure, the ladies had been taken on the fan-fetching expedition, but Ursula Dunn made it quite clear that her coachman was expected to sit in his box and hold his tongue. She could not abide servants who chattered. Frustrated, Beau had returned to an afternoon of hot, sweaty stable work. He knew he would see Nell when he took the ladies to the Assembly that evening at the Old Ship, but the limitations of his position as coachman were beginning to sink in. How did one woo a woman when one could not so much as exchange a word with her? And how did one go about it smelling of horses and hay? Well, there was no point in wasting time bemoaning what he had no control over. There was bound to be some aspect of the situation he could effect.

It was as he stood, sleeves rolled back for a quick sponge bath at the washstand by his dirt-clouded window, that Beau noticed the view he was allowed of the upstairs chambers in the main house once the night lamps were lit. He could see dimly, despite dirt on the one set of windows and lace curtaining on the other, directly into the room where Miss Quinby readied herself for the evening's festivities. Such a sight gave him pause, and he stood, mouth agape, the sponge dripping in his hands, trying to make out what little he could through a layer of grime. He used his sponge to clear a spot in the dirt, only to discover that most of it was accumulated on the outside surface of the pane.

Eager to avail himself of the best possible view, and

frustrated thus far in accomplishing that goal, he undid the latch on the window frame with wet hands, only to find that the window did not budge, for when it had been painted fresh the previous year it had been painted shut.

With a sigh that fogged the pane to an even dimmer state, he peered at the muzzy silhouette that moved about in the room across from his, content enough to know that it was she, and that she was near, and that he had the privilege of perhaps exchanging a word or two with her again this evening.

It was only as her light was extinguished that he remembered that he was now her coachman, and that as such, he must not keep her waiting, for the ladies had been most specific about the time the carriage was to be brought around to the door. He made himself presentable with a speed that would have left his valet gasping, for Lord Beauford had always been meticulously careful in the rendering of his toilet. Not so this evening. The duke threw himself together with more dash than splash, set his weather-worn coachman's hat upon his head, and flew down the steps to find that Toby held the horses ready.

Beau regretted his slapdash appearance when he drew the carriage around to the front of the house. Both of the ladies came down the steps looking elegant in their evening finery. Unaccustomed to wearing the same secondhand shirt and coat two days running, Lord Beauford felt diminished before their eyes. It surprised him that the cloth one carried on one's back could affect one's self-esteem so profoundly.

As if she read his mind, Ursula Dunn settled into her seat with a slightly jaundiced eye directed at her coachman's borrowed attire. "We must see you fitted for a suit of livery, Mr. Ferd. I am quite prejudicially opposed to the color of your waistcoat!"

Beauford, himself quite fatigued with the faded robin redbreast effect of his borrowed garb, yet felt his pride had been dealt a tremendous blow. With bowed head he agreed. "As you wish, madame."

"What do you think, Nell?" Ursula ground home the point.

Nell seemed withdrawn this evening. She met Beau's eyes with a distant look that could not but remind him of his position, and then fixed her attention on his waistcoat. "I think you are quite right, Auntie. Mr. Ferd will look much more handsome in some other color."

In that moment, Beau felt that he had set himself an impossible task. How might he now induce this lovely, mournful creature to consider him in any way other than as a pair of hands hired to do as they were bid? This feeling was not to be dispelled by an evening in which Miss Quinby participated in an assemblage of her peers while he stood outside and held the horses.

However, there was a singular incident that occurred on their way to the Old Ship that renewed hope and shored up his resolve. As he tooled the carriage onto the main street, a frenzied barking followed them.

"Bandit!" Nell exclaimed. "Mr. Ferd, I think you had best slow down so that we might take up your dog."

Ursula Dunn was not so tolerant. "We shall do no such thing. I think you had best lock the creature up when we intend to go out, Mr. Ferd. We cannot have him chasing after us everywhere we would go. It is not at all attractive."

"Yes, madame," Beau said obligingly, knowing how much Bandit would object to such a scheme.

"We should pretend Bandit is our carriage mascot," Nell said cheerfully. "Aurora has written me that they are all the rage in London this Season. Lady Aston has a fawn and white pug that goes everywhere with her."

"Does she really?" Ursula enquired, much impressed.

"Yes, and Lord Whitcomb is not to be seen without his bull terrier, nor the Viscount of Falmount without his French poodle."

"All right, all right, Fanella. You may take the dog up this one time. I know how dotty you are about animals."

Nell chuckled and opened up the carriage door. "Jump, Bandit," she called.

To Beau's surprise, Bandit obediently did as she ordered, and settled himself happily at her feet.

Beauford was watching Ursula Dunn's horses, playing fetch with his dog, and wondering what it might be like to dance with Nell Quinby, when Charley Tyrrwhit arrived at the Old Ship. Beauford's attention was not wholly focused on his play with Bandit. He kept glancing up at the windows of the inn, where some evidence of the gathered assemblage of local gentry was to be witnessed in the form of music and laughter and figures moving against the light.

"There are definite advantages to being a duke and not a coachman, are there not?" Charley asked softly. His question startled Beau, who had been too lost in thought to notice his approach.

"I a-a-am feeling rather an outsider," he admitted, and he waved the fetching stick at a small group of local boxmen and footmen who had gathered together by one of the waiting carriages for a smoke and a chat. They threw sidelong glances at him even as he spoke. "A-a-as things stand I belong to neither group."

"Well, I will not waste pity on you," Charley said. "There is absolutely no good reason for this preposterous charade."

"Perhaps," Beau said thoughtfully, unhappily reminded of the responsibilities he shirked in remaining here. "But I m-mean to see it through. There is some comfort to be derived in knowing that my station is but temporary. Comfort, too, in the knowledge that I shall never again lightly a-accept the services of my own servants. Their life is so very different than ours, Chaz!"

Charley laughed. "Oh, ho! Developing a social conscience, are you?" His expression went serious. "Do you know I have never heard you sound more like a duke than you did just now?"

A slow, sad smile transformed Beau's face. He knew he was not in the least like his father. It was one of the reasons he was so reluctant to assume his position as the seventh Duke of Heste. He tried to make light of the moment. "It is the hat talking." He ran his finger along its brim.

"A hat you may take off at any time," Charley reminded him. " 'Tis my opinion that you have set yourself an impossible and nonsensical task in winning a lady's heart without all of the persuasions available to you. I wager you a pony you cannot do it this way." He tapped the amber knob of his walking stick against the scarlet waistcoat that Mrs.

Dunn had only too recently avowed she could not bear. "And I do not mean a broken-down nag of a pony, either."

Beau nodded ruefully, as again his gaze strayed to the glowing windows above their heads. "I will not a-a-accept your wager. 'Tis all too likely you should win. I would a-appreciate your locating Gates for me. I require a valise to be packed with several of my plainest shirts, as well as fresh undergarments, tooth powder, a-a-and the like. He will know what is needed."

Charley sighed. "I suppose this means I have not convinced you to give up this foolishness?"

Beau shook his head. "No, for while I have begun to wonder if I shall be wasting too much time on the wrong side of windows, merely watching the life I mean to take part in, I a-a-am not ready to a-abandon my role as of yet. There is something far too exhilarating and liberating about my masquerade. I shall play out the charade a little longer."

Charley chuckled. "I leave you to it. No sense in arguing points with a thickhead who prefers the company of a mongrel to that of his peers."

"Ah, Fanella! There is a gentleman with whom you are familiar." Aunt Ursula crowed. She had consumed more than one glass of punch, and Nell noticed that her aunt's spirits seemed to rise in direct ratio to the amount of spirits she consumed. "It is Mr. Tyrrwhit just come in the door. It would do you well to befriend that fellow, you know, for he is very well connected."

Nell, who took almost as little joy in her first evening's entertainment as did her coachman downstairs, regarded the newcomer with interest. If anyone here might carry on a conversation that would interest her, perhaps it was this man.

Not that Nell did not enjoy the company in which she had immersed herself. The collection of local gentry, with its sprinkling of nobility, was nothing if not polite. Neither did she lack for partners, either for the country dances, the fetching of refreshment, or the sharing of light conversation. To the contrary, as one of the prettiest young women in the hall, Fanella was much sought after for the dances and her head fairly reeled with the new names and faces she must remember, as her aunt introduced her to one after another of her acquaintances. And yet Nell was too preoccupied with thoughts of the mysterious and contradictory Mr. Ferd, who she had fruitlessly vowed to henceforth ignore, for any in the assembled company to make an indelible impression.

Perhaps, like a child, she yearned for what was denied her. Perhaps she was drawn to the forbidden as Eve was to the apple, for certainly a coachman was a gentleman of inappropriate background and occupation for someone such as herself. She burned with guilt over the all-encompassing fascination that Beau Ferd's presence provoked within every fiber of her being. Such feelings were not at all proper, acceptable, desirable, or commendable in her, just because her family had fallen on bad times—perhaps especially for that reason. And yet, he, above all others, seemed to understand her, and the warring emotions she suffered at this point in her life, better than anyone else. She read empathy and compassion in his eyes. It was a beautiful thing.

Nell felt that her interest in—indeed her conduct thus far with—Mr. Ferd would have been quite unobjectionable, even somewhat amusing, had he proved, as she had been convinced, a nobleman simply masquerading as a coachman. But now, with his own straight-faced insistence that he was a coachman and nothing more, Nell felt consumed with two warring emotions—guilt for overstepping the bounds of polite society in striking up such a friendship and fascination in the pull of forbidden fruit.

The enigmatic riddle that Mr. Ferd posed for both her heart and her brain rudely intruded on all her thoughts. Imagination succeeded in wreaking havoc with every conversation in which Nell was engaged, for she could not help thinking what Mr. Ferd might have said or done had he been there. She kept searching the faces she met for some hint of the look that so entranced her with Mr. Ferd's pale blue eyes—that look of kinship, of deep compassionate understanding and admiration that so warmed her heart whenever their eyes chanced to meet. His particular shade of cerulean was not to be found. Neither was the look. Even Mr. Crawford—a fat old gent who told her aunt she was a pretty minx and Nell that she must marry him—did not cast his bleary eye on her with anything equaling the admiration and kinship she had grown accustomed to witnessing in Mr. Ferd's pale gaze.

Nell was drawn to the window on more than one occasion, to look down on the row of carriages waiting in the road. She wondered just why it was that a coachman, of all people, could make her feel so very attractive and witty and intelligent. There was no mistaking just which of the ill-lit forms beneath her belonged to Mr. Ferd, for there was only only driver who entertained himself in playing fetch with a dog. How odd it was that the most intriguing person to whom she had of late been introduced, stood outside.

Her thoughts were thus engaged when Mr. Tyrrwhit at last made his way to her side of the room.

"Miss Quinby!" he politely saluted her. "And just what, may I ask, so captivates your attention that your eyes are drawn more often to the window than to the fair company gathered in the room around you?"

Nell blushed. "I am watching that dog down there, sir, and wondering why he should have been so unfortunate as to lose a part of his ear. Mr. Ferd does not appear to be a man given to cruelty."

Mr. Tyrrwhit regarded her with a queer expression. "Nothing could be further from the truth. Bandit would be missing far more than his ear had not Beau snatched him from the very jaws of certain death." He scowled at the memory as she waited patiently to hear more. "The tale is not a pretty one. The telling of it is sure to offend the squeamish."

Such a remark could not fail to intrigue. "What tale?"

Charley looked at her doubtfully. "How familiar are you with the sport some men enjoy in dog fighting?"

"Familiar enough to know that I consider such sport as abhorrent as bull baiting and cock fighting," she said firmly, her expression very serious. "Was Bandit a fighting dog?"

"No, quite to the contrary. Bandit was to have been used as the bait, or fresh meat, in a blooding before the big fight between two young pit bulls."

Nell was confused. "What is this 'blooding' you refer to? I am not so familiar with dog fighting as to understand."

"Are you certain you wish to hear this, Miss Quinby?"

Nell glanced once more to the window. "Pray continue. I shall refrain from embarrassing you with an undue show of emotion."

Charley sighed. "The bait, or fresh meat, that I refer to is a live creature—a kitten, a puppy, a chicken sometimes. Weaker and less aggressive than the fighting dog, the bait is offered up as a sort of sacrifice that the fighting dog might get a taste for killing."

"Oh, my!" Nell's hand flew to her throat. Her eyes swam in tears. "Bandit was to die in this manner?"

"Yes, I'm afraid so. He would have, too, had Beau and I not happened by in search of a friend who, I blush to admit, quite likes to attend dog fights."

"What happened?" Caught up in the story, Nell was inclined to regard their new coachman as something of a hero for rescuing any creature from such a fate.

"It all happened in a moment. I had no idea what Beau was about. He simply reached into the pit and caught a puppy by the scruff of its neck, lifting him above the nose of the other dog. As I recall, the bulldog objected vociferously to the maneuver."

"And you were allowed to leave with Bandit, without further objection?" Nell asked, amazed.

Mr. Tyrrwhit grinned. "Not exactly. We were quite fortunate in that the friend we had come looking for arrived at the time we were to be set upon with cudgels and whips. Dog fighting crowds are not known for their tolerance of such interference, but because he is a man of some reputation and stature, our friend did manage to extricate both ourselves and Bandit from the incident."

Nell could not help but wonder who this mysterious unnamed friend might be. "It is fortunate for Bandit that you cultivate the friends that you do, Mr. Tyrrwhit."

Charley smiled as he looked out the window. "Indeed, Miss Quinby. I consider myself even more fortunate than the dog."

Chapter Nine

Beau saw Nell turn away from the window, and it occurred to him that perhaps Charley had the right of it. He was foolish to continue his charade. He would much rather be dancing than standing in the street. Watching Miss Quinby swing about on the arm of his best friend was small pleasure indeed. He had never been terribly fond of dancing, but to have the option of participating taken away, and as a result of his own actions, seemed oddly unjust.

Thus Beau returned to the window in his allotted room that evening filled with a restless energy that was not dispelled by the effort required to put carriage and team to bed for the night. The restlessness, he knew, was rooted in his frustrated desire for Miss Quinby's company. She was so near, and yet a great chasm of his own making yawned between them. Did he fruitlessly waste his time and energies in remaining here?

With the energy of a man with a mission that must not be abandoned at the first sign of trouble, he took up to his room with him a chisel and a pick, both meant for the use of maintaining a horse's hooves, but now put to good use releasing his window from its prison of paint.

His efforts were rather noisy, but when he was done, the sash went up without a squeak. Beau leaned out, proud of his accomplishment, and drank in the cool night air. He could see the lamplit windows of the main house clearly now. Fanella was in her room. There was movement against the light.

An unexpected pounding on his door caught him like a schoolboy peeping in a keyhole. Beau reacted abruptly, banging his head smartly on the window, as he withdrew into the room again.

It was Toby who knocked, and without waiting for permission to enter, stumbled in, half-awake, to demand, "What the devil are you banging at this hour, Mr. Ferd? We're up at four, don't you know?"

Beau was not at all accustomed to anyone questioning either his actions or the hours he kept. He rubbed the knot on the back of his head and strove for an appearance of nonchalance.

Toby blinked at him groggily.

"Terribly sorry," the duke apologized to the stable boy, all his mad desire to peer out the window squashed. "Terribly thoughtless o-of me to disturb your sleep. I required a-a-air."

"Air?" Toby was mystified.

"Yes," Beau turned to lower the window sash. As he did so, his jaw dropped open and his breath caught up in his throat.

Opposite him, silhouetted against the light in her window, Miss Fanella Quinby was taking down her long, dark hair. She went at it with both hands, her arms raised to pull free the combs and pins that held the wealth of tresses in place. As a result of her arms being uplifted, the shapeliness of her upper torso and neck were admirably revealed.

It took no more than a moment for the last of the pins to be removed. Leaning forward a little, she reached back to untwist the knot of hair at the base of her neck. Shaken out, it swung down over her shoulders like a heavy silk veil. The shape of her silhouette, the attitude of her head, was so changed by the release of hair that Beau stood completely mesmerized, his lips parted to facilitate easier intake of air, his hands frozen on the window frame, without any memory as to what it was he had meant to accomplish with them.

Toby crossed the room to stand at his elbow, yawning and rubbing at his eyes with the heels of his hands. "Air, sir? And what was wrong with the air already stirring in your room?"

Blinking, Beau turned his back on the window, his body blocking the breath-taking view. "It was old a-a-air. Quite stifling. I required fresh. Now that I've got it, you shall not hear a-a-another peep out of me, I promise."

Eyelids drooping with fatigue, Toby took himself off to bed.

When he stumbled downstairs the next morning in answer to Brampton Beauford's cheerful whistling, Toby, had he but chanced to look up, would have been surprised to see that the window above him was not only open to the cool morning air, but that it had been scrubbed so clean that it sparkled, inside and out. The window was not the only thing sparkling by the time the stable lad and his new head coachman went down to breakfast some four hours later, for the duke enthusiastically made inroads on the daily chores, whistling as he went. The curricle was polished until it too shone inside and out, and the harness freshly blacked with, of all things, the same inexpensive liquid boot blacking that Toby used on his own footwear.

"Are you sure this will do?" Toby asked dubiously when they began the task. "Mr. Terry, our head coachman in Ipswich, cooks up his own concoction of harness blacking. It takes an hour's worth of simmering to be done, and he is most insistent that it should be made up with mutton suet, and not beef or pork mixed in."

"Ah!" Beau said with unruffled composure. "It must have been some of Mr. Terry's very own mixture that was stinking up the tack room. I'm afraid his potion had gone rancid. I tossed it out this morning."

"But Everett's boot blacking, Mr. Ferd? Do you not think it too common? Surely it must be inferior to one's own mixture."

"Not at all Toby. Something so readily available saves us both trouble and time, and seeing as how Everett's is good enough for the Prince Regent, it is good enough for me."

"Priney's own coachman uses this? Are you certain, sir?" Toby looked dubiously at the quite ordinary can of blacking.

"A-absolutely certain! I have myself personally seen him with just such a can in his hand. A-and very smart the prince's harness always looks, if you will notice."

Toby's eyes went very round. "You have met him, sir?"

Beau smiled. "Yes. Bandit has, as well."

Bandit thumped his tail agreeably.

"We should not both be here today were it not for the prince's coachman. Whisked us out of a very touchy spot, he did." Beau smiled to think how young Toby's eyes would pop if he were told that Bandit was not only on ear-scratching terms with the prince's head groom, but that he would not be wagging his tail so happily had it not been for the intervention on his behalf of the prince himself.

Nell jerked up out of a dream of Mr. Ferd and his rescuing of Bandit from the horrors of a dog fight. That her last thought at night and her first in the morning should concern their new coachman disturbed her sense of propriety. Surely if she were to become infatuated, it should not be with a servant. And yet he was like a riddle to which she would find an answer. She could not help wondering about him at all hours of the day and night, a far more pleasant pastime that pondering either her uncertain future or the recent unhappy past.

Going to the window, she pulled back the lace curtain and flung open the window to see what kind of day she met. Her eyes were involuntarily drawn to the back hedgerow, beyond which stood the mews. With the window open, she faintly heard the gentleman who invaded her dreams laughing and calling to Toby, the groom, from the stableyard.

The shrubbery, which one must pass through in order to reach the stables, would not allow Nell to see exactly what it was that the two were doing, but as splashy sounds came from the stableyard pump, she deduced they were happily engaged in washing up for breakfast. With thoughts of her own morning toilet brought to mind, Nell was about to turn away from the window when a flash of color caught her eye. The box hedgerow was broken in the middle by an arch cut into the greenery, into which the wooden gate was set. Through this gap, she caught an occasional glimpse of what could be nothing but bared flesh.

Such glimpses, so brief and insignificant as to be unidentifiable in exact origin, were yet sufficient to capture both Nell's interest and attention to the exception of all else, including the passage of time.

It was not until their ablutions had entirely ceased, and

the young man and the boy came quickly through the gate, drying their hands on a rag they wadded up and passed between them like a ball, that Nell recalled herself enough to realize that she stood, clad only in a sheer muslin chemise, with her hair still untouched by the brush and hanging down about her shoulders, exposed at the window for all who cared to look up.

Nell froze. In moving she was far more likely to be noticed than if she stood perfectly still until the two below her had passed. Hand pressed to the windowpane, she willed them not to look up.

But her will, it seemed, was not strong enough. No sooner had Mr. Ferd closed the gate and turned to catch the rag, which Toby had let fly with an exclamation of fun, then he glanced at her window. Beau Ferd looked away again as if he had not seen her, to cast away the rag ball. Just as swiftly, he looked back again, and this time left Nell with no doubt as to his having realized she stood watching them. His jaw came unhinged, and when the flying rag was next lofted his way, he missed entirely the catching of it.

Breath and pulse racing, Nell stepped back from the window as he bent to retrieve the rag, but she could see, even from her retreated position within the room, that Mr. Ferd's eyes rose hopefully once more to the window where she had been standing, before he and the boy, the rag ball on the fly again between them, passed out of her line of sight.

The fact that she had been seen, and in such a state of undress, shook her. She should never have been so careless. To breakfast she went, pulse racing, palms sweating. Safe in the still dining room, where she alone took food from the sideboard while her aunt breakfasted from a tray taken in bed, she twitched and turned at every sound that radiated from the kitchen in the expectation of some kind of confrontation with her own foolishness. She was however, left undisturbed, and that in itself made her frown. She could not help noticing the servants' dining area seemed to be a much jollier place than the dining room, which echoed with stillness by contrast.

Nell had never before minded this arrangement, though breakfast had always been a time when the family came together at home. Today, with the thought in her head of Mr.

Ferd numbered among those who laughed and chatted in the kitchen, she felt very much alone as she buttered her toast and sipped lukewarm tea. It concerned her no end that a male servant in her aunt's employ should have been privileged with a glimpse, no matter how brief, of her watching him clad only in her nightclothes. She would have enjoyed discussing the predicament with Aurora. How was she to face Mr. Ferd again after such a mortifying embarrassment?

She need not have concerned herself. There was to be no further encounter with Mr. Ferd over breakfast. When the kitchen no longer rang with voices and the clatter of crockery, Nell found the absence of further confrontation strangely anticlimactic following so hard on the heels of the morning's incident.

She ran lightly up the stairs again to see if she might catch a glimpse of Mr. Ferd as he made his way back to the stables. From the window nothing more was to be witnessed than the closing gate in the hedgerow and the sound of Mr. Ferd's very recognizable whistle, this time warbling one of the country dances that had been played the night before at the Assembly.

Nell could not stop thinking of the flashes of bare flesh she had witnessed through the hedgerow and Mr. Ferd's slack-jawed expression in seeing her standing above him in the window. The scene played and replayed itself in her thoughts. Disturbed by her own wantonness, she went in to her aunt, who would, perversely, content herself with no other subject that the fitting of Mr. Ferd's new livery. Nell did her best to concentrate her mind on the dressing of that young man, and not his undressing.

Beau made it a habit to remove his shirt before beginning any work in the stableyard. When one had only a single garment with which to cover one's back, and no valet to see to the washing of it, said garment was best guarded carefully. It was much easier to scrub dirt from flesh than from muslin. The shirt had been removed that morning in washing down the carriage and in blacking the leather trappings. It was off again now in the currying of the bay horse that Ursula so longed to find a match for.

"Good day, your grace. It appears that Mr. Tyrrwhit did not exaggerate." It was Gates who spoke from the drive that led through the mews. He held before him, like a trophy, a fat brown valise.

Beau glanced up without any hesitation in the movement of the currycomb he was wielding. "Ah, Gates! I was never more happy to see you. What is it that Charley does not exaggerate? The state of my sanity, perhaps?"

Gates allowed himself to smile. "It was the state of your wardrobe we discussed, sir. I bring you shirts, and it appears from your current disposition that you are in direst need."

Beau slowed his work on the horse for a moment. "Indeed, they will be welcome. What else do you bring me?"

Gates approached the bay, set the valise gingerly down, and then, apparently dissatisfied with its arrangement amongst the dirt and straw, picked it up again.

"Clean nethergarments, your grace, and one or two other necessaries that I thought you might desire—tooth powder, a comb, soap for yourself and your clothing, today's newspaper, a book that you have been reading, razor and strop, several plain neckcloths, and a spare pair of boots. You must make up a list of your requirements if you find that I have forgotten something."

Beau set aside the currycomb for a brush and regarded his valet over the back of the bay. "You are, as always, completely aware of my needs, Gates. Have I ever properly thanked you for that quality?"

Gates's stoic countenance took on a slightly confused aspect. "Your grace?"

"No, I can see by your expression that I have not." Beau was quite seriously contrite. "Well, I am genuinely pleased to see you here, and not only because you bring me fresh linen. Did Charley tell you about the gray?"

Gates's confused look intensified. "Is it a gray, sir? I had been informed it was a bay you were seeking?"

Beau laughed. "Quite right. It is only on account of the gray that we seek a bay. A bay that would pair well with this one." He slapped the back of the freshly curried horse.

Gates's scrutinized the animal. "Do you require the markings to be of a similar nature, your grace?"

"No, I am more concerned that this animal should be of a similar age, height, and temperament, than with the number or arrangement of its stockings or facial markings. As for the rest, I trust your judgement implicitly with regard to health, conformation, and soundness."

Gates allowed a hint of a smile to lift the corners of his mouth. "I am flattered, your grace. Is there anything else you would have me do?"

"You may take that valise to the room at the top of the stairs, if you so please."

"Yes, your grace."

"One other thing, Gates."

"Yes, sir?"

"You must refrain from calling me 'your grace' as long as I am engaged in this charade."

"Yes, your . . . but, what must I call you then, my lord?"

"Not 'my lord.' That is no more to the purpose than the other. I should prefer that you refer to me as Mr. Ferd."

"Mr. Ferd, sir?"

"That's right."

Gates nodded, still confused. "That was the room at the top of the stairs . . . ." He paused, concentrating, for such informality went very much against the grain. ". . . Mr. Ferd?"

The words were a trifle wooden, but Beau was mightily pleased. "Just so, Gates."

Gates returned within moments, his face a picture of dismay.

"Am I to understand that I heard correctly, and that it is the room at the top of the stairs that your grace occupies?" he asked, aghast.

"I find no fault with your hearing, Gates, other than the fact that you have again addressed me as your grace, when I have just r-r-requested otherwise."

"But, my lord."

Beau was laughing now. "Gates!"

Gates sighed. "But, sir, that room is not fit, sir, no matter what it is that I call you, sir. The sheets have not seen soap and water for . . . I shudder to think how long your gra—"

Beau gave him a warning look.

Gates frowned and took a deep breath. "Mr. Ferd, sir."

* * *

Nell stood uncertainly in the gateway from the back garden that led through the shrubbery to the mews. She hesitated to continue her errand because she could see the new coachman from the shadowed spot where she stood. While it was expressly to see Mr. Ferd that she made her way here, she had not anticipated seeing quite so much of him, nor of his having company. There, before her, was the same back that she had so long regarded on the trip down from London. She was quite familiar with its shape, its breadth, the contours that had shaped the jacket and greatcoat that had once covered it, and yet, unclothed, it was a creature unfamiliar to her. There was something so changed in tone and texture, so provocative in the disposition of musculature, that she could neither step forward nor retreat.

How did one approach a young man stripped to the waist when one meant to ask a favor of him? Was it best done in the company of another? She thought not. She ought to go away.

And yet she hesitated. Nell had not, in her short lifetime, had opportunity to witness more than a handful of bare masculine torsos, and certainly none so attractively muscled as this one. Her interest in such a sight had been whetted that morning with the flashes of bare flesh she had glimpsed through the hedgerow. Now, with so much of him to observe, her eyes grew very round, as did her half-open mouth. Her breathing seemed suddenly unnaturally loud in her throat.

The man who stood conversing with Mr. Ferd as he finished sponging down the bay was none other than the same Mr. Gates she had met on the coach trip from Godstone. He had struck her then as having the manners of an upstairs servant. She saw nothing now to change that impression. Mr. Ferd seemed highly amused by their conversation, while Mr. Gates seemed to find nothing humorous at all in what was said. He did not stay long. And yet even with him gone Nell did nothing to announce herself. Instead, afraid she would be seen, she whirled back out of the line of sight and pressed against the shrubbery, one hand at her throat and the other pressed against her breast, where her heart seemed to beat an unusually erratic tattoo against her ribcage. Twice in one morning she had allowed her own wicked desire to consume her better judgement! Nell was surprised at herself!

Realizing that the blood no longer circulated so very well in one of her feet, so long had she stood, statue-still, in observing the object of her desire, Nell disengaged herself from the hedge to shake out her foot. She had every intention of quitting the vicinity. Circulation returning, she peeped around the greenery to see if her going would be observed.

In that instant, the coachman turned his head to look directly at her. "Miss Quinby!"

She froze, horrified.

Beau Ferd dropped the hoof he had been examining and advanced, his nakedness provoking such mortification in Nell that she knew not where to look.

"I do beg your p-pardon," he exclaimed. "I'd no idea you frequented the m-mews." He strode to the gatepost over which his smock shirt was tossed, and thrusting both arms within the fabric, pulled the covering down over his head.

In the moment that his face, and thus his gaze, was buried in cambric, Nell found herself unable to resist staring at the thatch of curling hair on his chest. There was something awe inspiring in observing sweat-sheened flesh as it rolled over swells of muscle that ran beneath the skin all the way down a man's abdomen and into the lacing of his britches. There was something strangely vulnerable and at the same time frightening in the tuft of dark hair that nestled in each armpit. Nell, her face flushed crimson as his head emerged from the neck of the smock, thought she would never again be able to look at any gentleman without wondering how he might compare to such a baring.

She was surprised and disgusted by the forward nature of her own curiosity and could not imagine how she was now to converse with a man she had seen so exposed.

"Did you wish the carriage brought a-a-around?" he asked, returning both the tone and focus of their exchange to the mundane. "You know you have but to send word, and I will have a conveyance r-ready in the blink of an eye."

Nell, her breath coming too fast, leaned upon the gate. Its

hinges let out a little squawk and swung toward him. She backed away from her prop, her gloved hands alone remaining in contact with the splintered surface. Her eyes could not resist the temptation of rising to the neck of his newly donned smock, which hung wide enough to reveal a hint of the curling hair it hid. Her embarrassment was acute when one ash-blond eyebrow rose ever so slightly, and when, with a hint of a mischievous smile, he reached up to tighten the string that gathered the fabric about his throat.

One dusty boot he thrust onto the bottommost rung of the wooden barricade between them, while his bare, work-reddened hands he leaned against the splintered upper rung, one on either side of her own.

As if their both coming in contact with the same piece of wood were somehow improper, Nell quickly withdrew her hold on the gate. Blushing, she clasped her hands behind her back and tipped down her face, so that a good deal of her expression was hidden by the brim of her bonnet.

He smiled at her, and it was another of the slow, disarming smiles that had so enchanted her in their trip down from London. She could not stop herself from dimpling in return, though there was something in his pale blue gaze that reminded her she meant to distance herself from the effect that this young man had on her better judgement.

"My aunt means to have you fitted for your livery before noon," she said. "Can you fetch us at eleven?"

He removed his booted foot from the gate. "A-as you say, miss." There was something curious and watchful in his pale blue eyes, as if he expected her to say more.

She turned to go, feeling as if there should indeed be more said between them.

"We shall expect you at eleven, then," she said thickly, and left with far more haste than grace.

Chapter Ten

Beau's eyes met Nell's in the pier glass before which he stood, arms extended shoulder height, while Mr. Treedle, the tailor, took the measure of him, his hands flying about with a length of tape. She blushed and looked away.

Ursula Dunn stood beside her niece, fingering two lengths of brown cloth. "What think you, Fanella? Which of these becomes the bay the best?"

There was something so very ludicrous in such a question that Beau could not resist smiling. His eyes sought Nell's, to see if she shared his appreciation for the ridiculous.

She did. Her eyes danced merrily. "Perhaps we should have the horse in front of the mirror in Mr. Ferd's stead, so that we might match the shade exactly."

Ursula Dunn looked up from the cloth. "Oh, do be serious Fanella," she said tartly.

"I am serious, Auntie." Nell's lip curled a little, as she shook her head in mock gravity. "The fashion of color can be quite cruel if one is not careful. I have heard that a member of the Whip Club by the name of Mellish is considered dashing with four matching white horses and snowy livery, and yet Tommy Onslow is not allowed into the same club because his matched blacks and funereal livery are deemed too sober. As for Lord Petersham, he is become a laughing-stock of sorts, for while all his horses and livery are a perfectly matched brown, word has it that his predilection for the color is based in his love of a certain married female of the same name."

Ursula Dunn's eyes flashed dangerously. "Fanella! Is it Catherine who has filled your head with such gossip?"

Nell shrugged, her cheeks blooming roses of embarrassment.

"Cat does follow all of the exploits of the more notorious whipsters with the interest of a scholar."

Such a revelation could not fail to interest Beau. He wondered what, if anything, the youngest Miss Quinby might have had to say about him.

"Your sister Catherine's time were better spent in other pursuits," Ursula said censoriously.

"Oh, I don't know, Auntie," Nell laughed. "We should never have known the least little thing about Aurora's duke had we not had Cat to fill us in on his status."

Beauford's interest was heightened.

"That is quite another matter, Fanella, and well you know it. One cannot begrudge your sister knowing a little something about the man who may very well hold the financial well-being of your entire family in his hands."

The duke's eyes narrowed in puzzled interest at Ursula's reflection in the mirror, then flicked with greater interest to observe Fanella. Until this moment he had had no ideas such power was his. What had he to do with their financial well-being?

The brilliance of amusement dimmed from Fanella's eyes. The teasing lilt no longer tugged the corners of her lips. "Is this Season of Aurora's truly so important, Auntie?" She asked. "How does a duke that we have never so much as laid eyes on hold so much power over us? Do you and mother seriously think he might marry Aurora and make us all rich enough to afford matching horses and livery?"

Beau burned with sharp-edged amusement, for he knew the answer to that question far better than Ursula Dunn.

"Marry her?" Ursula smiled and rolled her eyes heavenward. "God be pleased such a wondrous thing should come to pass. No, Fanella, neither your mother nor I are foolish enough to aspire to such heights, even with Aurora's wealth of good looks. Despite a history of good family, and the high hopes of his own sister, the Lady Beatrix, the duke is quite above our touch. The importance, you see, of Aurora's meeting with him has less to do with his own unattached state than with the marital status of his circle of friends. If he will but introduce your sister to his peers, and bestow upon her brow some stamp of approval in being observed dancing or chatting with her on some occasion of note, her status will be set. Somewhere among the Ton, your mother and I are quite convinced, Aurora is sure to win favor. Can you fault us for hoping he may be a young man endowed with means enough indeed to afford matching horses?"

Nell's frown deepened, but before she could respond, Mr. Treedle, finished with his measure taking, bowed unctuously before his client. "Madame, if you are still desirous of perfectly matching the bay, perhaps I might suggest that we could carry a few of the more likely bolts of cloth out to the horse."

"Splendid idea!" Ursula crowed, more than willing to be distracted. Pointing out no more than a dozen possible choices, in corduroy, worsted wool, jean, merino, and velvet, she led the way out into the street, followed by the heavily laden tailor and his apprentice.

Nell refrained from joining the exodus into the street.

Beau could not resist observing, "The mountain would not come to Mohammed, so Mohammed went to the mountain. Do you not intend to consult the horse as well, Miss Quinby?" He was surprised that he should suffer feelings of guilt for spoiling the carefully laid plans of so many. His troubled gaze met hers in the mirror as he spoke. He was buttoning up his waistcoat, which had been removed at the tailor's request, and there was something both in look and action that echoed the moment that morning in the stable-yard when he had been required to pull on his shirt with this same young lady intently regarding him.

"I've no great desire to see how well the mountain matches Mohammed," she said lightly, her eyes fixed rather absentmindedly on his hands as they did up the buttons of his waistcoat. She reached out in a sweetly unconscious gesture to assist him in finding the armhole as he shrugged his shoulders into the secondhand coat. He wished he might have as unconsciously assisted her family's search for financial security.

Something in his eyes gave away the deep nature of his thoughts, for when she caught him looking at her in the mirror, her blank look sharpened. She swiftly abandoned her hold on his apparel. Self-consciously, she stepped away from him.

Beau was disappointed but not surprised that she should drop both her visual and physical hold on him. There was something deliciously provocative in donning one's clothing with a lady reaching out to assist.

The huge brown eyes in her reflected image darted a look at him. Her eyes and mouth seemed suddenly serious.

"I am wondering if you would be so kind as to do me a favor, Mr. Ferd?"

He turned away from the mirror to regard her directly, ready to grant her every desire. Her lips had never appeared more provocative than in this moment, caught up as the lower one was, in the grip of her teeth, as if she meant to bite back her request.

"That would depend on the complexion of said favor, Miss Quinby. How may I be of service?"

She frowned, her gaze drawn to the window through which they both might observe the tailor busily draping cloth over the back of the bay, where each shade was carefully regarded with critical eye through Mrs. Dunn's quizzing glass.

She sighed. "This favor is of a sensitive nature. I dare not ask it of anyone else. I must warn you that should it be discovered that you have helped me in it, my aunt would most assuredly cast you off without reference."

He studied her profile with interest as he turned back to the mirror to straighten his collar and tie his dreadfully crushed cravat. Her dark hair and eyelashes seemed limed by light from the window. What was she plotting?

"What is this favor?"

She peeped a look at him as if she knew he would not be pleased by what she asked.

"There is a man . . ." She caught at her lip again.

He frowned.

She rushed on in the face of unmistakable censure, continuing, ". . . a Captain Jeremy Stiles, stationed here, among the Tenth. He is an old friend of my family's. I must locate him . . . speak to him . . ."

Her request annoyed him. He found he was no longer entranced by the disposition of her lower lip. "I will not help a-any young lady throw herself a-a-at a-a-a man," he said sternly.

"What?" Nell looked at him in dismay. "I am not bent on seducing Captain Stiles," she said carefully, and then blushed and lowered her gaze. "I am intent on the far more shameful task of begging him for the loan of some monies, and as I cannot very well go barging into the barracks asking his direction, I had thought that you might be so good as to locate him for me."

Beau felt a little ridiculous. "You require money?"

"Yes," she said ruefully. "I've none to speak of, and Captain Stiles may be flush enough to loan me what I require."

"Why do you need money? Perhaps I could—"

She allowed him to go no further. "You are very kind, Mr. Ferd, but I could not allow myself to be so indebted to you." She chuckled. "Do not forget that I know how much Aunt Ursula pays you. On such a salary you cannot afford to be loaning me money for a broken-down horse."

"Horse? Is this horse a brown and white piebald, with a blaze like a splash of milk running down one side of a face, in which one eye is chocolate brown and the other a pale cerulean blue?"

She stared at him a moment, lips parted. "You recognized him, did you?" She searched his eyes for any signs of mockery. There was none to be seen. "I mean to buy him back if I can scrape together the money."

Beau considered for a moment telling her there was no need to trouble her head further about the old horse, that he had bought Boots himself and shipped him off to his sister. He squashed the impulse. In telling her anything, he must tell her all. Beau was not ready yet to destroy the fragile connection he enjoyed with Fanella Quinby in informing her he was the lying Lord Brampton Beauford, seventh Duke of Heste—an inconsiderate, if rich and influential clod who would prove an embarrassment to her sister's chances of success rather than a boon.

"I will locate this Captain Stiles for you," he offered.

Knowing full well that his errand was useless, Beau set off that evening to carry it out, in the realization that he wove himself an ever-tighter web of lies to tangle himself up in.

Captain Stiles was not to be found at the barracks that housed his regiment at the edge of town. Neither was he at the Old Ship or the Castle Taverns. The next logical place to look was Raggett's gambling house. There, Beau was fortunate enough to find the room bright with the uniform of the Tenth Hussar.

Said uniform was, Lord Beauford thought privately, the gaudiest peacockery he had ever laid eyes on. No other regiment could lay claim to such ostentatious color and ornament, with less likelihood of seeing battle. The Hussars were the Prince of Wales's own Dragoons, and it was Priney himself who had a hand in the design of their accoutrement.

From the top of the rakishly tilted, brimless, scarlet and black, cut-cone hat, with its wide, gilded and scarlet tail that swept down over one shoulder to dangle about its wearer's scarlet and gold ribbed waistband, to the unusual silver-spurred and silver-tasseled canary yellow Hessian boots, there was no escaping the surfeit of gold and silver braiding, gilt, and tassels, until one's eyes came thankfully to the blank relief of skin-tight, chalk-white pantaloons.

Lord Beauford could not help calculating just what such lavish accoutrement must set its wearer back in coin, and when this sum was considered in juxtaposition with the more than two thousand pounds it took to buy into the position of captain, one might say an officer wore his wealth with pride.

"Captain Stiles?" Beau enquired of the first uniform he confronted.

The young man pointed unhappily to a table. "Over there. Not here to play him at cards, are you? Man's had the devil's own luck this evening. My empty pockets attest to it."

Beau approached the table with interest. There were three officers of the Hussar seated amongst the players, but only one of them a captain. He was the most handsome of the three—a tall young man with chestnut brown hair; a trim, waxed mustache; and dashing long sidewhiskers—

who looked up from his cards with a trace of irritation when he was addressed.

"Captain Stiles?"

"Who cares to know?" Stiles insisted with cool, scornful hauteur.

"B-B-Beau-ford, sir." In the midst of introducing himself it occurred to Beau that he must remember he was now plain Mr. Beau Ferd, and not Lord Beauford. The slip of his tongue proved providential, for the pause had been just long enough between the first and second syllable, so that he might continue the myth of his new and simpler moniker.

"And who might B-B-Beau Ferd be?" Stiles quipped, echoing his stammer.

To have his speech cruelly mimicked was not a new experience for Beau. To be denigrated for the handicap of his faltering tongue was something he had spent a lifetime learning to accept. He knew that Captain Stiles, no better than any cruel schoolyard bully, strove to prove his own superiority in ridiculing him before his compatriots. It was childish behavior, and far too often encountered. His father's advice not to waste time bemoaning what one had no control over had always stood him in good stead when he had encountered such an attitude. He thought of the advice now, and remained calm.

Captain Stiles's mockery brought a laugh from his inebriated friends. Beau swallowed the pride that swelled in his throat and resisted the inclination to give this cocksure young man a smart setdown. It would not serve him well to involve himself in a brawl with three of the prince's hussars. In the mildest of tones he responded, "I, sir, am coachman for Madame Dunn."

"And does Madame Dunn dun me, along with every other tradesman in Brighton? Tell your employer she shall be paid. I am come into some money this evening." He clicked one of the stacks of coins on the table before him with a smile.

Again, the captain's friends found him vastly amusing.

Somewhat less entertained, Beau pressed gamely on. "I have been sent by Mrs. Dunn's niece, a Miss Quinby, sir, who desires speech with you."

As his mates guffawed again, Captain Stiles's smug expression underwent a profound change. Drunken condescension was replaced by drunken interest.

"Here, here, man. What do you mean bandying about the name of a lady in a taproom?" He took Beau's arm rather roughly in his own, and dragged him out of hearing range of his drinking cohorts, an arduous light in his ale-bright eyes. "She is here, man? In Brighton?"

Beauford calmly removed Captain Stiles hold on his person. "She is currently residing with her aunt—"

Before he could go on, the Captain was finishing his sentence for him, "Aunt Ursula! Of course. How very clever of Aurora." Disregarding his own advice about bandying a lady's name about in a taproom, and the sudden change in Beau's expression, he chortled gleefully to his companions, "Listen up, chaps. Aurora has given up on chasing off to London after all. Rather than dance attendance on a duke, she has come to Brighton!"

The two recipients of this happy news lifted their cups, shouting out, "Au-ROAR-ah," as if her name were a battle cry.

"Begging your p-pardon, sir," Beau interrupted, amused he should be privileged to hear this slighting opinion of himself from a man he had never so much as been introduced to until this moment. "It is Miss Fanella Quinby who wishes to speak to you."

"Nell?" Stiles repeated, aghast, as the battle cry of the other Miss Quinby's given name continued to resound from the rafters. "Aurora came not with her?"

Beau shook his head.

"Blast!" Captain Stiles said with feeling, and whirling on his fellow officers, drowned out their happy chorus with a fierce shout. "Hold tongue, will you? A man cannot hear himself think, much less engage in conversation." He rounded on Beau, scowling mightily. "You, c-c-coachman," he teased. "Do you know I have heard that the Duke of Heste speak no better than you do? Can you picture it, man? The fairest young woman in Christendom, beholden to a man who cannot string two words together."

The duke was filled with a loathing of this man's contempt for him, filled with a need to give him a scathing setdown. He was saved from his own foolish pride when a familiar voice said lazily from the next table. "But sir, the Duke of Heste is not in London at all."

Charley Tyrrwhit leaned his chair away from the table, blowing a cloud of smoke from his pipe.

"Not in London?" Stiles blustered. "And where else would he be then, man?"

Beau gave his friend a warning look.

Charley smiled blandly. Turning his gaze to the ceiling as if to find an answer, he said, "Was it here in Brighton I have seen him?"

"Never say it is so." Stiles chortled. "That would be too rich."

"No, you are quite right," Charley agreed, with a quick wink. "It was at the races in Epson, this Tuesday last."

"I hope to God you've the right of it." Stiles raised his cup.

"Without doubt, sir. You may depend upon it. He was there." Grinning cheekily, Charley turned back to his cards.

Beau longed for the door. What if he should encounter someone else who might recognize him? "Miss Fanella Quinby?" he prodded Stiles gently. "What shall I tell her was your r-response?"

Stiles was smiling, well pleased with Charley's remark. "Tell her I'll make a point to call on her . . . if only to hear what word she may have of Aurora."

Beau sketched a bow and made his exit. As he went, he heard, like a rowdy echo, the name of the fine young woman that his sister Beatrix had been so set on his having to wife, as it was toasted to the rafters: "Au-ROAR-ah!"

Chapter Eleven

Nell wondered on the following morning if she had been in error in exposing so much of her intentions to Mr. Ferd, regarding money and Captain Stiles. Her doubts were erased however, when, as a direct result of his efforts, she ran into none other than the captain as she came down the steps of Mr. Donaldson's lending library, where her aunt had engaged herself in a game of loo. Nell had herself obtained several books pertaining to Greek and Roman mythology from which she intended to derive a costume for the masquerade ball that was to be held in the Promenade at the end of the month.

Captain Stiles came from the establishment across the street, Raggett's, which had been pointed out to her by her aunt as a place to avoid. It was a high-stakes gaming house, and no place for a young woman of good repute.

"Halloo, Miss Quinby," Stiles called out, recognizing her immediately.

With a smile and a nod, Nell paused beside the carriage that Beau held waiting for her at the curb. Stiles crossed over to her side of the street, dazzling in the glittering wealth of sunlit silver lacings that adorned so much of his stunning uniform. Nell could not help thinking that in the distinctive canary boots and scarlet fez, Jeremy Stiles resembled nothing so much as a rooster as he strutted toward her. She was at a loss to see what it was that Aurora found so irresistibly attractive in him. Her parents, especially her father, had been adamantly opposed to Aurora's infatuation with Jeremy. She wondered what her father would have thought of Mr. Ferd.

Stiles, with a rueful swipe of one palm along his bristling jawline, tipped his scarlet hat and saluted her hand.

"Pardon my rough appearance, Miss Quinby. I have been, I am ashamed to admit, at cards all night. I am only now on my way back to the barracks. Having been informed at some point between yesterday and today by your coachman that you were come to Brighton, and glimpsing you just now from the window of the club, I made haste to quit the game to come and speak to you. Do forgive my evil looks. Are you enjoying your visit to the seaside? How is your sister liking London? I was disappointed, as you may well imagine, to hear that she had not accompanied you here."

Nell, who knew all too well how disappointed he must be, smiled on him with pity as she handed her books up to Mr. Ferd.

"You know Aurora," she said. "She was disappointed in not coming to Brighton, yet we can be happy in the knowledge that she enjoys herself in such a lively place as London."

Captain Stiles, it seemed, could not be at all happy in such knowledge. He frowned. "I have heard that the duke she was sent to dazzle is gone to the races rather than play host." He relayed this information with such a keen look that Nell had no doubt that he was highly interested in hearing more on the subject.

Having only that morning received a letter from Aurora containing the same information, Nell was a little surprised that Jeremy Stiles should know so much. Such information, were it to become common knowledge, could do much to ruin her sister's chances at a successful Season. It would appear to some, she was sure, that the Duke of Heste—thoughtless, callous creature that he must be—had slighted Aurora in his avoidance of her company. Such a slight could do nothing to enhance poor Aurora's penniless stature in the narrowed eyes of the Ton, who might go so far as to believe her a fortune hunter.

"It's true that the duke is not to be found in London," she said with studied nonchalance, "but that he might meet Aurora was, after all, no more than his sister's intent. Most men do prefer the races, or cards, or the company to be found at their clubs, to playing host to a party of women, and fitting in with a sister's plans. Do you not agree?"

"I might agree with you, had I never laid eyes on your sister, Miss Quinby."

Nell laughed. "Well, then, we shall have to assume that either the duke is not so readily impressed with Aurora's charms, or he has, as you say, never laid eyes on her."

A faraway look took possession of the captain's eyes, and Nell, assuming correctly that he was thinking of her sister, felt that there could be no better time or opportunity to ask him for the money she required to buy Boots. Surely a gentleman so enchanted would see clear to loaning her the negligible sum she required.

"Captain Stiles, I will come right out and tell you that there was a most particular reason why I am so very pleased to meet up with you today. I have reason to hope, that you, of all my acquaintances in Brighton, might loan me a small amount to money."

Stiles's faraway look disappeared, replaced by a stiff awkwardness that wilted the hope Nell had allowed to blossom.

"I am sorry to impose on our friendship," she began, but he would allow her to go no further.

"No, no, Miss Quinby. It is I who must apologize. I am in no way able to grant a plea I can see it pains you to make. It is not that I would not be happy to advance you some monies, had I any. The sad truth of it is that I have unwillingly parted with all of this month's pay just this past evening, in a rather unlucky turn of luck."

Nell knew that her face clearly displayed her disappointment, but she could not under the circumstances remain completely calm.

He seemed anxious to make amends. "Is there any way, other than pecuniary, that I might be of assistance?"

Nell was about to refuse him—the very words had formed themselves upon her tongue—but she realized it served her better to make light of her financial predicament. "Yes, you can, Mr. Stiles. Tell me what it is you mean to wear to the coming masquerade. I am having a dreadful time of it, deciding whether I prefer the guise of Iris or Psyche."

Beau listened from his bench as Nell tried to recover lost pride in a trivial conversation about masquerade costumes. He could not understand why Stiles, his pockets full of winnings, did not readily grant the girl the paltry amount she required to buy an old nag.

Even as he puzzled over such stinginess, Lord Beauford was lowered by guilt, for he, far more than Stiles, cheated Miss Quinby of her happiness. He had but to tell her the truth, had but to tell her who he was and what he had done to see to Boots's comfort, and her mind would be relieved of this compulsion to borrow money she had no way of repaying.

The whole point in his buying the horse had been misguided gallantry if he did not ease the pain from which her tender heart so clearly suffered. His act of compassion was become cruel torture so long as he held silent.

He must tell her, then, who he was. He must undo this strange charade, ceasing to function as confidant and coachman and assuming the heavy mantle of responsibility so blithely shed. It was time he became duke again. Perhaps it was not too late to undo the damage he had done Miss Quinby's sister, the beautiful Aurora. He wondered if Nell could forgive him this. The truth he held would seem a double-edged sword. What he would say to bring Miss Quinby comfort was also sure to make her hold him in aversion.

With all honorable intention of revealing himself and that cutting edge of truth, Brampton Beauford stepped down from the curricle as soon as Captain Stiles took his leave, in order to help Fanella stow her books and step into the carriage. Where to begin? How did one go about telling a decent young lady that she has been victim of a hoax?

"Thank you, Mr. Ferd." Nell seemed subdued as she accepted his assistance. "Have you been waiting long for me?"

All of my life, were the words that sprang immediately to mind when he turned to her, doffing his hat. Something of what he was thinking must have revealed itself in his eyes, for she looked at him quite keenly, lips parted in surprise.

"I don't mind waiting for you," he said earnestly. "Any luck parting Mr. Stiles from some of his soft?"

Her forehead knitted with concern. "Jeremy has none to be parted from." Despair was like an ache in her voice.

Beau winced. He must tell her now, tell her about the

horse, and who he was. It was the only decent, honorable course he could take. "E-E-Even had he loaned you the blunt, there would have been no horse there for you to spend it on," he blurted. The horse was as good a way as any to begin.

"What mean you?" Her earnest brown eyes lifted to meet his.

"The piebald is no longer e-e-engaged in pulling the bathing box." There, that was a start.

She blinked at him. "Is he not?"

"No." And your coachman is a duke, he thought, but could not make the words come forth.

"I would see this for myself. Are you absolutely certain?"

"Yes, I—" He would have told her then, but in her impatience to know more, she interrupted him.

"Whatever has become of him, then? Do you think Boots has been injured, perhaps died?"

"No!"

"Then, perhaps he has been sold."

"Yes, I am—"

"Well then, there is nothing for it, but I must go and make enquiries with the boxman tomorrow morning when you carry us down to take the cure."

"Miss Quinby."

"Hmm?" Her thoughts seemed far away.

"There is something I must tell you."

She looked up, and then past him. "Now is not the time. Here is my aunt." She bent her head over the book plates she had been showing Captain Stiles, and said in a carrying voice. "Which of these do you think would make the better costume, Mr. Ferd?"

"Psyche suits you." He picked up her cue without a hitch. "A shawl might serve a-a-as wings."

"Oh, never ask a man such a question, Fanella," her aunt admonished, accepting Beau's hand in the scaling of the carriage steps. "A woman is far better judge of such deceits."

Beau could not suppress a wry smile. Ursula Dunn would seem to underestimate the truth as much as he would appear to have trouble delivering it.

Chapter Twelve

Lord Brampton Beauford, Miss Fanella Quinby, and Mrs. Ursula Dunn set out the next morning, as usual, for the salt-water cure. A fool's errand, Beau thought—an errand that might expose him as fool. With every hour that passed, his lie grew and fed upon itself. The line between reality and fiction blurred. There were unexpected risks involved in living out a falsehood. He had begun to feel a fraud in his assumed identity.

As the ladies descended at the beach, Nell shot him a rather speaking glance and then directed her gaze meaningfully toward the bathing boxes. He understood that was where she meant to go, but by the time he got the curricle situated, she had already accosted the dipper of the box that had once employed her old horse, Boots.

The dipper was not in a mood to be helpful. She was shouting, arms planted firmly on her damp, swaddled hips. "No, I'll not tell you what's become of the nag. It's you and your interfering ways that has seen to it we have been forced to find another animal."

Beau stepped between Nell and the woman.

"Madame," he addressed the dipper, as she eyed him with unleavened animosity, "Calm yourself!"

The words did not have the desired effect.

"Calm myself, he says," she hooted derisively. "I'll show you calm."

Before she could go on, the voice of the boxman interrupted her, as he climbed down off his seat to intervene.

"Leave off, Peg. I'll handle this."

Beau watched with admiration as Nell coolly drew herself up, her spine pikestaff stiff, her demeanor completely unrattled by the rude welcome she had received.

The dipper drew herself up, too, loathe to quit the confrontation, but with no more than a severe look, the boxman underlined his former directive and Peg, with a sniff and a defiant twitch of her hips, left off.

"You'll be askin' after the pie, I'm thinkin'," the boxman said politely.

Nell nodded regally.

" 'E's gone."

"Gone?" Nell repeated patiently. "Yes, I can see that he is gone. But why?"

"Sold. Same day you was last here about him." The boxman turned away, as if all that needed to be said, had been.

"Miss Quinby," Beau attempted to interrupt.

Nell would have none of it. "Wait!" she insisted. "Can you tell me who bought the horse?"

The boxman paused.

Beau opened his mouth. The truth he had abused had caught up with him and now meant to slap him in the face.

The boxman spoke. "Sure, and he was a small fellow, dapper dressed. Said his name was Bates . . . nah, that were not it. Yates, mayhap. No, no, I have it now . . ."

Beau winced in anticipation of Mr. Gates identity being revealed. It would seem he should never have an opportunity to redeem himself.

"His name were Cates." The boxman asserted. "Yes, that were it. I am sure of it."

Beau blinked. This was an unexpected reprieve.

"Do you know what this Mr. Cates meant to do with the horse?"

The boxman gave Nell a queer look. "Whyever should I ask him that? I am not a prying man, and he offered me good gold coin."

"And can you give me Mr. Cates's direction?"

"Nay!" He said, to Beau's further relief, and then quite spoiled everything by suggesting gruffly. "Carriers will like as not have it."

With this tantalizing lead to follow, Beau was not in the least surprised when Nell insisted she meant to go to the carrier's with all possible haste.

But it was not to be.

* * *

Once again, Aunt Ursula interrupted, scotching Nell's plan in the simplest and most unobjectionable of ways. "Fanella!" she cried, approaching on the arm of a young man. "Only look who I have bumped into."

"Mr. Bledsoe." Nell acknowledged the newcomer, whom she had met at the last Assembly.

"Miss Quinby." The young man tipped his hat. "I did enjoy our dance last night."

Ursula smiled. "I have only just been telling Mr. Bledsoe how much we should like to go sightseeing, and he has been kind enough to offer us his company in viewing the Long Man that I mentioned to you only yesterday."

"How kind," Nell said, well aware what it was her aunt was doing in carting this young man along with them. She was making good her promise to snare Nell a husband.

Thus began the first encounter with a long line of potential suitors Ursula Dunn thrust upon her attention. So thoroughly were Fanella's efforts engaged in fending off matrimonial candidates from that day forth that there was no opportunity for further exploration into the mysterious buyer of Boots.

So diligently direct were her Aunt Ursula's methods as she went about her self-assigned task of matchmaker that Nell lived in fear that she might soon be labeled a fortune huntress.

Mr. Bledsoe did not suit. Despite the fact that his father had been knighted, and he stood to inherit a goodly sized country house in Howe, he did not at all suit Nell's notion of a husband, and so she was quick to tell her aunt.

"He seemed a quiet and pleasant young man to me." Ursula defended the young man. "I will concede that he was not 'above the average' intelligent, but he spoke quite knowledgeably of crop rotation and the price of wheat."

"He had no conversation at all, Auntie," Nell said simply. "Considering Mr. Bledsoe showed a singular lack of knowledge on all other subjects, we are fortunate that Mr. Ferd was endowed with some information as to the Long Man's origins, otherwise we should have left our sightseeing excursion as ignorant as when we set out."

"Well, I am sure we shall enjoy ourselves far more to-morrow."

"Tomorrow?"

"Oh, yes, did I not tell you? A Lieutenant Colonel Smythe of the Tenth Hussar, who is far more inclined to conversation than Mr. Bledsoe, has offered to reveal to us the Oriental wallpapers in Brighton Pavilion."

Nell resigned herself to her aunt's machinations. Thursday progressed with no more success than Wednesday. Far more verbose than his predecessor, Lieutenant Colonel Smythe was as inclined to reveal quite inappropriate gossip about the infamous goings-on at the Pavilion as he was to discuss wallpaper.

On these outings, and again on Saturday in a walk along the high white, chalk cliffs known as the Seven Sisters with a Mr. Salcomb, Nell found herself measuring her companions against the yardstick of none other than her coachman, Mr. Ferd. It was a ridiculous comparison, she knew, and yet how could she entertain the thought of marriage to some fellow when she could not find it within herself to like him even so much as a coachman?

Aunt Ursula was unperturbed by Nell's fastidious taste. "You are like your father, Fanella," she said at one point. "He was a most particular man when it came to whom he chose to befriend."

Nell was uncomfortable with such a pronouncement. Meanwhile, Ursula reveled in her self-appointed role as matchmaker. Virtually every interesting sight within the surrounding countryside was considered a fair means to achieve the end of allowing her niece to better acquaint herself with connubial possibilities.

All the while, it was Beau who handed Nell in and out of the carriage and who tooled her aunt and the prospective marriage material safely about the countryside.

"Our Mr. Ferd looks quite unobjectionable in his new livery," Ursula commented to her niece.

"One might safely say handsome," Nell concurred.

Their Mr. Ferd was the only constant in the parade of men. An exemplary coachman, he saw to it that the excursions went smoothly. Never once did he get lost in the largely unmarked country lanes they traversed, and the local landmarks he was kind enough to point out with some informed remark as to their significance. The horses never came up lame, and the carriage, which he kept spotlessly clean, was never out of commission. When picnic baskets were to be put together, or lugged about the countryside, it was Mr. Ferd who saw to it. When refreshments were required along the way, Mr. Ferd seemed to know the most pleasant inn in which to find them. He bespoke rooms for their comfort with aplomb, and provided extra coats and hats when the wind blustered, spare walking sticks when the terrain proved difficult, and parasols for the ladies when the sun proved too strong or when clouded skies came on to rain.

And, as the days passed, and every one of them in each other's company, if only peripherally, he and Nell developed a communication of sorts—a language of shy smiles and telling glances. The two seemed to find amusement in the same quirks of personality exhibited among Ursula's chosen companions, and warm, laughing blue eyes more than once locked on mirth-filled brown.

It was a fleeting contact, this flirting language of their eyes, and as if to broaden their scope, Beau did, on every occasion that was offered him, extend their contact with a slight but speaking pressure on Nell's hand as he helped her in and out of the curricle. It was always he who seemed to be conveniently available when Nell required assistance in clambering over a rocky spot in the pathway, or in fording a shallow stream. He held her parasol, helped her into her coat and slipped it from her shoulder.

Nell, in turn, made a point of speaking to him whenever fate allowed. She offered no more than simple exchanges—a daily greeting, a question about the weather, a comment on the horses or the roads. None of it was absolutely necessary, or even very important, but there was something compelling, both in the timbre of her voice and in the focus of her eyes, that spoke volumes.

This strange, almost wordless exchange was, Nell knew, entirely inappropriate behavior, and yet she could not refrain from communicating with the one person who seemed to best understand how violated her sensibilities were by such a wholesale marketing of her future. She began to wish fervently that her aunt would tire of this husband hunt.

Beauford was not at all surprised that Ursula Dunn had contracted the headache. His own ears were ringing with memory of the incessant chatter from the recently widowed Mr. Wentworth, who had insisted on bringing his half-deaf mother with them on the long road to Lewes, and into whose ear horn he had been forced to shout each remark repeatedly before it was understood. Ursula, who had to the astonishment of both her niece and her driver, found it within herself to label Mr. Wentworth "an agreeable prospect if only he might be separated from his mother," tottered down out of the curricle when she had done so with both plump hands pressed to her forehead.

"I am in need of a little lie-down in a darkened room, Fanella," she said rather breathlessly, "with a dram of hartshorn and water, and a vinegar compress. My head is splitting."

Beau thought Nell looked as pulled as her aunt, but she made no move to leave the curricle. "Do you mind if I run to the shops for some furbelows I require for my masquerade costume, Auntie?"

Ursula shook her head, and then seemed to regret mightily having allowed herself such violent movement. She flapped a limp hand. "You go on, dear, and no need to hurry back on my account. I shall enjoy having the house all to myself for a while."

Thus, for the first time since his employ, it was just the two of them in the carriage, he and Nell, and though the space between them seemed immense, and there was no hope for conversation as they clattered into town, there was a strange expectancy that clutched at Beau's chest, a feeling that something important was about to transpire.

Nothing untoward happened as they drove sedately in to the shops, and Nell purchased the necessary trimmings for her costume. Neither was there anything unusual in her request that they return by way of the Marine Parade, for it was by far the most picturesque road to take. But Beau was a little alarmed when, having caught sight of Captain Stiles among a group of blue-coated young men, she leaned forward to say, "You will stop the carriage, please, should we happen to receive the slightest encouragement from Captain Stiles. I am still waiting to hear what he may have found out concerning the fate of poor old Boots."

As Beau knew all too well what had become of Boots, he could not be disappointed when they rattled past the captain without receiving so much as a nod.

Fanella's disappointment was palpable.

"Oh, bother! I am of the opinion he has no intention of keeping his promise to me." She sighed, and so defeated did she sound, that Beau dared turn to face her, with a hint of contrition softening his tone, for he felt in part responsible for the lowering of her spirits, "Have you the headache as well, Miss Quinby?"

She nodded weakly, as though with such an admission, all the strength had gone out of her. "It would seem I am in need of hartshorn and water as much as my poor aunt."

"You have endured a very wearing afternoon," he observed. "Are you perhaps bothered today more than usual by the loss of your father?"

For a long, telling moment her eyes met his. Something in their depths acknowledged his understanding of her situation.

"Yes," she swallowed hard. "However did you know that?"

He loved getting lost in her eyes, as he was lost in them now. There was a level of communication shared in the deep, dark, silence of their exchanged glances, that had nothing to do with words. "It has crossed my mind on more than one occasion that had he not died, you would not be obliged to suffer through this business of locating a husband."

She dashed a tear from the corner of her eye. "It is terribly selfish, I know, but I feel somehow abandoned by my father. He had, of course, no intention, either of dying, or of leaving me with such a feeling, but I cannot quell the violence of my foolish thoughts and unstable emotions."

"I understand," he said softly. The truth of it was he did understand. One's feelings ran a gamut of hills and valleys in coping with such a loss. Blushing, she dropped her gaze. "Best take me home, Mr. Ferd."

With little desire for this rare opportunity to be alone
with her to end so tamely, Beau said, "I know of a place so
beautiful to behold that it must soothe even the most trou-
blesome headache. Shall I take you there and tell you what
little I have discovered with regard to your old horse?"

She hesitated a moment. "Is it far?"

"Not far."

"I should like to see such a place, does it exist," she
agreed. "I had no idea you had learned something more
with regard to Boots."

He turned the horses northeast, along the very road they
had passed over twice that same day—the road that went
across the downs, through Falmer to Lewes. He took the
horses as far as the top of the first great foothill and reined
them in. They were long shy of Falmer, in a desolate, tree-
barren landscape, with nothing but rolling green hills on either side.

"This is the same road we took this afternoon," said Nell
with a hint of alarm. "Do you find this isolated spot beautiful? I do not."

He turned to look quite keenly into her dark eyes. There
was a hint of fear there. Beau did not like her to be afraid,
either of him or his intentions. "It is a familiar road of no
particular beauty that we shall soon see transformed by a
different light." His voice was calm and impersonal, as
non-threatening as he could manage. With great skill and a
minimum of backing, he turned the horses full circle, until
the carriage faced back the way they had come. It was
clear, when he had accomplished this feat, why he brought
her here.

From such a vantage point, at this time of day, the sky
was magnificent. It stretched from horizon to horizon in a
pale wash of azure, the clouds faintly tinted with coral and
mauve, the sun a newly minted guinea, burnished to an eye-
watering shine.

They were facing the sun-gilded crest of hill that led gently down to the cluster of buildings that was Brighton. The
town, caught up in the strangely mellow light of the sinking
sun, seemed touched by the hand of Midas, while the Channel stretched beyond like a sheet of hammered pewter.

"Strange how something so simple as light can transform

an ordinary place into something quite extraordinary." Nell was awed. She sank back against the cushions with a sigh.

Beau could feel her every movement in his hips and thighs as the carriage swayed upon its springs.

"You are very kind, Mr. Ferd," she said softly, "to think of bringing me here. Sometimes things most remarkable are right under our noses, if we do but open our eyes in the right moment to see them."

"Indeed." He turned to look at her. "I could not a-a-agree with you more, Miss Quinby." Very properly, he turned his back to her again and let silence and darkness creep around them.

"Do you mean to keep me in suspense, Mr. Ferd, with regard to Boots?" Her voice, a little concerned in its anticipation, carried softly to him.

"No, I um . . ." Beau knew this was the perfect opportunity to tell her who he was. He had waited for days for just such a moment. And now that moment was come, and the words he had rehearsed in his head were all flown, and he hated to spoil the happy perfection of the view. He did not, could not, turn to look at her. "I have . . . um, discovered the horse's whereabouts."

The springs creaked as she sat up, her voice alive with excitement. "Have you really? Tell me then, tell me all."

Beau squinted at the beauty of the sky confronting him. This was no way to get into heaven. "You will be pleased. I think, to hear that Boots is become the property of a family with three children who are learning to ride."

Nell's voice was low and breathless. "You are certain?"

He closed his eyes on the view. Why should the truth prove so difficult? "Yes," he said earnestly, and though he longed to turn and read her reaction, he resisted the impulse. "I have it on good authority."

She made a happy noise somewhere between a sigh and a laugh.

"I feel as if a weight has been lifted from me." Her voice lilted with pleasure, colored by relief. As if the sky were touched by the sound of it, the widening bands of rose and gold and turquoise blue intensified in hue. The shadows lengthened and the indigo of darkness settled in the low-lying areas.

Nell said nothing as the sun slipped into the clouds. She made no sound at all, and Beau, battling with his conscience, was equally tongue tied. The last warm spark of the sun's brightness hovered on the brink of quenching in the sea before he turned, ready at last to reveal himself.

He swallowed the words before they could slip his lips.

She was crying. Pale face lifted to the sky, lips parted, her huge, dark eyes seemed unearthly bright as, awash in tears, they reflected the dying aura of the sun. Moisture glistened on the dark fan of her eyelashes, moisture wet the sweet curve of both cheeks. She wept openly, silently, unashamedly, and with such an expression of contentment that he knew that each precious drop was an expression not of pain or disappointment, but of an overflowing joy, an overwhelming appreciation of the beauty she witnessed and the relief she felt in the fate of her old horse.

She did not look at him.

Much moved, and feeling very strongly that he intruded on something private, Beau turned his back on both Nell and the truth once again.

A chill stirred the air as the sun left nothing but its afterglow in the sky. Nell sniffed, and leaned forward to whisper, as if speech of any greater volume might shatter the delicate spell. "That was sublime!"

Beau was pleased she should say so, but no words she might have chosen at that time could possibly compete with the speaking vision he had witnessed of her aspect, wet with tears.

"A-a-are you chilled?" he asked gently, his heart heavy with his deception. "I've this greatcoat, if you are."

She smiled and dabbed her eyes with a damp handkerchief. "Sounds lovely."

Checking the brake, he climbed down, his every movement rocking her through the bouncing of the springs as much as she had rocked him, through the unsettling display of tears. Leaping nimbly onto the precarious perch of the step, his weight giving the carriage and Fanella good cause to lean rather drunkenly in his direction, he swung his secondhand coat behind her as she ducked her head to accommodate its weight and length. For a moment, as he enfolded her shoulders in it and her head rose to a more natural position, it was almost as if he embraced her.

He could see, by the fluttering of her lashes and the ragged quality of her breath, that she was as conscious of his nearness, as he was of hers. Tension stretched between them like a wire. His hands stilled on her shoulders, and in the instant before he released his hold on her and stepped back off the curricle step, he bowed his head ever so slightly over the sweet crown of her hat to drink in the smell of her hair. His eyes closed for an instant. With the longing to announce himself and his feelings for her like a great weight on his chest, he pulled away and jumped down off the step, so that the carriage rocked again in a most unsettling manner.

"Thank you," she said, her voice trembling slightly, and in the dimming light he could see her both tuck the garment about her shoulders, and lean briefly into the fabric, eyes shut, as though to hide the tear stains on her cheeks.

There was something so intimate in such an action that Beau dared to hand her his handkerchief. As she took it, she clutched the hand in which he held it out to her. "Thank you, Mr. Ferd, for your effort to put my mind at ease about Boots, and also for the beauty of this view. The road does almost appear to be paved in gold in this light."

He returned, for an instant, the pressure of her grasp. "A-a-and in your estimation, Miss Quinby?" His voice dropped almost to a whisper, so that she leaned closer in order to hear. "Do you believe that gold paves the road to happiness?"

"I do not know." Her eyes took on a faraway look. "I do know that its absence has brought hardship to my family. I should like to do important things with my life, some of which involve money, or the influence that comes with it. I cannot in good conscience tell you that I hold myself aloof from its lure."

He made a show of busying himself with the lighting of the carriage lamps. "What important things do you think that you can accomplish with money?" He was genuinely curious.

She looked at him as if his question were remarkable. "How can you ask such a thing? There is a magic in money. Not only does it make one's own life quite comfortable, it has the capacity, when used judiciously, to enrich the lives of all those around one as well. Why you yourself pointed out to me how much difference one almshouse, built nearly a century ago, has made in the lives of the poor and disabled. Money! It was all that stood between me and the peace and happiness I would have bought for Boots. What a wonderful thing to have such power at one's fingertips."

Silence sat softly between them. What light still hung in the evening sky was caught up in the earnest planes of her face, lending her a painterly beauty of light and shadow that any artist who had regarded her would have identified as chiaroscuro, and the man before her regarded as the irrepressible glow of her spirit.

"These things you mean to do with money? They would make you happy, even if you did not love the husband who made that money available to you?" he asked in all seriousness.

"I think it would," she said slowly. "Yes. I believe that am I not fortunate enough to find love, I can find some fulfillment and satisfaction, some function and purpose in the works I may accomplish. I do of course realize that any husband indulgent enough to allow me free rein with my own allowance must be worthy of very high esteem."

"But love does not enter i-i-into the picture?" he pressed, disappointed in her attitude.

She bowed her head into the collar of his overcoat. "It would be ideal if it did, Mr. Ferd, but while I know little of love, never having fallen prey to its lures, I am well schooled, as are all young women of my acquaintance, in the necessity of finding a suitable match. The alternatives are extremely unpalatable."

The Duke of Heste stood back from the carriage, distressed by her words. Here it was again, marriage and money, clinging together like strange lovers. There was a moment in which he had considered telling her who he was. He might have her in an instant did he but do so, she had as much as told him so. But, then this entire charade as coachman would have been for naught. He could never then be certain which it was she loved—him or his money.

He did not reveal himself. Instead, he circled the carriage to light the second lamp. "Any road, when viewed in the right light, can a-a-appear golden and prove, in a-actuality, to be gilded by nothing more than a trick of light," he said softly.

"And what of yourself, Mr. Ferd?" she asked. "What road do you follow? Are you not to be taken in by the glitter of anything? Can you honestly say to me that you eschew wealth and power and marriage?"

He laughed. "I do in point of fact avoid them."

She looked doubtfully at him. "I do not understand."

It seemed suddenly vital that she should do so. Beau found himself articulating feelings he had never before found words to explain—words of understanding that he wished his father might have lived to hear.

"Money and power carry also with them great responsibility—a crushing weight of it a-a-at times. The fate of so many rest in the palm of a r-r-rich man, his blessing becomes a curse. The behavior of everyone who comes into contact with such a man is changed by his money. Money breeds jealousy and resentment and contempt. It creates grovelers and bootlickers and beggars out of decent upstanding f-fellows. How does a wealthy man discern between friend and foe, when both come, hands out, ready to ingratiate themselves on his good graces, hoping for the benefits money brings while a-accepting none of its burden. In marriage, too, consider how difficult it must be for a man with wealth to determine whether love is based on mutual understanding or the thought of mutual a-assets!"

Nell looked amazed by his outburst. "You speak with great passion in regard to this subject, sir."

"I do, for while I mean both to better myself and to marry, I will not change my circumstances blindly."

"And what do men look for in women, Mr. Ferd, besides a pretty face and a biddable nature? I have often wondered, but possessed myself of no brothers whom I might ask."

"I cannot speak for men in general, Miss Quinby, only for this man in particular." There was something intensely personal in what he meant to convey to her here in the twilight, something that changed the timbre of his voice as much as the loss of the sun changed the sky.

Even with the warmth of his coat about her, she shivered.

"Speak then for yourself, Mr. Ferd. What do you seek in a wife?"

He began softly, for he wanted very much for his words to fall kindly on her ears. "I seek a-a-a woman of great beauty. Not physical beauty that suffers under the hands of time, but a beauty of m-mind and spirit that grows and matures with the passing of the years. I seek, too, a female with spirit and intelligence a-a-and the patience to kindly ignore the failings of my tongue."

Her mouth formed a little oh, as if she chanced to find said tongue rather eloquent.

"Such a woman would have a neatness about her, a sense of taste and refinement. She laughs a-at life—and values honesty a-a-and compassion. She is one who recognizes what is morally right and has the courage to stand by it."

A small frown affected the angle of her brows. "This woman you seek sounds a paragon. Do you think she exists? And if she does, will she have you when you have found her?"

Beau laughed. "That remains to be seen. Money may stand in our way. Tell me, would you marry me, Miss Quinby?"

She frowned at him, as if she could make out neither his face nor his meaning with any clarity. Then she smiled, and gave her head a little toss, and said lightly, as if it were no great thing he asked her, "I do not think you should be happy if I did, Mr. Ferd. I am not at all the ideal female you have described."

With a bow, for there was something in her tone that spoke unmistakably of dismissal, Beau returned to his bench, touched up the horses, and took her back to her aunt's home.

All the way there, he thought of what she had said about the happiness that his wealth and power could bring. He had never considered his inheritance in such a light, regarding it always as more of a burden than a blessing.

Behind him, Nell seemed equally occupied with her thoughts. She allowed him to hand her down when they reached the steps that led up to her aunt's house, and she thanked him prettily for curing her headache, easing her mind with regard to Boots, and for loaning her his coat, which she returned to him. She would not meet his eyes in the light from the doorway however, and fled quickly up the steps and through the door as if making an escape.

It was not until he threw the greatcoat about his broad shoulders that the new Duke of Heste realized how devastated he would be if this fair creature did in the end refuse him, for trapped in the folds of fabric, almost overpowered by the smell of horses, and his own musky scent, was, very faint, a trace of her—of soap and violets, enticingly feminine. It was, he decided, the scent of dreams, and he would have them come true.

As a light bloomed in the window above and he chirruped to the horses to drive them back to the mews, Lord Brampton Beauford thought long and hard about truth, and half-truths, and his own golden road to happiness and dreams come true.

Chapter Thirteen

Nell felt both troubled and elated as she fled up the stairs to her room, where she paced about, flinging aside the confinement of her clothes that she might breathe more freely. Conversation with Mr. Ferd left her feeling strangely winded. Her dress lay in a puddle on the floor, and then, one by one, her petticoats, stockings, and corset. Only when she roamed about her room like an impatient ghost in flowing chemise, hair unpinned, could she breathe more easily. She had spent the entire week in conversation with a whole host of eligible bachelors. Why should the one man she might not have—a coachman of all people— make her heart leap and her stomach flutter? Why was it he who concerned himself with what mattered most to her? With no other gentleman did she plunge so fluidly into the very heart of discussion. Why did she long for the sound of his voice, his whistle, his step? Why did she yearn for blue- eyed looks that made her very backbone go soft? No other hand burned so hot against hers. No other set of lips would seem to beckon. In torment when he was beside her and even greater torment when he was not, Nell felt as if she had been knocked off balance. She hadn't the faintest no- tion of how to regain equilibrium. Was this what it meant to fall head over ears? Could it be that she tumbled headlong into love with a coachman? Unthinkable—and yet she thought of nothing and no one else.

The idea was preposterous, even frightening. Could she honestly see herself happy as a coachman's wife, with- standing the certain censure of family and friends in sink- ing so beneath her station? Was father turning in his grave? Nell paced the room wondering until, exhausted by the whirl of insistent thoughts, she extinguished the light, convinced that in so doing she symbolically snuffed out all feeling for Beau Ferd as well. The part of her mind that formed dreams was not so convinced. She woke halfway through the night to pace again.

It was, strangely enough, the easy intimacy of her conversation with Mr. Ferd that made Nell profoundly uneasy in his company the following day. She had emotionally undressed herself before this young man. There was something terrifying in such nakedness. He had gone so far as to ask her if she would have him. Unsure just how she should go on with a coachman she had so stripped herself before, Nell sought safety in withdrawal, both in person and in speech.

Such a distancing, she reasoned, was not only prudent but necessary, as an affirmation of all they had discussed. She had allowed herself to become far too familiar. She had allowed too much to be revealed to a pair of penetrating blue eyes. If she did not take very strict rein on both tongue and emotion, she would find herself embarrassingly compromised.

On the following morning, in order to accomplish this desired detachment, Nell carefully avoided the unspoken language in Mr. Ferd's pale blue eyes when he asked how her head was.

"Fine, thank you," she lied, for she felt far worse this morning than she had the night before. Coolly, she turned her back on him as her aunt outlined her requirements for the carriage that day, and with every fiber of strength she resisted the impulse to watch him go. With a great show of self-control she refused to look out of the window as he crossed before it, and tried very hard not to listen as he cheerfully whistled a bit from Beethoven's second symphony in passing through the garden gate.

Such restraint required a great deal of concentration. Nell had not realized just how great a toll such effort took until her aunt turned to her over their luncheon to ask, "Are you feeling quite all right, Nell? You are looking most dreadfully pulled, and I have yet to hear a single lighthearted or teasing remark pass your lips. It is most unlike you. Perhaps you had best forego Mrs. Lowden's tea this afternoon in favor of a bathing cure. I shall send Mr. Ferd back with the curricle if you like."

Nell could not help but blanch a little at the prospect of an afternoon in which she and Mr. Ferd should have the curricle to themselves. She meant to avoid him, not take herself off alone with him again.

"I do believe I shall cry off from the tea, Auntie. There are some letters I have promised myself I shall write."

Ursula Dunn patted her cheek. "Quite right, my dear. I had forgot you are unaccustomed to so much activity. A quiet afternoon with nothing to do is just the thing to calm your nerves. We cannot have you losing all your looks right before the prince and his crowd descend upon the town, now can we?"

Nell spent the better part of two hours in the composition of three letters. The contents of one could not help but remind her of the young man whom she had sworn to ignore. So distracted did she become that she could not content herself with a nap. Knowing Mr. Ferd had returned with the carriage, she sent word to the mews, requiring him to take her to the beach that she might follow her aunt's suggestion, in taking the salt-water cure.

He greeted her at the door at the appointed hour, his demeanor so natural and friendly, that Nell felt herself remarkably stiff and awkward by comparison. So caught up in this sensation did she become that she forgot that she meant to mail her letters, until they had reached the beach in weighty silence.

"My letters! I intended they should meet the mail. Perhaps you had best turn the horses," she said, as he opened the carriage door.

He smiled. "Shall I deliver them for you?"

It was impossible to sustain the remoteness of her tone when a gentleman looked at her with such a sweetness of expression. Nell could not but dimple as she handed the letters over to him. "The one on top requires that address you promised me, for Boots's new owners. You do not mind writing it in for me, do you?"

Beau did mind. He had not expected Nell to dash off a letter so soon to his sister Anne. Such a letter was sure to be the undoing of him. On his way to the posting office he pulled the carriage to one side of the coastal road, that he might stand on the little spit of land that hung out over the sea, while the bay and the gray stood patiently champing their bits. He looked out to sea for an answer to the question, and debated with his conscience the fate of Nell's letter.

The missive was tucked in the inner pocket of his new livery, the pocket over his heart. His right hand touched upon the crisp edge of paper, his fingers thrumming with the beat of his pulse as he waited for his brain to decide what next to do. The name on the letter was written in his own lean, flowing script.

Should he allow the flimsy bit of ink and foolscap to meet its destination when the words it contained surely meant the undoing of his disguise? It would be an easy matter to tear the things to pieces, to burn it into nonexistence, or merely to allow the wind to carry it away into soggy oblivion in the waves below. And yet Beau found himself reluctant to add even this small mite to his long list of transgressions. Deception was not an art in which he had planned to become accomplished, and yet he was fast becoming master.

He looked again over the edge of the cliff, to the dizzying surge and swell of gray-green water below. Was it perhaps another scrap of his integrity he proposed to fling into the sea? His lies begat more lies, his deception more deceit.

His hand slid empty from its place within his jacket. It was time to put an end to the lies and deception, he thought. Time to see if the spider was caught in the web of his own making. He must resolve this matter before the missive found a reply.

Turning his back on the sea, he set out to post the letter.

Having thus threatened his own future peace and happiness, Beau went on to the room rented in his name, to collect what correspondence he had himself received. There was a pile of it—letters from his sisters and from Gates, and a great packet from his solicitor. With thoughts of his responsibilities weighing heavy on his mind, and his stack of letters heavy in his pocket, he returned to the beach to await Miss Quinby's pleasure.

The day, his new bay-brown livery, and the news he read in his letters, seemed unbearably stifling to Lord Beauford. Gates's letter informed him a bay horse had been located. Beatrix wrote in a tirade from London, with regard to his absence and its insult to Aurora Quinby. Anne, startled by the unexpected delivery of Boots, wondered if her brother was hoaxing her. His solicitor demanded an immediate response and the courtesy of his signature on the documents enclosed. As he read, the brightness of the sun wilted both the duke's shirt points and his spirits.

There was no breeze to cool the sweat on his brow and upper lip, and beneath the folds of his neckcloth; the packet from his solicitor, full of documents that required immediate attention, did nothing to relieve his discomfort, for it could not help but remind him that he was very much a fish out of water.

The imp of mischief that had led him into this strange life gave way to the voice of reason that kept sounding in his head. He had responsibilities he must return to. His father had entrusted him with a great deal of money and power. It would be criminal to continue ignoring his duty. The life he had abandoned was sure to seek him out if he did not return to it. The letters were proof enough of that.

He glanced up from his reading now and again to look out over the sparkling expanse of water into which he wished to do nothing so much as plunge himself, in pursuit of a certain blue bathing box in which even now Miss Quinby was disrobing.

Removing his hat, the new brown coat and waistcoat, Beau neatly folded them across the curricle seat on top of his mail. The book he kept in the carriage to read as he waited further secured his clothing from the whimsey of the wind. He loosened his cravat—all of which provided little relief. He was still most uncomfortably warm. He wondered, and not for the first time, just what it was he meant to accomplish with this bloody charade. Why did he stand here pacing about in the heat, when he might just as easily enjoy his leisure in the water below?

The answer to that question stepped out of the blue bathing box. Beau forgot for the moment how very uncomfortable he was. Miss Fanella Quinby paused at the top of the steps that led down out of the box, her attention riveted in turn by a woman on the beach who had just sunk to the sand in a dead faint.

The stir amongst the little crowd that gathered around the poor unconscious woman was not based so much on the woman's fainting as on what she had observed to provoke such a response. The source of her distress had attracted the attention of a great majority of those who promenaded along the shore, and two that numbered among this crowd were women who succumbed to the spectacle in a like manner, sinking like scuttled ships into the arms of the nearest gentlemen.

There was a man of very little modesty and even less patience for the queues that waited entry into the men's changing rooms, who was stripping off wet clothes for dry on the beach, in front of God and everybody else. He was assisted in his endeavor by the ministrations of a woman who looked to be of less than gentle birth, who rather ineffectually held a large unfolded napkin in front of her companion's private parts, as he removed his soaked bathing attire, and was handed dry shirt and breeches.

Beau, who was feeling the heat again, was further annoyed by the fact that the fellow below, who had every reason to be sweating, looked cool as a cucumber and completely unperturbed by the sensation he created with his unblushing display.

There was, Beau had to admit, something most arresting in such an unexpected sight, but uppermost in his thoughts, and of higher priority to his consideration as he looked away, was discovering whether Miss Nell Quinby bore witness to it, and if she did, if such exposure inclined her to fainting.

It would appear there was little danger of Fanella so succumbing to nerves that she might be in danger of drowning herself. She stood now in the water, looking not so much shocked as curious and amused. So taken in was she by the scene unfolding on the beach, that she had no consciousness that her body, clad only in saturated flannel, was a spectacle as provocative in nature as the man changing clothes on the beach.

She had submerged herself, and stood waist deep in

water, her hair wet and sleek and hanging like a thick, dripping curtain over her right breast.

Her left breast was not so concealed from view.

Beau knew that it was the fashion among the more daring young women in France to dampen the fabric of their dresses, the better to reveal their charms. His sisters had more than once expressed their dismay at such lewd behavior. He realized now, as never before, why such activities alarmed the British sense of propriety.

Wet flannel covered Miss Quinby's charms no better than transparent gauze, and while the rare privilege of seeing her thus flushed his entire person with a heat of pleasure far more burning than the heat of the sun, with that pleasure came a sort of panic, that someone else might see this treasure publicly revealed and attempt to steal it away from him.

Panic soon had him in a sweat to abandon the carriage so that he might rush out into the water, to hide Miss Quinby's amazing breast from the lascivious attentions of any man gazing seaward save himself. As lathered as a horse before a race, he paced beside the carriage, his eyes locked on the young woman he had come to care so much about, his heart galloping, his breathing fast.

The dipper who accompanied Miss Quinby, a strapping, sun-browned woman of such an age that she might consider her role a motherly one, was encouraging Fanella to turn her back to the nonsense on the beach, but Miss Quinby was not entirely obedient. She turned readily enough, but curiosity kept turning her head back again.

Every time she turned, the astonishing outline of her raised left nipple was revealed.

Beau was beside himself.

Attracting the attention of a lad who agreed to watch the horses, Beau tossed his shoes into the carriage, stripped off everything but shirt and breeches, and picked his way out to the water's edge that he might walk into the waves.

Fanella returned to the carriage to find Mr. Ferd absent and a lad holding the horses. She dismissed the boy with the shilling he was promised and stood looking about for what might have become of Mr. Ferd. Had he abandoned her? The prospect gave her a moment's panic.

No, his hat, jacket, and waistcoat were neatly deposited on the driver's bench. The book he had the habit of reading when forced to wait for the return of his passengers weighed them down. The pile of clothes brought her to the blush, for they could not but remind her of the scandalous scene that had transpired on the beach. However, when some few moments had passed, and still no Mr. Ferd, Nell picked up one of the sun-warmed gloves that reached out to her from the top of the pile and fit it over her own small hand. There was something strangely personal in trying on the article of clothing, as if she had violated Mr. Ferd's privacy. Uncomfortable with the feeling it engendered, she set aside the glove and concentrated instead on the book that weighed down the clothing, curious to see what sort of written material was of interest to her unusual coachman.

She was not surprised that Beau Ferd knew how to read, although it was not at all common in a coachman to be literate, but to discover that the tome was a French work by Voltaire was startling. Mr. Ferd appeared to be more than halfway through in his reading of it, for several pages were marked. What surprised Nell even further, when she thought there could be no more surprises, was to find that the book opened on a number of pages between which flowers had been pressed to dry. One by one, she examined the specimens so carefully flattened between the sheets of vellum. There was no mistaking them. They were pinks from the posy she had given Beau Ferd to replace those she had crushed in his lapel on the way down from Godstone.

She shut the book with a snap when Bandit appeared, as if from nowhere, and shook violently, ears flapping, drops of water flying in all directions.

It appeared Bandit had leapt into the sea and that his master had followed him there. Beau Ferd, his face pink from exposure to cold water and bright sun, his hair slick and darker than she was accustomed to, his pant legs dripping, stood gazing at her as he wrung out his shirt sleeves.

"You and your dog are very wet, Mr. Ferd."

He nodded. "It was very warm." Blue eyes locked on hers, stilling her tongue. "Unbearably warm, f-feverishly so." There seemed to Nell to be a hint of the fever he spoke of in the blue depths she was in danger of drowning in.

"Sorry to keep you waiting," he said.

"No need to apologize. I have been diverting myself in examining your book." Flustered, Nell came very near to dropping it as she handed the volume back to him.

"Voltaire cannot be half so diverting as what transpired on the beach today." His eyes sparkled as brilliantly as the drops of water that glistened in his hair.

Nell flushed as her gaze dropped, and she utterly failed in trying not to stare at the damp outline of his thigh. "A dreadful display," she agreed.

"Quite." He offered a damp hand as she approached the steps of the curricle. "I have always understood how well a dinner napkin might protect one's lap, but must admit that I had never seen one as desperately employed as this afternoon's."

Nell would not allow herself to be amused. She took his hand and frowned. His glove was soaked from water dripping off his sleeve, and in grasping hers unkindly shared its moisture. Nell could not help but stop to stare at the rivulets of water running from clinging shirt cuffs and breeches legs.

Why did her hand feel so very much at home in his, despite its having been soaked? Disengaging his grasp, she peeled off her wet glove and wrung the moisture from it, with a feeling that he watched her every move with far too much intensity for such a mundane task.

"You partake of the salt-water cure, then, Mr. Ferd?" she enquired, and could not resist the temptation of looking to see if his clear blue eyes were indeed bright with some illness.

The feverish heat was still there, the intense, burning ember that fired his gaze as it met hers. Yet he had not, in any other way, the look of illness about him. His face fairly glowed with health and well-being. He regarded her with disturbing intensity, vibrant and alive and expectant, as if he stood on the brink of telling her something of vital importance and yet held his tongue in check. Said tongue darted over his lower lip, and it occurred to Nell, and not for the first time since she had met him, that Mr. Ferd had a most attractive mouth, the lips being full and firm and of a remarkably provocative pinkish hue.

"The waters beckoned," those pleasing lips now said.

"And are you feeling better?" she asked. "It is clear to see that Bandit is rejuvenated."

Bandit was rolling ecstatically in the grass. Beau Ferd smiled one of the slow, engaging smiles that so disarmed her.

"We are both feeling much better. Thank you for asking, Miss Quinby, and I do beg pardon, both for soaking your glove and for allowing Bandit to shake himself near your person."

"Never mind," she said, struggling to slip her hand back into the damp kid of her glove. "Did you mail my letters before allowing your hound and yourself to answer nature's call?" She gave up on the glove and tried very hard to look severe. In this she failed as miserably as she had in donning the glove, for there was something very unsettling in the way that Beau Ferd stood respectfully answering her, as water dripped in a most ridiculous manner from his soaked shirt, breeches, and a lock of wet hair that hung down over his forehead.

"Your words are on their way," he said. "In addition, I have news from Mr. Gates. He has located a bay for your aunt."

Chapter Fourteen

Ursula Dunn's nerves were all adither when she discovered that she was soon to have her matched pair of horses, did she but approve of the bay Gates had discovered. "We must send a note around to Mr. Tyrrwhit," she instructed her niece.

And so it was the next morning that Nell and her aunt were in expectation of both the carriage and Mr. Tyrrwhit, who had sent word that he would be delighted to accompany them. For the second occasion since coming to Brighton, Nell went to answer the knocker at her Aunt Ursula's front door, expecting to be met by their coachman, and found someone else in his stead. It was her sister Aurora who stood expectantly on the steps.

"Nella!" she cried, her beautiful face alight with glee, and before she could respond, Nell found herself engulfed in the sweet cloud of Aurora's perfume and wrapped in Aurora's soft embrace.

"We are come to Brighton, of all places, is it not wonderful?" Aurora chortled. "I was never more pleased than when Beatrix decided we must make an effort to locate her brother."

"It is wonderful to see you, Aurora," Nell said, disengaging herself. She stepped out of the door to look at the empty hackney waiting in the street. "But where is Lady Cowper? Came she not with you?"

Aurora tipped back her head and laughed. "You will not find her there, silly. He is merely waiting to be paid, and I haven't a penny with which to do so. Have you any spare coin?"

Nell, with very little of her own spending money for the

month left in her reticule, did not hesitate to offer it to her sister, so happy was she to see Aurora.

Aurora was equally pleased that they should be together again. Once the cabman was paid, she linked her arm through Nell's saying, "I cannot wait for you to meet Beatrix, Nella, for I am sure you will adore her as much as I do. She is quite the most independent young woman of my acquaintance. No sooner did we arrive than she directed me to seek accommodations, while she herself went immediately to inscribe our names in the ledger at the library. Otherwise, she says, we shall not be allowed to attend tomorrow's masquerade, and that would never do, for we have both of us the loveliest costumes to wear. Bea is of a mind that she must run onto her brother at such an Assembly. She is determined to find out what he has been doing with himself, and intends to peruse the pages of the register for any mention of where he might be lodging."

"The duke is without a doubt come to Brighton then?"

Aurora giggled. "Came to Brighton long ago, it would appear. Beatrix has only just run him to ground by way of his solicitor."

"Did he really leave town without a word to anyone else? I can scarcely credit such paltry behavior."

Aurora's eyes sparkled dangerously, and she lowered her voice to murmur with acidic humor, "I am of the opinion that the duke was too terrified to face me."

"What? What kind of man would not care to meet you, Aurora? Does he not like women?"

"I do not think it is that he does not like women so much as that they would seem to make him uncomfortable. Beatrix tells me that her brother still suffers greatly over the death of their father, and while she has never said so, I am of the opinion that I am not the only female the family has thrust under his nose, for Beatrix did go so far as to tell me that her brother's speech impediment is far more pronounced when he is presented to any young lady of good breeding."

It crossed Nell's mind that it was rather coincidental that another gentleman with problematical speech should cross her path, if only in conversation.

"The duke has a speech impediment?"

"Yes, isn't it dreadful?" Aurora's voice was full of sympathetic distaste. "Poor man stutters."

Nell thoughtfully narrowed her eyes as suspicion darted into her mind, and was as swiftly dismissed as ridiculous, for why in heaven's name would a duke take up position as private coachman?

As if her thoughts had drawn him into being, Mr. Ferd appeared at the end of the drive in her Aunt Ursula's sparkling-clean curricle. The horses were carefully groomed, their harness gleaming in the sunlight, and while their driver cut a bit of a dash, whirling into the carriageway with an artistic flourish of the whip, Nell could not convince herself that this might be the Duke of Heste.

"Aunt Ursula and I mean to go look at a bay horse this morning," she said to her sister. "Shall I encourage her to put off the errand, since you have only just arrived, or would you care to come with us? It is a bit of a drive, but our friend, Mr. Tyrrwhit, has planned to take us to a spot called Devil's Dyke for an al fresco luncheon."

"Tyrrwhit?" Aurora repeated, with bright-eyed interest, "You cannot mean Charley Tyrrwhit?"

"But yes. Do you know him?"

"I know of him. He is one of the duke's Whip set. However did you meet him? Do you think he might be able to tell Beatrix where her brother has gotten himself off to?"

"You may ask him yourself if you mean to accompany us."

"Well, it is decided then. I shall go with you to examine this horse, if only to meet Mr. Tyrrwhit, but we must drop by the courier's office on our way out of town to pick up my trunks and tell Beatrix my plan."

"Perhaps we had best do that now, for we've a quarter of an hour before Mr. Tyrrwhit is expected."

"Splendid! Let me just pop up to tell Auntie where we are off to, and give her a kiss."

Aurora darted into the house as Beau pulled the curricle to a halt in the drive and stepped down off the carriage seat to open the door for Nell. His eyes met hers as he did so, with one of the flatteringly appreciative looks for which Nell had so much come to depend. She allowed herself to return that look for a heartbeat or two longer than was ordinarily her custom, for it crossed her mind that with Aurora here, competing for such attentions, she must not expect such tribute to be directed her way quite so often.

"Good morning, Miss Quinby."

"Good morning, Mr. Ferd. My sister is just arrived, but she seems happy enough to accompany us."

He smiled. "And how is Miss Catherine Quinby? She does not come for the cure, I trust."

Nell laughed at such an idea. "No, it is not Catherine at all, but my elder sister, Aurora, that I mean."

He had been smiling when she mentioned Aurora's name, and Nell could not help but notice the marked change that overtook his features. She had no time to determine just what it was about his expression that struck her odd, for here was Aurora herself, come skipping breathlessly down the steps with a brilliant smile. Nell focused then most intently on Mr. Ferd's reaction to her sister, for she was curious to see what effect Aurora might have on him. In her heart of hearts, Nell feared that the look of admiration—that flattering, heart-fluttering look with which Beau blessed her every time their eyes chanced to meet—must change somehow with the intrusion of Aurora's incomparable beauty.

In that she was rather pleased to find herself mistaken, for Mr. Ferd looked more concerned than impressed by her sister's intrusion. He smiled pleasantly enough at Aurora, but he seemed rather repressed in her company, and expressed none of the glowing admiration in his eyes for Aurora that he did for Nell. In fact, his pale blue eyes looked almost frozen, while his tongue seemed locked in his lips, when Aurora beamed at him as he helped her up, and said in her endearing way, "Have I kept you waiting?"

He answered with a simple, subservient, "No, miss."

And then, from behind her sister's back, as he helped her into the curricle, there it was again, for Nell's eyes only—the look that set Nell's heart aquiver with the perception that he regarded her as something unique and rare and wonderful.

Aurora nudged her as the coach was set into motion. "What spell have you cast on Auntie's handsome coachman, Nella?" she whispered. "The young man does not seem at all inclined to take his eyes off of you."

Nell was amazed that this was her sister's immediate impression, for she had not thought that the looks she and Mr. Ferd exchanged were anything but discreet.

"I had not noticed," she lied, coloring with pleasure.

Behind the barrier of her fan, Aurora whispered in jest, "Your blush says otherwise, Nella! Anyone would think you had a *tendresse* for him."

Nell sank against the cushions, blushing rosily.

Aurora's cornflower blue eyes got very big above the edge of her fan. "Oh, my? It's best that I've come then, for it would appear that I must save you from yourself."

Nell laughed. "You pretend to come for my sake, then? I would have guessed at quite another reason."

Aurora archly rolled her eyes. " 'Tis true, I have lowered myself to come chasing after a duke who is so disgusted by his sister's matchmaking that he has fled London." She twirled her parasol provocatively at two gentlemen who quite brazenly stared and tipped hats to the lovely occupants of the open carriage as it swept past. "Do you know, Fanella, it would seem that you have had more opportunity to make the duke's acquaintance than I have, for Beatrix tells me that a shipment was made to her sister Anne from the Duke by Brighton courier some weeks ago. He has been here at least as long as you have."

Nell smiled, for Aurora was an incurable flirt, and she could bend the truth when it pleased her purposes without looking any the less innocent.

"That has little enough to do with why you are here," Nell challenged her with a laugh. "I am not so foolish as to believe that you would chase after this paltry fellow, duke or no duke, whom you have never met, when he refuses to so much as acknowledge your existence."

"Whatever do you mean?" Aurora very prettily fanned herself and feigned confusion with dancing eyes.

"Don't think you can pull the wool over my eyes. It is another young man entirely who lures you here. 'Fess up," Nell teased, "or I shall not tell you a word of what a certain young captain of the guard has had to say to me on the occasions we have had to meet and converse."

"Never tell me you have actually spoken to Jeremy? That would make me too jealous for words. What did he say, Nella? Do not tease me. Did he ask after me, or has he forgotten me entirely?" Aurora demanded with such ill-contained excitement she fairly bounced upon the seat.

When Fanella had told her everything—not once but twice, and in minute detail—Aurora sank back with a sigh. Quite forgetting that the coachman could hear her every word, she said, "We are a pretty pair, are we not, Nella dear? I would toss away the chance to snare a duke who is reputed to be as rich a Croesus, for all he may stutter, in exchange for a tent and sea biscuits, as wife of a captain of the Hussar, while you have sunk even further, in allowing yourself to become enamored of a coachman, who would come home to you smelling of horse and all over hay."

"Aurora!" Nell gasped, as the coach pulled to a halt before the courier's offices. She was horrified that her sister could have been so careless as to speak out loud within earshot of the very coachman she referred to, and with a nudge in Aurora's ribs she shot her a warning look as Mr. Ferd tossed the reins to the boy who stood at the curb for just that purpose, and hoped her sister would take the hint.

"Oh!" Aurora bit down on her lip, momentarily contrite. "He cannot hear me all the way up there, can he?"

Nell, her face awash with crimson, hoped that such were the case. Had she the privilege of viewing the lively twinkle in Beau's pale blue eyes, she could not doubt that he heard every word and was perversely pleased with the hearing.

Beau was not so pleased a moment later when he heard to his dismay that he was to fetch out the trunks from the courier's, not only for Miss Aurora Quinby, but for the Lady Beatrix Cowper as well.

"Lady Cowper?" he repeated stupidly.

"Yes," Nell interrupted chatter with her sister to inform him. "Lady Cowper will be staying with us."

"Oh, yes," Aurora confirmed, and then struck terror in his heart by saying with obvious pleasure, "Here she comes, even as we speak."

Flabbergasted to see that Beatrix was indeed approaching the carriage, and overtaken by the nasty realization that he had completely run out of luck and time, Beau leapt from the curricle, head down, and darted into the courier's office, with every intention of looking for a back door.

Behind him, he could hear his sister's voice, acknowledging Aurora's query of, "Did you have any luck locating your brother, Beatrix?" Her reply brought him skidding to a halt.

"I have not, I am sorry to say, located my brother in person," Beatrix admitted ruefully, "but I have managed to find out where he has booked rooms."

"Rooms?"

Beau cringed. Did this mean he could no longer retreat to his rooms?

"Yes." Beatrix laughed. "I am told by the landlady that he is never to be seen about the place, but the bags there are unmistakably my brother's, so I have decided that I shall not intrude on your aunt's hospitality, setting up residence in Brampton's rooms instead. He must come back to them eventually, and then I shall hear an explanation of his whereabouts this past week. See if I don't."

Nell had been staring at Beatrix Cowper throughout this exchange. The young woman did, in some manner she could not quite place, look familiar to her. She was stoutish, of medium height, dressed in the height of conservative fashion, and possessed of a look of intelligent determination. She had the confident air of someone who is accustomed to having her word trusted implicitly and her commands promptly obeyed.

Aurora introduced the two.

Again, Nell was struck by a feeling of familiarity. It was something about the tilt of Lady Cowper's head as they were introduced, something about the slow smile that touched her lips as she said hello. There was nothing at all familiar in her voice, however, and the fleeting impression of having perhaps seen her before dissipated like a fog as Beatrix cheerfully remarked that Aurora was forever mentioning her little sister Nella, so she felt as if they were already acquainted.

Beatrix listened to Aurora's plan to go and look at a

horse that very afternoon with some dismay, however, and politely declined the invitation to accompany them.

"My love, I cannot even contemplate such an excursion so hard on the heels of our having been on the road down here! I have a hundred and one details to attend to in relation to my costume for tomorrow's masquerade, and fully intend to have a lie-down before this evening. Are you sure yet another journey will not fatigue you?"

Aurora laughed and took up Lady Cowper's plump hands. "I shall not be too fatigued to enjoy tomorrow's masquerade." Her eyes sparkled mischievously. "We are going to look at this horse in the company of Mr. Charley Tyrrwhit, and I may be able to find out something with regard to your brother's direction."

"Charley's here? Well, if anyone might know where Brampton has gotten himself off to, 'twill be Charley. Tell him that I am to be found in my brother's rooms."

Nell stepped from the carriage. "I shall just nip in then, and tell Mr. Ferd our change in plans."

Nell's entrance stopped Beau from slipping out the back door. He could not so callously abandon her.

"Mr. Ferd?" she called out to him. "We shall not require Lady Cowper's bags after all. She means to arrange their transport to her brother's lodgings."

Beauford licked his lips. "Miss Quinby?" He must reveal himself to her now. He had no choice but to do so.

"Do hurry, Mr. Ferd," she insisted, without realizing he meant to speak. "I should not like to keep Mr. Tyrrwhit or my aunt waiting." She walked back out of the door, and opportunity was lost.

Beau hoisted Aurora's trunk onto one shoulder, clutched a valise and two hatboxes in his free hand, and took a deep breath. Time to face the truth. He followed Nell out into the sunshine.

There he was met by an unexpected but most fortuitous distraction. A bevy of uniformed young men surrounded Aurora and his sister. Nell readily joined in the animated conversation, which seemed to be focused rather specifically on the various costumes to be donned for the masquerade.

Using the trunk on his shoulder like a shield, Beau skirted his sister as she enquired of Captain Stiles, "Have any of you, by chance, seen my brother, the Duke of Heste, here in Brighton?"

Stiles laughed. "Can't say as I have laid eyes on any dukish-looking characters myself, unless he is perhaps the mysterious Green Man who haunts the streets of late."

Nell laughed. "You cannot seriously believe that the queer gentleman who wears only green from head to foot is anything but a likely candidate for Bedlam."

"Who knows?" Captain Stiles shrugged. "What does a duke look like but any other man? He could be standing right beside me and I would not know it. Why, only consider Beau."

Beauford regarded the man with trepidation around the end of the trunk as he lowered it into the boot.

"Beau?" Beatrix looked interested.

"Our coachman?" Nell asked.

Stiles was pleased to be the center of attention. "It is Beau Lascalle I refer to, the Great Pretender."

"And why, pray tell, is this Lascalle called Pretender?" Beatrix enquired.

"Have you not heard of him then? He is one of Brighton's more interesting fixtures. The prince himself labeled him pretender, for those two are as like as peas in a pod. So closely does Lascalle resemble the prince that the two are quite often mistaken for one another."

"If the likeness is so very pronounced I should very much like to see this Lascalle," Nell admitted.

"One can only hope one does not make the mistake of bowing to this Lascalle as if he were indeed royalty," Beatrix said.

Stiles chuckled. "Far better to bow to Lascalle than to slap a prince on the back and address him as Beau. There are one or two who have embarrassed both themselves and the prince by going so far."

Aurora laughed outright. "How very singular to go through life doubling as someone else. Almost as if one were split into two separate beings. It must be quite diverting to escape oneself, now and again."

"We shall all of us have opportunity to do just that, to-morrow at the Masquerade Ball," Nell pointed out.

"Oh, my, yes." Beatrix waved a dismissive hand. "Do not let me keep you, ladies. Captain Stiles, will you be a dear and help me with my trunks?"

And so it was, Beau narrowly missed detection.

Chapter Fifteen

Nell was not at all amazed to see Charley Tyrrwhit fall slave to her sister Aurora's charms on the drive to Poynings, where they meant to look at the bay. She would have been surprised had he not done so.

"So you wish to know about the Duke of Heste?" He seemed amused when Aurora pressed him for information.

Nell thought he had the look about him of a sleepy cat. Amused, condescending, his lips were caught somewhere between a smile and a sneer, as though he knew not whether to play with the beauty before him or eat her.

Nell's aunt, who sat beside him, was not privy to the look on Charley's face. "We know all we need to know," she interrupted with a bombastic righteousness that would seem to indicate that her mind was already made up with regard to the duke. "He has evidenced nothing but a rude thoughtlessness—I might go so far as to say downright snobbery—in refusing to so much as meet Aurora, when it was clearly his sister's intention that he should do so. Such a cut, indirect though it may be, has irreparably injured her chances at making an instant hit with the Ton. Tell me all you will of your friend. I am a fair woman, and would not like it said I hold him in complete disgust if there are some redeemable qualities to save him from such an opinion."

Nell's attention strayed, as it all too frequently was wont to do, in Mr. Ferd's direction. Their coachman appeared to be listening keenly to what was being said. His head was half turned the better to hear, and there was something in the rigidity of his posture that gave Nell the impression he did not wholly approve of their discussion. Nell wondered what he might have had to say were he to join in the conversation. But conversation from a coachman was as out of place as her interest in him.

Charley chuckled. "The Duke of Heste is neither devil nor angel, ladies. He is not at all proud or overbearing or rude; rather he is a man understated in his demeanor, quiet and collected and calm. I am sure he had no intention of slighting you, Miss Quinby, for he is a mannerly sort of fellow, and of slightly more than ordinary intelligence."

"You must tell us more, Mr. Tyrrwhit. What of his appearance and habits?" Aurora inquired.

"His appearance? Well . . ."

Mr. Ferd turned, but not to look at her, as Nell might have hoped. He shot a look instead at Charley Tyrrwhit.

Mr. Tyrrwhit did not appear to notice the interest with which he was regarded. He was squinting at the heavens, as if he recalled the duke's appearance somewhere in the clouds. "He is of average height and weight," he said thoughtfully. "His coloring is nothing out of the ordinary, and his features might best be described as . . ."

Mr. Ferd shot another squint over his shoulder. Mr. Tyrrwhit smiled. ". . . as even. His background and schooling are typical. He conducts his financial affairs in the usual way, does not gamble, smoke, or drink to excess, and he dislikes hunting."

Nell protested with a musical laugh, "You surprise me, sir! What draws you to fellowship with someone whom you would describe more in terms of what he is not, than what he is? Such a description gives us very little clue as to whether we should love or hate the man."

"Oh, but you must love him, Miss Quinby!" Charley said, a benign smile molding his lips.

"Does any woman love such an ordinary man, other than his mother?" Nell insisted.

Mr. Ferd appeared to stiffen on his bench.

Charley protested. "Never think the duke an ordinary man. He is not. He is kind and thoughtful; involved in any number of worthy charities; dotes on his family, cattle, and pets; indulges his servants to a fault; has an excellent sense of priority and an even better sense of humor; and I cannot name the chap I would rather have befriend me. He will most certainly run the family estate better than his father, may be counted upon to assist family or friend without question when ill befalls, and conducts his business without condescension or plays of power. He performs his social obligations with a minimum of fuss. He has a large circle of friends, and both of his sisters love him dearly, as do his nieces and nephews. There may be one other female . . ." he said, squinting thoughtfully at Nell. "The duke has been dangling after this one particular young woman of late. I think she may see something in him that she likes."

Aurora leaned forward. "What? Is the duke become secretly attached to someone? Is that his reason for quitting London with such haste? I know for a fact that Beatrix has no knowledge of this mysterious young woman you speak of. Who is she?"

Mr. Ferd noisily cleared his throat.

"That would be telling," Charley said. The catlike look had returned.

Ursula nodded. "Mr. Tyrrwhit is quite correct to refuse to tell you, girls. For while he may be certain as to his friend's feelings—"

He nodded. "The man is besotted. I am sure of it."

Ursula's head bobbed. "He cannot be certain as to the sensibilities of the young lady. If he were to connect the names, and she had none of him after all, it would be most unfair to both parties, for the gentleman might be seen as a cad and the young woman a heartless flirt."

"Or worse," Charley agreed.

Aurora was disappointed, but Nell not at all dismayed. "You say your friend is besotted?"

Charley nodded. His catlike attention swung in her direction. Nell got the uncomfortable impression that she amused him.

"How does one know when a man is in such a state?"

Beau closed his eyes in anticipation of his friend's response. Charley was enjoying himself immensely at his friend's expense. And well he might. Seldom was a fellow given the opportunity to tweak another man's nose while he sat within earshot and endured whatever slander might be brought forth, without the slightest demur.

"The poor old boy is making a complete cake of himself." There was an edge of laughter in Charley's response. Beau might have laughed himself under different circumstances.

"Cake? Can you be more specific?"

Dear Nell. She sounded so very serious.

Charley could no longer contain his mirth. "Oh, you know." He laughed outright in an explosive little burst. "He is trying to be something or someone he is not."

Nell shook him far more than he would have cared to admit when she went on earnestly. "Do you know, Mr. Tyrrwhit, I do not think I care very much for the duke, no matter that he is a friend of yours. I have no patience with men who feel the need to recreate themselves in the image of what they think a woman wants, in order to impress. In my opinion, any serious attachment must be based on honesty, openness, and the strength of trust."

"Ah, Miss Quinby, would but the duke himself might hear your words. He would be a better man for them. Do you not agree, Mr. Ferd?"

Beau did not turn from the managing of his team. "I am sure you have the right of it, Mr. Tyrrwhit," he acknowledged stiffly, realizing how wrong he was to continue to deceive these people. He must reveal himself. He knew it with a clarity of thinking that made his conscience hurt. He had built a relationship that mattered dearly to him on lies, and in so doing he knew no more about whether this woman loved him for himself and for who he really was, than had he never misrepresented himself to her. Lies were no foundation for trust, or love, certainly not commitment. Lies propagated more lies, until one began to question where truth left off and the lie began. Lies had one constantly looking over one's shoulder, made one wonder at one's own consistency in lying, and caused one to dodge truth, for it might undo the knotty business of the lie. Life had begun to stutter as awkwardly as his tongue. He tired of such a double existence. He had to tell Nell the truth.

"Do you know the duke then, Mr. Ferd?" Ursula asked.

"We are a-a-acquainted, after a f-fashion," Beau acknowledged, pointedly ignoring the gurgling choke that Charley emitted.

"Give us your impressions of the man, if you please," Nell coaxed.

Her sister agreed. "Yes. What think you of the duke?"

Beau squirmed beneath the increasing weight of his falsehoods. He was asked to describe himself now, and he could think of nothing commendable to remark upon. Charley had already painted a rosier picture than he himself might believe. What would a coachman have to say of him?

"Well, he has a good eye for horseflesh, and can handle the r-r-reins well enough, although he will never be classed as the neck-or-nothing jumper that his f-father was thought to be." He fell silent a moment, and his throat constricted. He had not thought of his father much in the days he had passed in Nell's company. He wondered what the old man would have thought of her. "A rare sort of girl," he could almost hear him saying, "with a rare knowledge of horseflesh."

Beau could feel the anticipation to hear more, prickling the hairs at the nape of his neck. He cleared his throat. "His grace likes dogs, I am told, and values his f-friends and family. A-a-above and beyond that, I've nothing to tell, other than that he has a-a-as much trouble expressing himself as I have."

"I understand that he has been spotted in Brighton," Ursula prodded. "Have you happened to see him while we have been here?"

Beau chewed a moment on the inside of his lip. Another lie to swallow. "Can't say that I have."

"Well." Aurora flounced a bit in her seat. "While I can no longer with good conscience say that I hate such a man, I am still in no mood to forgive his slight of me, no matter that he is a duke, and my dear friend Beatrix's brother besides."

"And no more should you," Charley advised, and in stretching his arm out, he managed to knock it up against Beau's elbow. "He is a rascal to have gone off without so much as making your acquaintance. I advise you to cut him dead should you have the misfortune of running onto him. Even a duke should not be allowed to get away with such frightful behavior."

* * *

The contemplative study that Beau fell into as a result of Nell's opinion of the man she supposed him to be did not lift until the carriage entered the long, rolling stretch of road that led from Clayton across the downs. There, his thoughtful expression was replaced by one of astonished panic.

Heading their way at a smart pace came a fast-moving entourage—five of the finest and most recognizable sets of satin-coated bits of blood and bone to be witnessed in all of England. The prime-blooded horseflesh was pulling the latest and most well-sprung vehicles that money could buy, and each of these remarkable equipages was tooled along the road by a skilled whipster, all of them kitted out in matching white greatcoats, and black Allan-brimmed hats, with flashy yellow posies the size of dinnerplates gracing their wide lapels.

The Whip Club, or the Four-in-Hand Club, as some had begun to refer to it, were on their way south to Brighton! Beau knew he was done for. There was no way he could run such a gauntlet without being recognized.

"Whoever might that be?" Aurora wondered while the horses and carriages were still some distance away.

Charley Tyrrwhit twisted in his seat to look. "Eee-gad," he gasped. "It's the lads, Beau!"

"They are moving at a most remarkable pace," Ursula observed. "Had we best pull over to let them pass?"

Aurora nudged her sister. "But who are they, that we should give up the whole road to them?"

Fanella startled Beau in answering, "Unless my eyes deceive me, we are privileged enough to witness the approach of a few of the members of Catherine's beloved Whip Club. I would guess that we see first Mr. Mellish, then Petersham. I do not recognize the fellow driving the showy blacks, but the man at the rear is most assuredly—"

"Lord Barrymore," her aunt provided, quite correctly.

Charley almost choked, he inhaled so abruptly.

"However can you know such a thing?" Aurora demanded of her aunt and her sister.

"Yes, how?" Charley wheezed. "I'd no idea you were familiar with the club members."

Ursula became slightly defensive. "It is no great thing, once one learns the idiosyncratic color schemes these gentlemen effect. It is Lord Barrymore who is to have my gray, and only see, the last of the carriages is drawn by perfectly matched grays. Is he come to look at the horse, Mr. Tyrrwhit? Is that why so many of your friends are come to Brighton? They cannot all be in need of the salt-water cure."

Beauford did not have to look over his shoulder to comprehend that Charley's amusement escalated at the same rate as did his concern. "The lads always come down for the Season here," Charley said jovially. "I daresay I'd best tell you . . ." He paused too significantly for it to have been an accident. Beau wondered if Charley meant to unmask him, but no, he meant to reveal something else entirely. Charley's voice dropped to a conspiratorial whisper. "The chap driving the blacks is Gentleman Jackson," he said. "And the chubby fellow behind him is none other than the Prince of Wales."

"Never say it is so!" Ursula gasped.

"And me with my hair a windblown mess," Aurora complained.

Beau wanted to laugh through his clenched teeth. His reputation was about to become far more of a mess than Aurora's lovely locks. There was no way he could run the gauntlet of his friends without his identity being uncovered. How could he ever have guessed that the end to his relationship with Nell would come in such an attractive and familiar package? His time as coachman was fast drawing to a close. Nell would soon know him for the liar he was.

Beau prepared himself for the inevitable. He had an excellent view of his friends' faces as they approached. Recognition dawned. Surprise accompanied the flash of hands as each gentleman in turn raised the rakish black hat. Potentially damning words slipped from one startled set of lips after another, like arrows launched to pierce his pride—arrows that might kill all chance of success where Fanella Quinby was concerned.

"Beau!" The word whisked past.

"Ho, it's Beau and Charley!" Another verbal arrow missed the mark.

"Hallo, chaps! Where's the dog?"

"Damn, so this is where you've gotten yourself off to!"

"Headed the wrong way, aren't you?"

Then, remarkably, they were past, and Charley was waving and shouting gleefully from the back of the carriage as though they had just won the Derby. "See you tomorrow at the masquerade, lads."

Beau's head reeled with the enormity of the close call he had just suffered. His eyes swung back to meet Charley's in stunned disbelief. He slipped through Fate's fingers for a second time!

Charley laughed gustily. "Gad, what a surprise that was, eh, Beau?"

When, having reached their destination, the women were engaged in looking at the attractive bay that was brought out for their inspection, Charley pulled Beau aside to wonder, in a loud whisper, "Lord, but that was a close shave! When do you mean to give up this dreadful guise?"

Beau laughed. He was feeling incredibly fortunate as he admired the way in which Fanella was examining the bay's ears, eyes, and hooves before directing the lad in taking him through his paces. She was possessed of a most discerning eye, this remarkable young woman!

He did not take his eyes off her as he admitted, "I have done Miss Quinby an injustice in so long perpetuating the lie of who and what I really am. You must realize that I would tell her all in this very moment, given but a moment alone with her."

"Damned pleased I am to hear it! I do not know what has taken you so long as 'tis. No more mucking about. Devil a bit at Devil's Dyke this afternoon, and I shall contrive to see that you have your moment alone with the chit," Charley vowed.

Chapter Sixteen

Nell was vastly pleased with the bay. She was pleased, in fact, with the entire day, for she and Aurora always got along splendidly and it had been far too long since she had shared female company other than her aunt's. Arrangements having been made for purchase and delivery of the horse, the hungry party set off on the relatively short drive to the Dyke House Inn, between the villages of Poynings and Fulking. There Mr. Ferd performed his usual magic in making baskets of food and wine and water appear before the group set off on foot onto the South Downs, to view that natural phenomenon of clefted hills that the local people credited to the workings of a saint in his confrontation with the devil—the Devil's Dyke.

The weather was perfect—warm and cloudy, with just enough of a breeze to cool the sweated brow one might expect as a result of such an excursion.

And yet Aunt Ursula could not content herself with perfection. Peering at the sky, she observed that it looked as if it might come on to rain later in the afternoon.

"Rain!" Charley Tyrrwhit scoffed. "Never," he insisted confidently. "Our luck is far too sound for that!"

Nell was pleased to notice that Beau Ferd took a long look at the sky and, apparently less certain of their luck than Charley, added three umbrellas to the load he already carried.

"May we assist in any way?" she asked, when Aurora would have set off after the others at a galloping pace.

The arresting blue eyes settled warmly on hers, blessing her with the admiration she so enjoyed witnessing there. "How kind you are," he said.

"Here, you cannot carry all of that," Aurora agreed, and

between the three of them, the burden was more reasonably divided.

Side by side the sisters set out, with Mr. Ferd right behind them. Nell was surprised when Aurora leaned close to whisper, "He has a most engaging smile. I should not wonder you are so taken with him, but dear sister, do guard your heart against his wiles. You must remind yourself the man is no more than a coachman."

Nell held her peace. She had done just that a hundred times and more since making Mr. Ferd's acquaintance. Aurora did not understand, and Nell had no idea what she might say to enlighten her. How did one verbalize a plethora of feelings and sensations that followed neither logic nor reason? Where might one find the words? She hadn't the faintest idea.

"This is it, then," Charley said, when they had walked as far as the beaten track would take them without plunging down into an abrupt swale, beyond which rose an odd V-shaped cleft in the hills. "Devil's Dyke!" He set down the basket he had taken from Aurora's hands. "It is all that stands between us and the ocean."

"And why is this dyke the devil's?" Aurora asked, peering intently across the swale.

Unable to stop her eyes from straying in his direction whenever he was about, it was Beau whom Nell watched, though Charley answered.

"According to local legend, the gap below us was dug by the devil, who wished to flood the low-lying areas of the Weald with the waters of the Channel."

"He was stopped"—Beau took up the tale—"by the light of a candle, held up by a woman who was curious enough to watch what the devil was about." The pale blue eyes settled on Fanella. "The devil mistook the candle for the rising sun and stopped his digging."

Aunt Ursula was gazing at the horizon, but it was not the Devil's Dyke, as it turned out, that so fascinated her. "Do you not think those clouds look as if they might hold rain?" she insisted.

Nell forced herself to look away from Mr. Ferd's pale, laughing eyes.

"Nonsense," Charley said. "We have been blessed with the devil's own luck today. It will not rain."

Fanella looked at the clouds and could not be so sure. It did look as if inclement weather might overtake them.

Charley was proved wrong. Their luck would seem to have run out. Rain it did. The al fresco luncheon was but half devoured when, with silent deceptiveness, fine, soft droplets began to mist down on them.

Raising one of the umbrellas Mr. Ferd had brought, with an I-told-you-so vigor, Ursula beckoned her nieces. "Come, my dears, we shall lead the way back to the carriage."

Raising the second of the three umbrellas, Aurora was quick to follow her, but Nell bade them go on, saying she would catch up to them as soon as the baskets were packed away. She stayed to help Beau and Charley stow away the remains of their feast. Charley remarked that perhaps he should go and see to the horses, for they had been taken out of the traces and must be put back in again in order to carry them safely home. Grabbing up two of the hampers, he left them.

Nell felt awkward, left alone with Mr. Ferd, even if it was only in the task of gathering up the remainder of their provisions. The two worked in relative silence, seeming to understand the other's intentions and purpose without a word said, as if they communicated on a level that required no verbal interchange. The work went quickly, and yet, for all their mutual cooperation, there was a growing tension between them, in the lonely stillness of the spot that had so recently been alive with voices and laughter. As if in concert with her increasing uneasiness, the rain began to fall with intent.

Beau unfurled the third and last of the large black domes, snapping it taut, just as Nell finished buckling the straps on the final basket. "There is something I would s-say, Miss Quinby, but first I think you had best take advantage of the umbrella."

He held it out to her, shielding her from the rain, and yet taking no shelter for himself. He was, in fact, more doused by the umbrella than not, for the rain it shed from Fanella's person ran down its sides and onto his arm, as he picked up the baskets that had to be carried back to the carriage. His hat brim too, ran moisture, and Nell could see, in looking up at him, beads of rain on his cheeks, and dripping from his hair.

"Do take cover with me, Mr. Ferd," she insisted. "This is an inordinately large umbrella. There is surely room to keep both our heads dry. Never say there is not."

As she spoke, warmth kindled in his blue eyes. In the midst of so much cold, damp rain, his pale eyes smouldered softly. The pansy-black centers swelled. Transferring both baskets to one hand, he stepped beneath the protection of the umbrella.

Rain misted down around them like a gray velvet curtain, closing off the outside world, until the periphery of their vision might discern shapes no more than five yards in any direction. Their shrinking universe seemed composed of just the two of them, the object that drew them together, and the dripping bead curtain of rain that ran down off the lip of the umbrella. There was little to look at but each other, but to look at one another while in such close proximity seemed somehow improper, so Nell found her gaze darting and sliding in awkward confusion.

Mr. Ferd seemed not at all unhappy with this new and much dryer arrangement of his person, but Nell, her heart pounding so loud she was sure he must hear it, her face flushing with her discomfort at standing so very near to this man that her skirt was in constant danger of brushing against his leg, could not feel at all settled. It was much easier to believe she cared nothing for her coachman when a proper space separated them, but with no more than inches, her resolve was not so firm. The rain seemed to have separated her from modesty and a proper sense of propriety, in the same way that the pole of the umbrella separated them from one another.

Mr. Ferd had removed his hat as soon as he stepped beneath her shelter, but his greatcoat began to drip from the moment he took refuge, and while Nell did not find herself too greatly incommoded by what little bit of water did happen to fall her way, he was immediately preoccupied with what he regarded as a problem.

"Now, what was it you meant to speak of?" she asked.

"Yes, well . . . terribly sorry." He pulled the dripping coat away from her.

"It is no great thing," she said, sincerely hoping that he would not choose to be drenched again rather than drip a little in her direction.

It would appear he had a better idea.

"Hold this a moment." He thrust the handle of the umbrella into her hands and began to shrug himself out of his greatcoat. "There is something I m-must tell you." Nell took the handle readily enough, but, as she was not so tall as he, her natural inclination was to hold the thing much lower than he did. This presented a problem. The ribbing of the umbrella thus dropped down to knock against Beau's head as he struggled with his coat. In consequence, he hunched his shoulders and leaned forward, while she, conscious of the resistance, tipped up her chin to see what obstacle the umbrella had met.

"I . . ." he was saying, "I am not . . ."

Their eyes could not help but meet under such circumstances. Come together their gazes did, for what seemed an eternity of anticipation before their lips connected as well, he bending his head further to meet hers, she lifting her chin a trifle, when she might have ducked it down, and thus averted what was sure to follow. Nell's eyes closed with the terrifying realization that while she wanted to be kissed, and kissed most particularly by this young man, more than anything else she had wanted within memory, it was very wrong in her to do so.

His lips brushed hers, soft and warm and gentle, like the rain. Arms hanging loosely shrouded in the half-removed greatcoat, Mr. Ferd had no power to hold her submissive to the meeting of their lips, and yet she did not pull away.

The kiss was plush as velvet, hot and surprisingly dry in the midst of so much dampness. The touch was fragile, glancing, and yet unbelievably powerful in the emotions it stirred. Nell flushed with an inward heat. She inhaled rather abruptly between slightly parted lips when he pulled away from her, the sound like a backward sigh, as if she meant to recall his lips to hers.

He drew away, in order that he might look at her, as if to

reassure himself that she did in fact not resist his very improper advance.

Nell looked back at him, her mouth alive with longing, her eyes liquid with fear that he had not found the kiss to his liking. With the sweetest smile she had ever seen, and a light of recognition, warming his pale eyes, he bent to kiss her a second time, as lightly as the first, this time planting soft kisses above, below and beside her mouth, in a manner so deliciously teasing that her own lips parted and sought his.

His kisses changed. They drank in her mouth as if it were wine, sipping and savoring. Shrugging himself back into the coat, and dropping both picnic hampers at their feet, his arms encircled hers, as if he meant to draw her into the coat with him. Such an embrace, seemed to Nell, to involve their bodies as much as their mouths. There was a raw urgency to the clutching of him, hands and mouth. She could feel the hard handle of the umbrella between them, so close were they pressed. She listened, breath stilled, to the raw sighing of his breath between each searching kiss. Hungrily, he explored her: cheeks, neck, chin, and forehead. Her lips felt moist and swollen, like ripe fruit. She let him pluck them with the sweet, heady heat of his mouth. She had never been prey to such feelings as those that coursed through her, and the very newness of such rampant emotion carried with it the pleasure of discovery and the spine-tingling sensation that she had leapt without looking into the forbidden.

Fanella's passion frightened her. There seemed to rise within her ribcage an uncontrollable, ballooning joy, tethered by no more than a thin thread of fear. The fear was of surrendering, of shattering her mild, uneventful life into a thousand irreclaimable pieces.

A second round of kisses rained down on her lips with frightening intensity. Foreign, forbidden kisses in which Beau's tongue, like liquid fire, darted along the ridge of her lips, probing their parting. Nell's anxiety grew. Surely this strangely invasive tangle of tongues was more than just kissing.

The umbrella brought Nell back to her senses. It slid awry between them. Unheeded at first, raindrops began to pepper her hat, her eyelashes and cheeks, while Beau's tongue, with growing persistence, thrust into her mouth. Nell drew in a startled and sobering breath.

Driving her hands against Mr. Ferd's chest, she pulled away from the unexpected lure that his mouth had become, her desire for him as palpable as the taste he left on her lips.

He blinked, looked down at her hands as they stiffened between them, and fell back from any contact with her, his pale blue eyes searching hers with a look of concern, as if it mattered very much to him what she was thinking in that awkward moment. What he saw brought a gentle, knowing smile to the lips that had so recently taken possession of hers. Nell found herself holding her breath, hoping he did not mean to surrender her so easily.

He bent to retrieve the umbrella.

Their separation, as he withdrew the warmth of himself and his greatcoat, was awful and strange for Nell. She shivered, her teeth actually rattling in her head, jolted by the sudden, debilitating awareness that she had placed herself in a damningly vulnerable position. Her emotions had robbed her of good sense and judgement. Desire had brought her to the brink of ruin. She must stop this madness, and stop it now. Her knees trembled weakly beneath her and her body craved nothing less than the warmth and solidity of his, to brace it.

What must Mr. Ferd think of her?

His face turned toward her as he stood, the dripping umbrella in his hands. The answer to her question was to be read in the sweetness of his expression. The message such an expression conveyed sang like a lark in the depths of her heart. He thought her as awesome and wonderful as she thought him! She could read it in the pale depths of his eyes, in the growing smile. He marveled at her, desired her, meant to have her. Such intent could be read in his look. Nell could not help smiling, but even as she smiled she realized that it was still up to her to stop this thing, to nip it in the bud before she was compromised beyond redemption. She shivered again, and a sense of sadness and loss cooled the flame of her passion. She forced herself to look away from him. She could not hold fast to her resolve and yet look into those azure eyes. There was a heaven in their depths that was not hers to claim, a heaven that might bring with it a hell, of her own making.

"Dear Miss Fanella Quinby."

Her back stiffened, as he lifted the umbrella to shield her from the rain once more. She held one small, gloved hand before her like a shield. "No!" she gasped, willing him to fall silent.

Never had the coachman bent to her will in the past. Neither was he bent now.

"Nell," he chided, ever so gently. She had never heard her pet name on his lips before, and the sound caused her hand to fall. He took it in his own. "You cannot hold up your hand a-a-and pr-pretend that naught has happened. You feel this as intensely as I do. I can read it in your eyes."

His voice was far too elated to be stilled. He wheeled away from her, the umbrella whirling in one hand, the other uplifted to the rain, which he allowed to wash over his face, over the wide-eyed expression of joy that transformed it. "This f-f-feeling is too wonderful to deny. You know it is." His pale blue eyes challenged denial, and when no denial voiced itself, he turned his happiness heavenward again. "Today is the a-a-answer to my prayers, and dreams, and heartfelt wishes. Today . . ." His boots jigged water from the puddles in the pathway. "Today, we will r-remember for the rest of our lives. We will speak of it when we are both old and gray, and our children's children dare a-ask about the wisdom of love."

"Mr. Ferd!" Nell did not recognize this wet, wild man. He had not the look of a reliable coachman about him at all, and he dared to speak of children! "Please, I beg of you . . ."

He had turned, and as she spoke, he raced back to her, and fell on both knees, in a puddle at her feet.

"Nay, say no more! I have something I would a-ask of you, and you will want to hear it, I am certain of it."

Nell's mind was racing. The rain had slacked off to almost nothing. Aurora and her aunt were doubtless wondering what had become of them. They must not return to find their coachman on his knees before her, as he was now.

"Get up, Mr. Ferd," she insisted. "Do get up, I beg of you."

"I will rise soon enough, my love, but for now, my knees are too weak to hold me. P-Passion will do that to the strongest of men, you know."

"Passion?" she whispered, and she could not hold her heart aloof from him in such a declaration.

"Yes, Fanella Quinby." Again, her name fell prettily from his lips. He smiled, his most winsome smile. "I find myself quite hopelessly in love with you." His voice was thick with emotion. "Will you marry me, Miss Quinby? Will you marry me, Nell, holding up the candle of your lips to ignite the flame of love that I have held back like the tide thus far, or would you refuse me, and allow the cold waters of your denial flood the fertile Weald of my heart, extinguishing the flame of my passion forever?"

Nell was amazed that of all things he might say, these were the words that passed his lips. He spoke poetically, his words uttered in all sincerity. A little noise issued forth from her throat, her lips paralyzed by their recent foray into uncharted territory.

He rose up from the pathway, allowing the umbrella to tumble away from him as he did so, and for the breadth of a moment, so close did his face loom to hers, she thought he meant to kiss her again. Such was not his intention. He meant naught but to gaze deep into her eyes. Stripping off one sodden glove, he lifted his index finger to caress her cheek, as light and as moving as his first kiss had been. His eyes followed the course of his finger, which traveled to her eyebrows.

"I do love you, my dear," he repeated earnestly.

Something in her gaze seemed to disturb him. He pulled back, and a look passed over his pale blue eyes, like a cloud through a clear sky. It was a look of fear, as if he read her thoughts, and stood now in dreadful expectation of disappointment.

His mouth no longer smiled.

"Do not answer my proposal in haste," he said huskily. "My heart is broken if you say me nay without giving it at least a modicum of consideration." He gathered his breath, as though to say something of moment. "I . . . I am . . . You should know . . ."

Fanella stood quite still, her chest heaving, her eyes heavy with concern for what she had done, and what he asked of her as a result.

He shook his head and went on. "The life I have to offer is not, I will admit, what you are accustomed to, but I am quite certain that I can make you comfortable and happy. You seem to know me, to understand who and what I am, far better than any woman I have ever before encountered, and yet there are some ways that you know me not a-a-at a-a-all." He broke off uncertainly. "I would have you know a-a-all of me. There is much I would tell you, should have told you long a-a-ago . . ."

He was looking at her lips again, a look that spoke of such piercing need, such blatant desire, that Nell found it difficult to swallow. Unable to bear the glowing hope in his eyes, that she must squash, she rested her head on his broad, damp chest, shaken by a desire to tell him that she would follow him anywhere, if he could but hold her safe from a life of poverty and social censure.

His chest rose and fell beneath her cheek. His voice rumbled in her ear. "I know that this must come as a surprise to you. I had not meant to rush into this thing like a bull after red flannel, but I must tell you, I am—"

"Fa-nel-la!" Her aunt's voice interrupted him. "Fanella! Where are you?"

Nell's head came up so abruptly, she slammed Beau's mouth shut on the very words he had struggled so long to say. "Oh, my! We must go," she said, conscience stricken.

Wincing from the pain of having clapped his tongue between his teeth, Beau caught up her hand.

"B-But wait, I must tell you—!"

"Fa-nel-la!" The sound drew nearer.

"Whatever it is, you must tell me later," Fanella insisted. Disengaging his hold on her, she set off resolutely toward the voice that called her back to reality.

Chapter Seventeen

All along the muddy road back to Brighton, Nell sat, sure that by some sign, everyone around her must realize what folly she had just committed. Her lips felt swollen, marked by what she had done with them. Her cheeks glowed with inner heat. Her pulse was erratic. Her stays felt too tight. What had she been thinking, to behave in such a foolish fashion? Kissing a coachman, wanting to be kissed by him again. It was absurd! Could she hope to find happiness as a coachman's wife? Such a prospect seemed highly unlikely, until her eyes strayed to the back of Mr. Ferd's neck, and then anything seemed possible, and her heart fluttered in her throat and forced her to smile. It was absurd how happy this man could make her feel.

He wished her to marry him! Ludicrous notion. And yet she could not turn away from the thought, away from the idea of a future with this man who made her heart leap. She stole another glance at the straight backbone before her. Dear Mr. Ferd looked cold—soaked to the skin. His poor hat steadily dripped a stream of water onto his coat collar. Nell was possessed of an unbidden desire to reach out to wipe away the wet, to feel the heat of his flesh against hers. Perhaps the idea of marriage was not completely ridiculous. Never had she felt so inclined to care for a gentleman before. Certainly she had never cared to kiss any man in the cravenly passionate manner she had surprised herself by just doing. Might another man fire such desire within her breast? She thought not.

He "could not bear life without her," he had said. Could she bear to think of a life without him? The life he offered her was one to which she was not accustomed, but he offered, too, his heart, his lips, his arms, and the intention to do his utmost to see her happy. What more did she want or need?

There was no one to whom she might turn for advice. All who cared for her would, without doubt, encourage her to abandon the mere thought of such a union. They would be amazed that she so much as entertained the notion of marrying beneath her station.

What would life bring to her as a coachman's wife? She liked horses, and the smell of stables did not sicken her, but she wondered if it might not prove daunting always to be fighting the smells and flies and dirt that accompanied such an existence. As wife of a man who must travel, might she not find herself lonely a great deal of the time? And what of the absence of ready money? Would she become discontented and resentful, forced to make do on scant means? She would make a miserable wife if such were the case. Survival without the extras in life, the frills and furbelows and geegaws that so captivated Aurora, would not be too terribly difficult. Late-night dancing, balls and fetes, and polite company she could do without, could she not? But what of the skills required to manage a household, no matter how small, without the benefit of servants? Could she keep a house in good order?

It devastated her tender heart to think what her mother would have to say to such a match. Father would have forbidden it in an instant. Mother, who would not leap so quickly to bar her happiness, had yet taken pains to make sure she was educated in the finer arts—watercolors and music, polite conversation, and needlework. She could not but be disappointed. Nell had been versed in the skills required of a woman of means, a hostess and a landowner's wife. What could her own children expect, should she be blessed with them, with their father a coachman and their mother misplaced gentry? She lowered her progeny as well as herself in taking such a social plunge.

It was ridiculous! She could not marry a coachman.

The decision wrenched at her physically, twisting her stomach into knots as complex as the ones she busied her mind untangling. Her heart needed no convincing. It was steadfast in its certainty that with Mr. Ferd at her side she could make a happy life. It was her mind that threw the barrage of doubts and questions at her. And yet she knew the value of good horses and cattle, and the way of balancing a budget. While schooled for a far different way of life than the one that was proposed to her, she might yet fit into it with some grace. Who was to say she and Mr. Ferd could not cut a comfortable niche for themselves in the coaching world? Mr. Ferd claimed excellent connections amongst the upper crust. Perhaps they might be used to good advantage.

She knew Beau Ferd to be a kind and thoughtful man, a plain, honest man who reached out without hesitation to help those who were in need. He was gentle and self-educated; he loved animals, laughter, and music.

To his detriment, he cared little for possessions or money, and yet she could not fault him in it, for his inner drive for advancement was not stilled. His work habits were to be admired. She could in fact think of no single vice that she had witnessed in the entire time she had observed Mr. Ferd's behavior, other than his recent inappropriate pursuit of her affections, and she was as much at fault as he where that was concerned. She could not help but be flattered that she would seem capable of driving such an exemplary young man to distraction. There was something undeniably wonderful about the passionate side of his nature. An irrefutable energy had leapt between them, from the moment she had first set eyes on him, and he had fumbled about beneath her skirts. Was it the heady lure of passion, or the promise of a lasting love that she had seen smouldering in his eyes?

She closed her eyes against the consideration and reconsideration of that single breath-stopping moment when the world and all its objections to such a match had been stilled. There was magic in the meeting of their mouths. She could not conjure up the memory of it without lifting a finger to graze ever so softly against her lips, in an attempt to reproduce the strangely mystic sensations to which she had so recently been introduced.

The thought of kissing Beau Ferd again flushed her entire being with a throbbing heat. Her pulse quickened as she considered the strange appeal of having a man's tongue thrust between one's lip. Her breath caught in her throat. Her heart and mind did, for the moment, abandon all hold on weightier and more sensible considerations. Never in her short life had she felt so wonderously desirable and guilty and improper in her happiness—all at the same time.

What struck Nell most profoundly in her ruminations as the carriage rattled and splashed its way through a countryside that had never appeared more beautiful to her, was the realization that she had known he meant to kiss her, had known and yet had not stopped him. She had seen the intention of the kiss in the softened quality of his eyes and mouth, in the steady advancement of his head to hers. She might have stopped him at any moment. She could have pushed away, for he was not such a brute as to force himself on her. He had, in fact, paused, his eyes searching hers, before he tilted his chin so that their noses would not knock against one another, and, eyelashes skimming his cheek, feathered his lip against hers.

She had done nothing to stop that first kiss, or the ones that followed. She had known what was coming, had anticipated it, full of wonder, barely daring to move, or even breathe, in the face of her own audacity. And she had enjoyed the sharing of their lips, thrilled to the closeness of their bodies. She could not deny that to herself or to him, and reading as much in her eyes, he had dared to kiss her again and again and again. The passion they shared left her ready to abandon all reason, all practical considerations. Falling in love, she decided, was not a practical business.

Marriage however, was generally nothing but a practical consideration. Marriage, as she knew it, was the joining of names and title, wealth and land. With her father's untimely demise, she was left with naught but her name with which to bargain a worthy match. Mr. Ferd would take that from her, too, along with all that it stood for. Was the love and devotion he offered in return enough to keep her happy?

Was she completely depraved to allow such freedom with her person if she had no intention of marrying this man? His request for her hand was nothing but honorable, considering the circumstances. Did she dishonor herself in refusing him? Nell knew she must come to a conclusion.

Yes or no, she must devise an answer for Mr. Ferd's proposal.

When Nell went to give him answer to his proposal of marriage, Lord Brampton Beauford, seventh Duke of Heste, was rehearsing the delivery of what he long since should have told her. He stood ankle deep in manure, and as flies buzzed about his grace's ears and a sheen of hard-earned sweat dewed his brow, he threw his weight into the shovel with which he was mucking out a stall as energetically as he threw his heart into verbalizing aloud what it was that he meant to say to his beloved.

"Bandit, old boy, I must tell her I'm a l-l-liar, and telling is far more difficult than I had anticipated." He sighed. Bandit, who had curled up near the wagon into which he was shoveling the manure, raised his head, ears at the prick.

Beau leaned on the shovel to think, and then stepped back to address the implement as if it were Nell. "My dear Miss Quinby, I a-a-am—"

A shadow filled the sunlit doorway to the stall.

"You are what, Mr. Ferd?"

Beau looked up guiltily to see none other than the young woman whose mouth fit so perfectly to his, blocking the light.

Nell stood in the shaft of sunshine that gilded the dust motes and penetrated the doorway, bathed in the glory of light, looking calm and collected, all in white. There was something angelic in her appearance, something perfect and pure and untouchable. Her dress, virginly high necked and high waisted, was in danger of being soiled should she choose to step any closer. The dress became a sort of halo, a shroud of brilliant, backlit white, an outward expression of the inner light Lord Beauford had always felt in Miss Quinby's presence.

Must he now reveal himself to her, with sweat dripping down his nose and his boots clumsy with straw and manure?

"Mr. Ferd?" Her sweet voice had an uncertain quaver that sent a chill down his spine. "Was there something you meant to say to me?" There was an intensity in the way she asked, and in the way she looked at him, that gave him the uncomfortably vulnerable sensation that she knew exactly what it was he meant to disclose.

He opened his mouth to speak the words that he had been rehearsing. No words came. With great effort, he managed to whisper. "I am . . . I am . . . desperately in love with you."

He smiled as he said it, all his love for her shining in his eyes. She surprised him by blinking and turning away.

"I have come here to respond to your proposal, Mr. Ferd," she said stiffly. And even as she said it, Beau, who in that moment felt completely unworthy of such a prize, lost all ability to say a word, for he could not convince himself that she meant to tell him anything but no.

She bit down on her lip a moment, straightened her shoulders, and drew a deep breath.

He leaned into the support of his shovel.

"I cannot deny the truth of what encompasses my heart, Mr. Ferd," she began.

Beauford frowned. What was she getting at?

"I have never felt drawn to a man as I am drawn to you." She regarded the toes of her kid boots.

The shovel slid unnoticed from Beau's flaccid grasp. This was not at all what he had braced himself to hear. He could not believe his ears.

"I have never allowed a man to so invade my dreams, my thoughts . . ." She blushed, slid a troubled look in his direction and continued, ". . . to so sway my better judgement with a kiss. I have never felt for any other man the rush of feelings that undo my sense of decorum whenever I am in your company. Did my decision affect only myself, I should readily trust you with my heart, my happiness, my very future, Mr. Ferd, for I cannot imagine a more honest, open, and trustworthy husband. But, such a decision . . ." Her voice faltered. She seemed unable to continue.

Beau felt as if he had just had a net dropped over his head. How in heaven's name could he now reveal himself to her? Honest. Open. Trustworthy. He was none of these! He advanced, mouth half open, mind reeling, and stopped within arm's length of a pristine white sleeve. He could not touch her, with mucky hands! He could not kiss her, reeking of manure. Above all, he could not sully her opinion of him in admitting himself devoid of all the qualities it would appear she most admired in him. He felt like a maggot, a dung fly, a flea.

"I fear that I must disappoint . . ." She regarded him intently, and Beau felt all strength, all joy, all hope, depart body, heart, mind, and soul.

"A decision to marry me concerns someone other than ourselves?" he pressed, his stomach tensing, as if for a blow.

She nodded, her expression troubled and unbearably sad. Her chin trembled. "I will not lie to you. My decision, with regard to marriage, has the power either to save my family, or to lead them into greater financial ruin than they already face."

Beau wiped his forehead on the back of his sleeve. Odd, how money figured into things, even when he went to great lengths to see it did not. "Miss Quinby—"

"No!" She impaled him with the intensity—he might almost have said the ferocity—of her gaze, as she batted a fly away from her face. "I cannot stay, Mr. Ferd. I cannot allow you opportunity to sway my better judgement. This has been the most difficult decision I have ever considered." She closed her eyes in order to gather herself together, for it seemed she was on the verge of tears. "I am sorry to disappoint you." She gave a watery sniff. Her hand lifted to dash away a tear. "I hope it may content you somewhat to know that I am heartbroken in refusing you, for I feel as if I deny myself all hope of ha-happiness . . ." As her words broke on a sob, she fled.

Beauford was left with the feeling that she took all light and hope and happiness with her. Unable to bring himself to pick up the waiting shovel, heart aching, chin set, he strode out of the stall, Bandit trailing at his heels.

Lord Brampton Beauford burst into his rented rooms calling for Gates. "I require a bath," he ordered when Gates showed himself, and added, "I also require a replacement coachman be found and sent to Ursula Dunn's residence."

Gates calmly responded to his summons, as if not in the least surprised to see him. "Yes, sir; how soon, sir?"

"Immediately."

A tiny furrow troubled Gates's brow. "A coachman might prove a trifle challenging to locate today, sir. Tonight, if you will recall, is the masquerade."

"I am a-a-aware of that f-f-fact," Beau almost snapped. "Is my costume ready?"

"But of course, sir. The difficulty lies in obtaining a replacement, sir, when all reliable coachmen have been engaged for many weeks in advance in preparation for this evening's festivities."

"Hmm," Beauford began to strip himself of his offal-stained attire.

Gates took up the clothes as they were removed and held them at arm's length. "Shall I have these washed, sir?"

"Burn them," Beau ordered impatiently. He knew he could not leave Mrs. Dunn and the Misses Quinby stranded, not when it was so important to everyone concerned that they attend the masquerade. But neither could he go on pretending to be the coachman he was not.

"Shall I ride to Lewes, sir, in search of a driver, as soon as your bath is prepared?"

"Excellent idea, Gates, but perhaps we may persuade Charley to play escort to the ladies tonight and save you the trip. I do not think I should know how to go about donning my costume without your assistance."

"You would seem to have gone along just fine as coachman, your grace." Gates sounded ever so slightly miffed.

Beau considered the morning's confrontation with Nell. "Not as well as I would have cared to," he said softly. "I have been like a fish out of water in many ways."

Gates knew best when to hold his tongue. He prepared the bath while Beauford, with no more than a towel wrapped about his torso, sorted through some of the mail on his desk. He was standing thus, half clad and still stinking to high heaven, when Beatrix and her maid came into the apartments.

"Beau!" Beatrix shrieked, her hand fluttering over her eyes. "Whatever do you mean, standing there so nonchalantly, without a stitch on?" Crossing the room to greet him, she would have offered him a peck on the cheek had not the stench turned her away, hand to nose. "My stars, but you do smell as if you should be drawing flies. Where in the world have you been, and what have you been doing, to reek so?"

"Your bath, sir." Gates announced, as if on cue.

"I should a-a-ask what you are doing, camped out in my apartments, were my bath not cooling even as we speak," Beau turned away from her questions.

Beatrix was not so easily put off. She trailed after him, stopping in the doorway to the room where the tub was set up. "But, Brampton, you must tell me, or I shall die of curiosity. Where have you been? Do you know how very angry I am that you went off without so much as a word, when you knew I was bringing Aurora Quinby especially to meet you?"

Beauford took the towels Gates handed him. "You're off to Charley's then?"

"Right away, sir."

"Excellent."

Beatrix stamped her foot. "Brampton, I will not be put off. Tell me."

"Yes, I knew you would be a-angry, Bea. I am sorry to have raised your fur. I a-am sorry, too, for any inconvenience caused Miss Quinby. You will be p-pleased to hear that I have only just come from a flower stall, where I have ordered a large bouquet of roses to be sent round to the Misses Quinby, along with a note of a-apology."

"But you still have not told me where you disappeared to, Brampton."

Beau frowned at her. "I have been hunting, Bea. Now go a-away and let me bathe in peace." He closed the door in her face and turned the key.

She did not go away, or allow him any peace.

"But, what were you hunting, Beau, at his time of year?" Her voice came muffled through the door.

Beau stripped off the towel and stepped into the bath with a sigh of pure pleasure. He had forgotten just how lovely hot water could be.

Beatrix rattled the doorknob. "Brampton!"

Beauford scowled at the door. She would never go away until her curiosity was sated. "I have been hunting peace and happiness, Bea. Do go a-a-away, or I shall be sorry I returned."

There was a moment of silence beyond the door. "Did you find any?" Bea's voice sounded strained.

"Any what?"

"Peace and happiness, Brampton. Did you catch any on this silly hunt of yours?" Her voice sounded cross and quavery, on the verge of breaking down. "I have been worried sick about you."

Beauford stopped lathering himself with the sandlewood soap he favored. She did not ask the question lightly. He had been a brute to go off without so much as a word to her.

"I miss him too, you know." The voice on the far side of the door had taken on a childlike quality.

Guilt flooded over Beau. Bea thought he sought peace and happiness solely because of their father's passing. The soap slipped through his fingers. Funny, but that was exactly how this adventure had begun. He had almost forgotten. He fished about in the water for the soap. Somewhere along the London to Brighton road, his father's death had become more a part of the past than the present.

"I know you miss him, Bea. I'm terribly sorry to have troubled you by leaving no word as to my whereabouts. 'Twas unconscionably r-r-rude of me. I will not be so foolish again. I promise you."

"I should think not." The starch had returned to her voice. "I will ring a peel over your head should you so much as try."

He heard her step away from the door and then come back again.

"The peace and happiness, Beau. You did not tell me. Did you find it?"

Beau smiled wistfully. "I think I did, Bea. The trick will be to hold onto it. Tell me, do you mean to go to the masquerade this evening?"

She sounded surprised he should ask. "Of course I do, and you must go too, for Miss Quinby will be there, and you can apologize to her in person."

Beau was scrubbing at his face and hair with great determination. "My idea as well," he said, before submerging himself. He meant to come clean, in more ways than one, to both the Misses Quinby.

Chapter Eighteen

Fanella was masquerading her mood as much as her person that evening. She was a butterfly, well and good enough—fragile, inconsequential, blown and battered by the wind of change. Yet she seemed to possess none of the lighthearted joy with which a butterfly should be embodied. Her masquerade as Psyche felt dreadfully inappropriate. With a heart weighed down by her recent refusal of Mr. Ferd's offer, Nell felt not at all inclined to float and flutter. She had not suffered such misery since her father's passing.

The heaviness of her spirit was in no way lightened by the arrival of an enormous bouquet of roses and pinks, addressed to the Misses Quinby from none other than the Duke of Heste. Aurora squealed with delight on their delivery. Well she might, for in the included note the duke apologized profusely for leaving London with such haste he was never privileged enough to meet her.

Nell was not so easily impressed. The duke's snub of Aurora was part and parcel of her reason for denying her own pursuit of happiness. Glaring at the flowers, Nell wondered if the blooms had come but a day earlier might she not make a happier butterfly tonight. She sighed, as if in sighing she might expel the tight sadness that bound her breast. She could not catch a glimpse of her outfit without wincing. The cast-off blue ball dress of her aunt's that had been artfully transformed into the garb of a butterfly creature was of the exact same shade of blue as Mr. Ferd's eyes. The last thing she wanted to contemplate was the memory of those pale blue eyes. It was a shame not to enjoy her creation, but it could not but in every way remind her of what was now lost to her.

Her bodice, in plush gray velvet, seemed as soft to her fingertips as Mr. Ferd's lips on hers. She could not keep her hands from it. The costume had, from the very start, been her coachman's suggestion. He had recommended she choose Psyche as her model for the masquerade ball on a day that now seemed so very long ago. Now he would never see the pinch-pleated embroidered gauze shawl that draped her shoulders and tied at the wrist to look remarkably like wings, just as he had suggested it might. Mr. Ferd had left them, had taken himself off with what her aunt termed "mysterious haste." Nell was not so mystified.

His leaving left her dreadfully unhappy, but no one would know it in looking at her. She masked her sorrow behind a smile, and stepped into her costume and then into the coach, and at last into the crowd along the Promenade, with convincing enthusiasm. Her aunt was fooled, her sister was fooled, even Mr. Tyrrwhit, who served as escort now that Mr. Ferd had vanished, seemed to be fooled.

Nell could not fool herself. The idea that she might never see Mr. Ferd again left her miserable. She could not stop herself from looking for him in the masquerade crowd. She did not blame him for leaving. She had refused him. What else could he do but leave? And yet her heart refused to be reasonable. The sadness she hid behind her butterfly mask intensified. She felt the loss of her Mr. Ferd almost as strongly as she had felt the loss of her father!

Nell wished nothing more than to withdraw from the push-and-shove frivolity of the masquerade. The crush of the crowd separated her from her aunt, and the crush of Aurora's admirers parted her from her sister's side. Charley abandoned her too, that he might see to the fetching of refreshments.

Left alone, there was a spot along the Promenade that Nell gravitated toward as if it were home. It was beneath two crossed strings of twinkling Japanese lanterns, near the area that had been designated as outdoor ballroom. There, above the whirl of paired dancers, light had drawn a great cloud of moths, and Nell found something compelling in the parallel dip and sway.

She stood lost among the fluttering wings, wondering if she might ever again feel so lighthearted as the glittering revelers who cavorted about her. She stood quite still, no flutter in her wings save that raised by the breeze that played with the transparent blue layers of gauze that made up her skirt. As they floated weightlessly about her, she felt in an odd way as if she were become part of the dancing cloud of moths. She lifted her right arm, as if to catch up one of the passing insects. The pleated gauze of her shawl floated in the wind. The moths danced just out of reach.

She dropped her arm, dismayed to realize that as she stood watching the moths with complete fascination, she was herself become the object of intense scrutiny. A young man in costume had stopped, an island in the stream of humanity that flowed around him, as he turned his masked visage her way. It was difficult to say for certain, so all-encompassing was his mask, but she got the feeling he stared at her to the exclusion of all else.

In his left hand the gentleman held a stick. Suspended from this stick, partially hiding his face, was a fearsome beast's head, all fur and fangs. When this stick-mask was lowered, however, the gentleman's face was further disguised by a second half-mask tied to his face. In contrast to the beast mask, this half-mask was pale and smooth and youthful, the face of a perfect and symmetrical being with shadowed eyes.

A wig further obscured the stranger's identity. Full and long and brown, it hung in shining curls about his shoulders. Atop the wig perched an old-fashioned green felt hunter's cap, with a dashing red and black feather curling off the brim onto the wig. The gentleman swept the hat from its perch upon the wig and executed a courtly bow.

It was a handsome disguise, a dashing masquerade. A quiver of arrows hung from a leather thong across one shoulder, alongside a lean, ash bow, unstrung. Nell had no idea who the gentleman might be. She wondered if such a thorough disguise hid one of the many fellows that she and her aunt had taken on excursion. The gentleman seemed to be waiting for some sign of recognition.

It began to make sense to Nell why this man should stare at her so discourteously, with carefully leashed expectancy. He was Eros, or Cupideo, the mythological counterpart to her Psyche.

As she stood there, undecided as to her direction, the masked man closed the distance between them, his right hand darting out as he approached, quick as a frog's tongue, into the cloud of moths that wheeled in the light above her head.

Nell, who felt very forward in having been caught with her attention so unwaveringly fixed in his direction, no matter that she was Psyche and he Eros, could not help but wonder if a moth had in fact been snared.

He extended his balled fist. She could not turn away and pretend to ignore him, with the mystery of the moth's fate yet to be revealed.

Turning his hand with the flair of a magician, he slowly opened his fingers. A dazed but whole moth sat for an instant in the gloved palm before flitting up to join its brothers.

"However did you do that?" Nell breathed.

"Psyche"—Beau Ferd's voice was altered by his mask, but not so much that Nell could not recognize him—"do you so soon forget the magic of E-E-Eros?"

Nell's eyes widened. "Mr. Ferd!"

The smooth, boyish mask regarded her. Nell was used to being able to read this man's expression. Here, her searching gaze was met by nothing more than a perfect paleness, and an absence of all emotion.

"Ah, but I am not Mr. Ferd at all."

She did not track his meaning. "Whatever do you do here, Mr. Ferd? It is most improper in you to come uninvited to this masquerade. You must leave before you are discovered."

He took up her hands, in no hurry to depart, and whirled her in a brisé, in time to the music. "I will not leave until we have spoken, Miss Quinby. There is something I must tell you."

Dizzied, both by the dance movement and by Mr. Ferd's unexpected appearance, Nell felt more than ever like one of the moths that whirled above her head. "Mr. Ferd, please do go away," she pleaded, "for while your costume is very clever, it will not do to have you unmasked."

The expressionless face remained unperturbed. "I am far more in control of my own destiny than you presume, Miss

Quinby, and far better at disguises than you would credit me."

"But to what purpose?" Nell looked fearfully about, sure that they would be discovered at any second by her aunt or her sister. As it was, she could see Charley Tyrrwhit frantically waving in their direction. He was pushing his way, rather rudely she thought, through the crowd that separated them.

Beau did not notice his friend. "I have gone to the trouble of donning this ridiculous outfit in hopes that I might have a moment alone with you. There is something important I must tell you, something I have been meaning to tell you for some time."

"Mr. Ferd, this guise of yours is the ultimate in foolhardiness. Only think of the consequences should someone else recognize you." Nell could not take her eyes off of Charley Tyrrwhit. He was plowing through the dancers now, his passage creating eddies in the regularity of the whirling sets.

Beau caught up Nell's hand as it flew toward her throat, as lightly as he were capturing another moth. He drew her toward him, close enough that she alone might hear him, close enough that the sheer gossamer of her costume fluttered against the obstacle of his cloak, close enough that she forgot all about Charlie Tyrrwhit.

"I am not who you think I am, Miss Quinby." Beau's voice was huskier, more urgent than ever before it had sounded in her ears. "My being here is not a whim, conducted without f-f-forethought. It is the culmination of a great many evenings' contemplation, while standing in the street beside your aunt's curricle. You have witnessed my d-desire, and would not d-d-deny the power of our mutual passion."

"Oh, but this will not do, Mr. Ferd," Nell began, her breast rising and falling very rapidly. She felt like weeping. Why did Mr. Ferd set her mind whirling again, now that her mind was made up? Must the firmness of her resolve be tested every time they encountered one another, and with every word he uttered?

She looked about for assistance. Mr. Tyrrwhit was almost upon them. The revelers fell back out of his way as if compelled by some unseen hand. And suddenly it all made sense, for there was Bandit, wriggling through the feet of the people in front of Charley, on a beeline for his master.

Bandit gave Beau away. Fate personified, in the form of a ball of black and white fur, he thrust his way through the crowd. One minute Beau was trying to explain who he was, and the next, the dancers before them were parting with hilarious alarm to allow the running dog through, with Charley, and Mellish, and the Prince of Wales hard on his furry heels.

There was no fooling Bandit with clever disguises, no fooling the prince either, once Bandit came to Beauford's heel and could not be shaken.

"My Lord Beauford," the Regent boomed jovially. "What a splendid disguise. I would never have known you but for the dog."

In the heartbeat it took for Nell to turn and recognize the prince, horrified realization took possession of her features. Her mouth dropped open in a little oh. She went white about the lips, her wide-eyed gaze going from Beauford, to Bandit, to the prince, and then back again.

"You are the Duke of Heste?"

He nodded.

Her eyes closed, as though she would shut out the sight of something that pained her. Then, wings fluttering, she pushed away from him, through the growing crowd.

Beau would have followed. Indeed, he made an effort to do so, but his bow and Mr. Mellish got in the way, the former catching itself up on the raised lance of some fellow kitted out like a knight, while the latter dragged on his other arm, demanding to be informed what the great mystery was about his recent disappearance. Then both Bandit and the prince began to bark—Bandit, because it was his nature to do so, and the prince, because he seemed to think Bandit was expecting some sort of exchange. With the knee-weakening impression that happiness had just flitted from his grasp, Lord Beauford froze, unable to move or coherently explain, resembling a stunned moth caught in the palm of fate.

* * *

Nell whirled through the press of costumed partygoers, half-blinded by the welling moisture in her eyes that threatened to spill over into tears.

Directionless, she plunged by a knot of people that included her sister and Beatrix Cowper. Aurora reached out to touch her arm.

"Nella!"

Blinking furiously to clear her vision, Nell looked up.

"Miss Quinby. I see you have been chatting with my brother." Beatrix Cowper, clad in a multicolored robe, with a helmet on her head, also many hued, to depict her role as Iris, turned to Aurora with a smile. "Come, my dear, it is high time you met the scoundrel. He has only just returned from some sort of hunting trip this afternoon. I do not know exactly what it was he was hunting, but in chasing it he was all over muck. A sight to behold, I assure you."

A hunting trip? Was that how the duke described his recent activities to his sister? And had she herself been the quarry?

Nell took up her sister's hands in both her own, and with a look that spoke volumes, begged a moment of Aurora's time. Beatrix Cowper regarded her with some dismay, but she did not demur when Aurora stepped out of earshot, hissing, "Whatever is the matter, Nella? You are white as a sheet."

"He was our coachman," she choked.

Aurora, who had come dressed as her namesake, Eos, the dawn, flicked out her fan, which beautifully depicted a sunrise, so that she might speak to Nell behind cover of it. "What has the coachman to do with anything? Why do you interrupt to speak to me of him? You heard Bea. She is about to introduce me to her brother, the duke."

Nell felt like shaking her. "You have met him, Aurora."

Aurora looked at her keenly. "I don't understand," she said, her back up.

"Lady Cowper's dear brother, the Duke of Heste," Nell said impatiently, "has been masquerading as our coachman."

Aurora's cornflower blue eyes flew wide. "No!"

"Yes!" Nell dragged on her hand. "Come, we must be going."

Aurora tore loose from Fanella's hold long enough to wish Beatrix a hasty good-bye. Aunt Ursula was then hailed, the services of one of her friend's coachman obtained, and before the evening was truly begun, the three women had put the Brighton masquerade behind them.

Chapter Nineteen

The following morning, Nell sat quite still beside Aurora in the crowded post coach bound for Godstone, hoping her own motionless state might still the gush of tears that insisted on racing down her cheeks.

Why had he lied to her? Why did all the men she placed her trust in, lie? Were they never to be trusted?

"Why should a duke pretend to be a coachman?" Aurora whispered the question, for the Quinbys were not alone in the coach.

Nell glanced up. Two older women bound for London shared the interior of the coach. They seemed to regard her and her fair sister with haughty disdain. With good cause, Nell thought, for she and Aurora had spent the better part of the journey so far with heads bent together, whispering, and now here she was, weeping in public.

Aurora had a great deal on her mind, and all of it must be discussed sotto voce.

Nell was too stunned either to join in Aurora's latest speculation or to silence her. She felt a fool. She felt betrayed. The enormity of the identity of the young man who professed to love her rocked her far more profoundly within than the post coach did without.

"Was it some sort of jest, a cruel prank, the mischief of a young man still tasting wild oats?" Aurora was whispering again, voicing the questions that Nell had already heard in the back of her head. Aurora did not give a fig for the black looks she encountered from their traveling companions. "Was there perhaps an elaborate bet arranged between himself and his Whip Club cronies?" she hissed. "If so, I've no very high opinion of the lot of them. 'Tis a twisted scheme."

Nell sighed. Persimmon faced, Cat would have called the two females facing her. Nell could not blame them for their dour looks. It was very rude of her and Aurora to continue their private conversation for such a long time. The old tabbies would think the worst. She almost laughed. They were entitled to think what they might. This was the worst. She could imagine nothing to surpass the excruciating embarrassment of her situation.

She bent toward her sister's ear. Perhaps she could put an end to the whispering. "I find it too unbelievable to think that I should be singled out as the target for such a plot, if plot it is," she hissed. "The duke had never set eyes on me until we met in the lane leading to the White Hart Inn."

Aurora tossed her golden head. "Yet, 'tis odd that on the very day I was to be introduced by his sister, he introduced himself to you instead. Can fate be so fickle?"

Nell had not thought of it that way. Perhaps this madness made more sense than she had at first supposed. Lord Beauford had known that a Quinby was to be introduced to him with the hopes of attracting his attention, perhaps attracting an offer of marriage. She herself had more than once confirmed as much within his hearing. Was this offer of marriage from Beau Ferd, the coachman, a young man's attempt to foil both his managing sister's matrimonial schemes and the pretentions of a pair of penniless young ladies? Was the man she had fallen in love with really capable of such cruel mischief?

Nell was shocked and sickened by the turnings of her mind. She felt numb with the enormity of the lie that had been perpetrated against her. All of her hopes and fears of the past day and sleepless night, wondering about the future she must decide upon, were like ashes in her mouth.

In a daze she rocked along, blind to the passing scenery, blind to the censorious looks from the females with whom they shared the interior of the post coach. Her mind was too overcome with the hugeness of the lie perpetrated against her to think of, to notice with comprehension, anything else.

This incredible revelation explained a lot of things that had plagued Nell's better sense. It explained the expensive gloves Mr. Ferd wore. It explained a vocabulary that was far more extensive than what one might expect of a driver. It explained Mr. Gates, and the strange friendship between Beau Ferd—she must remember to think of him as Lord Beauford—and Charley Tyrrwhit. It explained—Nell felt suddenly soulless—it explained Beethoven, and a whistling coachman who would share his music with a postboy.

Why had she not trusted her instincts? She had questioned the coachman's identity from the start. She had at one time asked him outright if he were not a gentleman. She remembered now that he had evaded the question, answering it with a question of his own.

She had suspected something was amiss, and pushed her suppositions away. She had abandoned all sense, and allowed her sensibilities, her growing desires, her naïveté, and her trusting nature to reign. She had believed that Beau Ferd, not the Duke of Heste, loved her, that he meant to honor his vow to cherish her for the rest of his life. How much—how little—could she trust him, now that she knew him for the liar he was?

Doubt cut through Nell's numbness like a knife as she considered the possibility that this love she felt to the very core of her being was nothing but a lie. And like a knife, this possibility wounded her so deeply that Nell felt physically weakened and shaken. She had clung to the stair railing last night, that her legs might not surrender beneath her to that weakness, and having made her way upstairs, flung herself down upon her bed and wept like a child. She clung to the idea of returning to the safe haven of her mother's arms with equal tenacity today. Her chin wobbled and tears stung her eyes, but she did not give in to her weakness. Yet so long did it threaten her composure that it made her angry in the end. Like a wounded animal turning to defend itself, she focused her anger, her suffering, on its source. She began, deep within her heart, to hate the man who had misrepresented himself to her as the kind, soft-spoken Mr. Ferd. Each time she thought of the kisses that had been coaxed from her lips she was stabbed afresh by the sharp point of a duke's deceit.

As she stared out the dusty window of the coach, something powerful and savage rose within Fanella's breast, something angry and vindictive that wanted nothing more than to inflict pain in return for this torturous rending of her heart.

"He kissed me," she said softly, wiping her hand across her lips, as if to wipe away the memory.

Aurora's cornflower blue eyes widened in disbelief. "What?"

The two women who shared the coach perked up. For the first time, Aurora had not bothered to lower her voice.

"He kissed me," Nell was careful not to follow her sister's example.

Angry color blazed in Aurora's cheeks. "He must be made to pay," she spluttered, her volume still far too loud. "He must make an offer for you. Mama will see to it that it is so."

"Hush, Aurora. He did offer for me." Fanella's words stopped Aurora's tirade cold.

"Oh, Fanella! Did he really?" Aurora gasped, holding in the sound of her astonishment with some difficulty. "But, my dear, this is wonderful! Mama will be so pleased. She had expected me to snare a duke, and here you have snatched him right out from under my nose."

The two women opposite them exchanged a telling look.

Fanella sighed. "I'm sure such an offer is not to be taken seriously," she said in a very small voice, leveling a sober look at Aurora. "I would not have you breathe a word of it to anyone."

"Not even Mother?" Aurora hissed.

"Especially not Mother," Nell insisted.

Chapter Twenty

Beau was turned away from Ursula Dunn's door on more than one occasion by the very housekeeper he was used to take meals with as Mrs. Dunn's coachman. The woman gave him the same fish-eyed stare, nose in the air, every time he came to call on Fanella.

"The ladies are not at home to callers," she said with righteous indignation, and before he could get anything more out of her pinch-purse mouth, the door was slammed in his face. As he made his way down the steps for the third time in as many days, Toby called out to him. He was standing in the ivy-bound gate to the mews.

"She's gone, sir."

"Mrs. Dunn?"

"Nay, Miss Nell Quinby, sir. It's she you're after, ain't it?" He winked knowingly. "I am also guessing you wouldn't mind me telling you where she was off to."

"I will not argue with that. I really m-m-must speak to her, you know."

Toby nodded wisely. "Miss Nell's gone home to her mum's, with the sister. Left two days ago."

"Two days ago? Good Lord! Thank you, Toby. I must be off."

Beau set out that afternoon for the cottage near Godstone, where the Quinbys had taken up residence. He went with misgivings, and just as he had been at Ursula Dunn's, he was turned away.

"She's no desire to speak to you, my lord." Aurora met him at the door, stiffly polite, like a mastiff who would refrain from biting him if only he would leave them in peace. Meticulously correct, she escorted him to the gate.

On his way there, Beau stammered out his apologies, both for his pretending to be a coachman, and for leaving London before being introduced to her.

Aurora tossed her head. "You have wounded my sister's heart, my lord, far more than mine. You have confused if not destroyed her trust." She smiled in a brittle way, as if her lips objected to such an arrangement. "She has told me that she was ready to become a coachman's wife, despite the fact she knew it would have broken our mother's heart for her to do so. She has told me, too, that she refused your offer because of her feelings of responsibility with regard to my family's welfare."

Beau nodded. "A-and yet she would refuse me still, when I might do much to improve the state of all of your a-a-affairs."

Aurora looked at him with unguarded surprise. "It was not some heartless jest, then, this proposal?"

Beau blinked at her, amazed he should be asked such a thing. "A jest? A-am I sunk so low in your sister's estimation?" He observed some movement in the second-story window that looked out over the hedgerow, and focused on it with interest.

"I am quite h-hopelessly in love with your sister," he admitted candidly. "My intentions are honorable, if not my methods."

Aurora softened. She too glanced up at the window above them. "Do you mean to try to win her back again?"

He regarded her intently. "Have I any hope of doing so?"

The eldest Miss Quinby held out her hand to him, one eyebrow archly raised. "You will never know, my lord, until you try. You have my best wishes, and my belief that Nella still cherishes some feeling for you. She would not suffer so, if she cared nothing for you."

Beau winced. "I would relieve that suffering, you know. Do you think p-p-perhaps we might arrange my introduction to your mother?"

Aurora tilted her head, to regard him, as if for the first time. "I do not think that is too unreasonable a request," she agreed. "As long as you are the one to explain to her all that has transpired."

Beau frowned. "She knows naught of this?"

Aurora shook her pretty head. "She will never know unless you tell her. Nella will not say a word, and she has sworn me to secrecy as well."

As a direct result of having explained himself to Nell's mother, Beau set up residence at the White Hart Inn for a fortnight. For as many days, he was cordially invited to visit the Quinby cottage. Each day, he went in hopes of speaking to Nell. With him came flowers and baskets of hothouse fruit and boxes of specially blended tea. But while Mrs. Quinby served him an untold number of cups of that very tea, along with biscuits, scones, crumpets, and jam, and Cat grilled him about every detail with regard to the Whip Club, as well as the horses he rode and drove, and Aurora kindly sat and chatted with him and made a point of informing him as to her absent sister's well-being—Fanella, whom he yearned to see, ignored him completely.

She went for walks whenever he was expected, or took the pony into the village on errands. They passed one another in the lane on more than one occasion, but in each instance she pretended not to see him as he raised his hat and called out to her.

"I return to London tomorrow," Beau informed Aurora when the weeks had flown. "I can leave my responsibilities untended no longer."

Aurora bit her lip in disappointment. "I see," she said. "I am sorry . . ."

Beau held up his hand, and in it a folded screw of paper. "No a-a-apologies, please. I a-a-am not surprised I am so reviled by your sister. I am discouraged, but not yet b-b-beaten. Give her this, if you will. Perhaps she will be more inclined to read of my contrition than to hear it from my lips."

With hope like a dying ember in his heart, Lord Beauford returned to London.

While he himself no longer came to the Quinby Cottage, deliveries began to arrive almost daily in his stead; more baskets of hothouse fruit, and flowers, as well as current copy of news from London, and fashion plates, sheet music and books of poetry. And with each delivery came a creamy envelope addressed to Fanella, bearing the seal of the Duke of Heste.

These letters, like the one he had left in Aurora's care, were not opened. Fanella refused to so much as acknowledge the correspondence. She would have refused the fruit and flowers but her mother would not allow it.

"I quite liked the duke, Fanella, my love," Mrs. Quinby explained. "He is extremely well mannered, and generous in the extreme, and while I will not force you to accept his advances, my dear, neither will I do anything to discourage the suit."

The fruit was eaten, the books read, the news and fashion plates examined with interest, and the flowers placed in vases, but none of it by Fanella's hand. She made a great pretense of ignoring all of it, until the day that a packet of sheet music was delivered. Even then, she did not make any effort to pick out Mr. Beethoven's works herself on the pianoforte, only listened very keenly when Aurora had a go at it. But, as the first few bars filled the drawing room, the same music that she had heard ringing through the trees in what was left of old Anderida, she fled the room, tears in her eyes.

The mounting pile of letters from the duke Fanella stacked very neatly, one atop the other, on the table by the window in her room, and when they threatened to tumble down, so many were there, she bound them up in three neat piles, with blue ribbon, and tucked them away in her stocking drawer.

Her mother tried on more than one occasion to reason her into reading them. Nell, in all other ways an obedient daughter, refused. Aurora pleaded with her to reconsider. Nell turned a deaf ear. Cat scolded. She was dying with curiosity to know what so much correspondence from any gentleman could have to say. Nell ignored her. The letters remained unread.

Her obstinacy made sense to none but Nell. She had entrusted her heart to a man whom she thought honest, and no more than a coachman. She had refused his offer of marriage based on that lack of position. To reverse her tact, based solely on this change in status—to allow herself to be taken in by a lying man because he was a duke, seemed inconsistent and foolish. Nell had no desire to seem foolish. As a result, she behaved with utmost foolishness. She read none of his letters, nor did she answer them.

When no responsive epistles were forthcoming, Lady Beatrix Cowper took up her pen to address both Nell and Aurora, expressing her dismay in the way things had worked out. She extended an invitation to all of the Quinbys to come and winter with her in London, for she had no desire for word to continue to fly about that their two families were at odds with one another. Gossip was such a nasty business.

Aurora and Cat were thrilled. Nell was not. Her wounded pride, and the ache in her heart, left her unbent to kindness. She could not find it within herself to agree to such a plan.

Cat was furious, and Aurora ready to argue the point, but Mrs. Quinby quieted them both. "You must give your sister time to stop hurting, time to see clearly the sagacity of such a plan," she chided gently. "Fanella cannot fail to realize in the end that the best way to go on is in making just such a visit."

But Nell did not come to such a realization. Safe in Godstone, she backed away from any thought of facing up to Lord Beauford or his family. And in her safe solitude, her spirits sank to their lowest ebb. She was as miserable now as she had been following the death of her father.

Respite came in the form of a great packet of gossipy letters from Aunt Ursula, who was missing her nieces' company most dreadfully. The packet extravagantly included separate letters for everyone. Two were addressed to Nell. The first was written in Ursula's crablike scrawl, and recounted her overwrought feelings with regard to the duplicity of the Duke of Heste, whom she admitted she could no longer judge too harshly. Although she had snubbed him, refusing to so much as receive the flowers he had sent her, the duke had gone to great lengths to find her an excellent coachman for the duration of her stay in Brighton, whose wage he had paid in advance. And the lovely new bay was so well tempered and such a perfect match to her own, that she could not completely revile the man who had made him available to her.

Aunt Ursula empathized with Nell's disappointed hopes,

and decried the nasty gossip that should be circulating about both of her unfortunate nieces. Tearfully, she recommended that if her darling niece would not reconsider the duke's offering of marriage, which she understood to be real enough, she must at least take advantage of Lady Cowpers's invitation to stay the Season in London. Such an honor could not but do all of the Quinbys' standing some good. In addition, she suggested that perhaps Fanella would be interested in the offer extended her in the enclosed letter, which she had seen fit to forward.

This second letter was from a Lady Anne Elliot, who thanked Nell prettily for her own correspondence with regard to the old horse, Boots. The horse was, she said, quite content in his new home, his task no more than to pull a cart on occasion for the children, whom he seemed happy to allow to straddle his broad back. She was welcome, the letter told her, to come and visit old Boots whenever she should so desire, and in addition, she was encouraged to write and inform Lady Elliot if she knew of anyone responsible who might be looking for a position as companion to a wealthy peer, who was quite as dotty about animals as Nell appeared to be. There was an opening she knew of that must be filled.

Nell's sisters vociferously encouraged Nell to go.

"Go on, Nell. I should very much like to know what has become of Boots," Cat insisted.

"Yes, do go," Aurora agreed, with perhaps a little too much enthusiasm. "Some time away from home cannot but lift your spirits."

"It will take your mind off of . . . other things," her mother suggested with an odd little smile, and then she offered to write a letter to Lady Elliot announcing Nell's imminent arrival.

Realizing that her obstinate refusal to forgive Lord Beauford had been more than trying to her family, Nell got the feeling that they would all be glad to see the back of her for a time. So she packed her bags and sent them away by courier, all the while thinking that she had been behaving in a rather juvenile fashion since her return from Brighton. It occurred to her, if only for an instant, that perhaps it would be best if she agreed to a Season with Beatrix Cowper. The white-hot embers of her hurt and anger might cool, given limited exposure to the man she still thought of as Beau Ferd.

For now, once again, Cat navigated the dogcart along the lane to the White Hart Inn, and Nell, her thoughts touched by poignant memories of the last time she had traversed the same road, climbed aboard the post. Aurora had kindly packed a hamper with treats for the trip, and as she hugged Fanella and pressed the basket into her lap, she whispered, "You must return to us our old happy Nella, my dear. Have a good trip, and give old Boots a hug."

It was not until the coach was well under way that Nell opened the lid of the hamper, and saw that Aurora had rifled her stocking drawer. Topping the fruit and sandwiches were three blue ribbon-bound stacks of unopened letters.

As though a viper had been revealed to her, poised to strike at her hand, Nell snapped the lid on the hamper closed again. And yet, as the miles flashed by and memories of her coaching experiences with the man she had called Beau Ferd welled to the surface of her mind, Fanella found herself drawn time and again to opening the basket lid that she might peek at the creamy promise of the letters. What did he have to say to her? She could not deny some curiosity.

Kill the cat or no, in the last leg of her journey, Fanella threw open the basket, filled her lap with letters, and set out to discover what it was that the Duke of Heste had to say for himself. She was shaken and speechless by the time she had finished. Lord Beauford wrote with beautiful and touching eloquence. More than once she was forced to ply her handkerchief, for she could not hold herself aloof from the emotion he poured so freely onto each page. The letters, read one after the other, could not fail to pierce the swollen boil of her anger. The love in them reached out to her in a wealth of deep feeling and profound thought. Yet another facet of this truly perplexing man was revealed to her.

"I wanted you to see me for myself, and foolishly stripped off a part of that self in an effort to achieve that end," he explained. She could almost hear his voice. "My

actions had something to do with my father's death. I am
not sure why, but there was within me a need to do something wild and reckless—something that redefined me," he
wrote.

"I wanted to believe that someone might care for who
and what I am without title and money and connections. I
did not realize that my dishonesty might alienate the very
person I sought. I am sorry for the deceits you have suffered on my account," he claimed in another.

"A young woman should not be lied to by the very man
she means to entrust herself to, for the rest of her life." The
lines welled up off the page, like a healing balm. They were
the words she had been wishing to hear above all others,
and had avoided for fear they would not be written. She
read them again. Could it be that the strength of her reaction had something to do with her own father's passing?

"Can you not accept my apology?" he asked when four
letters were sent and still no reply. Could she not?

"Will you not let me hear forgiveness from your own
sweet lips? You do but deceive yourself if you are convinced you can no longer care for me," he scribbled after
fourteen had been sent and still no response.

"Can you not care for a duke as much as for a coachman?" His tone was reasonable, even in the last of the letters. "You have always seen what lay within my heart and
head, within my very soul, duke or dustman, coachman or
king. I have read the knowledge in your eyes, and in your
acts of kindness. Do you think I am changed so much by
the power of a name? Do you mistrust your feelings so
much as to end all chances of our happiness? Can you no
longer find any place for me in your heart? I love you, my
dear. I always will. I should like above all else for you to be
my wife. I have begun to make changes in my household
with just such a future in mind. Please give me some indi-
cation as to your feelings in this matter.

"The last thing in the world that I intended was to hurt
you, to injure your sensibilities in any form or fashion. My
undying love I pledge, along with a profound desire for rec-
onciliation."

She could not fail to be swayed.

Nell sat quite still when she had finished reading. The

last letter expressed regret that she had not seen fit to respond to his correspondence. Lord Beauford politely informed her that it was no longer his intention to plague her with communication, he had been informed, she refused to read. He would, in addition, refrain from pestering her with his presence, should she be so inclined as to accept his sister Beatrix's invitation for a Season in London. He wished her all the best, and signed himself off, as he had in each of the letters, as "Duke or Dustman, Coachman or King," Beau.

Nell carefully folded the letters away again, and bound them up with their blue ribbon, as tears misted her eyes. She began to think herself very foolish in having so cut herself off from Lord Beauford as to make it very difficult ever to face him again, much less admit to him that she found it much more difficult to fall out of love with him than falling in love with him had been.

Chapter Twenty-one

On arriving at her destination, Nell found it a great relief to have her thoughts redirected from their obsession with a certain bundle of letters by the kindly reception from her hostess, Lady Elliot. Anne Elliot met her with an embrace such as one might expect of a relative, and announced that her bags had arrived before her and had been unpacked in the guest room she was to occupy.

"You must relax a moment, my dear, and take a cup of tea with me, before setting off to witness Boots's transformation."

Nell was in no way inclined to refuse such an offer. She was exhausted, both by the trip and by the gamut of emotions she had suffered in plowing through the correspondence of a gentleman whose connection to her she had so long let lie fallow. She would cherish those letters for the rest of her life, no matter that she could not bring herself to respond to them.

"You will not recognize him, my dear, when next you set eyes on him," Lady Elliot said as they settled into two comfortable chairs with a steaming pot on a table in between. For a wildly disordered moment, Nell, whose mind kept wandering back to the man she had once thought to be a coachman, thought this lady referred to the duke. Her mind was soon disabused of this notion. "Your Boots is another animal entirely from the poor beast my brother Brampton first packed off to me," Anne clarified.

Nell focused her attention on the purpose of her visit. "I am so pleased you have seen fit to care for the old dear—"

Lady Elliot filled her cup. "I know, my dear. My brother Brampton, you see, was quite struck by what happened that day on the beach in Brighton when you wanted to rescue the poor horse from the bathing boxman."

Nell blushed. "I'm afraid I made quite a spectacle of myself."

There was something in Anne Elliot's slow, engaging smile that reminded Nell for the briefest of moments, of Beau Ferd, or Lord Beauford, as she must remember now to think of him.

"A moving spectacle to hear Bram tell it. Moving enough to prompt his buying of a horse he had neither need nor space for. I was never more surprised than when the poor emaciated beast was delivered to my door, and yet I do not know why I should be amazed. My brother was always the sort of boy who brought home wounded creatures. I should not be too surprised that he was touched by your distress. I can remember a time when a hare, at least two birds, and a stoat were kept in his room."

Nell thought she would much rather meet such a man than continue to dwell on the failings of Lord Beauford. "I should like to thank your brother personally."

Anne's eyes sparkled. "My brother is anxious to see you again, Nell. May I call you Nell?" She beckoned her four-year-old daughter out from under the tea table, where she had been quietly playing with a set of lettered blocks. The solemn, fair-haired child regarded Nell with wary approbation when her mother asked her if she would be so good as to lead Nell down to the stables, that she might meet Uncle Bram, who had promised to show her where Boots was kept.

"He would have joined us for tea," Anne assured Nell, "but Brampton will not renege on a promise, no matter how trifling, and he has promised to teach my son, Andrew, how to handle a whip before he returns to London."

Nell's hand was taken up in little Betsy's small, sweaty clasp, as the child led her through a garden and out into the stableyard, where the cracking of a whip was to be heard, along with the rumble of male voices. Nell regarded the child with the interest of a woman who might have borne sons and daughters to the Duke of Heste. She wondered if children were meant to be a part of her future. She wondered where the Duke of Heste fit into it as well.

The whip sounds ceased. The rumble of male voices quieted. There was no more sound than that of a single set of footsteps approaching them, and the whistled trill of a tune, that Nell could not fail to recognize as one Lord Beauford had used to teach a postboy the rhythm of Beethoven. She stopped in her tracks, despite persistent tugging from Betsy.

There was no mistaking that whistle, no mistaking the black and white ball of fur that came bounding out of the paddock to the left of the stables. It was Bandit, whom she had never thought to set eyes on again. She bent to stroke the eager animal, her mouth gone completely dry, and could not bring herself to look up, or rise, until a highly polished pair of riding boots came to a stop beside Bandit's thumping tail.

Lord Beauford had ceased his whistling, and leaned upon the crooked, silver-laced handle of an umbrella, whose point bit into the dirt near Bandit's hind leg.

Her eyes rose to meet the pale blue gaze she had once trusted so implicitly, passing over the trim, natty garb of a man who had at his disposal the finest tailors money could buy. She paused for a moment in her regard, to focus on the fresh posy of pinks that bloomed in his buttonhole. She wondered if this duplicitous fellow still kept the ones she had given him pressed between the pages of Voltaire. She hoped he did.

Beneath the brim of a fine, gray beaver his pale gaze swallowed her up with a hungry, almost fearful pleasure, from the top of her not so fashionably bonneted head to the hem of her skirt.

"I a-a-am e-e-ever so pleased to see you, Miss Quinby!" His delight spilled into the pronunciation of her name.

Nell gave no such display of joy. She was too stunned. The last person she had expected to see here was the Duke of Heste, the sentiment of whose letters still burned fresh in her memory. She had only begun to release her anger toward this man for past deceits. Surely he did not expect civility from her when he insulted her with fresh pretense.

"My lord Beauford," she dipped a stiff curtsy. "We play at charades again, it would seem. Shall I call you Uncle Brampton this time?"

A winsome smile touched his lips. "You may call me anything you like, Miss Fanella Quinby, if only you will speak to me."

Her mouth set itself in a hard line as she tried to stop the trembling of her chin. "Even liar?"

He flinched, and, glancing at the solemn little girl who stood watching their exchange, said softly to her, "Run ahead with A-Andy, Bet. He has just gone down to the pasture with his whip. We shall follow in a m-moment."

The fair head bobbed, and after a long dubious look at Nell, the girl trotted away. Nell felt shamed to have shown her temper before the child. She met Beau's pale blue regard, feeling pained and foolish.

"You may call me liar if it pleases you," he said evenly.

"It does not please me." She bit down on her lip, reminded of all the beautiful sentiments this man had expressed to her in his letters. How did one cross a bridge of lies and deceit to reach a place where such words might be believed? How did one assuage the pain? "I am wounded that you have resorted to false pretenses yet again, to lure me here."

He rubbed at his forehead, and flicked a lock of hair from out of his eyes. "Sorry about that. I had, a-a-as you must r-r-realize, exhausted all conventional a-a-avenues of communication, to no a-a-avail."

Nell frowned. There was some truth to what he said. His stammer was far more pronounced than usual. She felt somewhat responsible for his agitation. "I should be leaving," she said, backing away from him. Anger and sorrow tore at her voice, confusion ruled her heart.

A sadness pulled at the corners of his mouth. "You came to see Boots. Do not go without having put your mind at r-r-est a-a-as to his condition."

"That too, was not a lie?"

He sighed. "See for yourself." He waved the umbrella in the direction his niece had gone.

Nell could not help but be reminded of a time in their

past that involved yet another umbrella. Taking a deep breath, she set off in the direction he indicated.

"The position mentioned in your sister's letter, that of a companion, was that too a lie?" she asked, expecting the worst.

He hesitated.

"Is it?" she insisted.

"There is a p-p-position," he said haltingly, his voice following her. "I had hoped that you might be willing to fill it."

She whirled around to face him. "I did not come seeking your charity."

He sighed. "Well, if you think it a charitable deed to serve as my life's companion, I welcome your generosity."

She blinked in dismay, completely disarmed. Her anger seemed unable to find a target.

He reached out to lend support to her elbow.

"I did not lightly ask for your hand in marriage, Miss Fanella Quinby," he said earnestly.

"Oh!" she snapped wretchedly, wrenching her elbow from his grasp so that she might precede him down the pathway at a headlong clip.

Troubled and confused, she rushed through the woods to a blindingly sunny green meadow where she shielded her eyes against the glare to observe three children as they ran and played with a golden horse. The horse was Boots! A fatter, glossier Boots. His head came up knickering recognition when she called his name.

The children were as happy to see their uncle as the horse was to see Nell.

"Uncle Brampton, Uncle Brampton," they cried gleefully, each of them seeking his attention in a different manner. Two young lads were playing leapfrog. "Look here," called one, bounding to the top of the stone wall that enclosed the pasture.

The eldest caught up his whip, taking care to flick it in a direction away from the horse and his siblings. "I think I'm getting the hang of it," he crowed.

The little girl who had led Nell to the stables was tuck-

ing flowers into the horse's mane whenever Boots lowered
his head to crop grass. "Doesn't Boots look pretty, Uncle
Brampton?" Her big blue eyes regarded Nell with some
concern. "She has not come to take him away, has she?"

Beau looked at Nell.

Nell shook her head, so troubled by what had just transpired in the woods that she empathised most acutely with
the child's unwarranted fear. "No," she assured the girl. "I
have only come to see how my old friend is doing. I am
very pleased he is your horse now. By the looks of him, he
is very happy here. It was kind of your uncle to send him
to you."

Her remark brought a long look from Lord Beauford.
She could feel his pale blue eyes on the back of her head.
Too overwrought to face him, she made her way to
Boots's side, where she stroked the horse's gray-flecked
ears and nose. This confusing gentleman who claimed he
still wished to honor his promise of matrimony, had been
very kind to see to Boots's well-being. Despite his lies, he
had always been kind and considerate, duke or dustman,
coachman or king.

For some reason she could not fathom, Nell felt like
weeping. Without meeting Brampton Beauford's eyes she
said softly, "I should like to leave now."

He offered her his arm.

She took it.

They were facing into the sun as they set out.

"Shall I put up the umbrella?" he offered.

Nell was too rattled to comprehend he meant to shade
her from the glare. "Do you think it looks as if it might
come on to rain?" she asked, perplexed, for the sky was
free of clouds.

Beau looked at her and not the sky. "Not a chance of it."
He shook his head sadly.

She felt as if she had missed something vital in what he
had just said with regard to the umbrella. Her eyes strayed
to the furled object. Could it be, she wondered, that he too
thought of nothing more in that moment than the last time
they had been caught together beneath a single umbrella?

Was his passion for her honest and true, as he said? She did not like to think his affections for her, had been but a masquerade. What purpose was there in such deceit? He was not an unkind man. That much was evident on his handling of Boots, and Bandit, and in his relationship with his niece and nephews. That much had been made clear to her in his letters.

As they reached the section of pathway that passed through the wooded area, he startled her, reaching out swiftly, as if to catch a moth in the air above her heart. He stood looking at her, the ball of his lightly clasped fist before her.

"What is it?" she asked, for she had been aware of no insects in the air.

With the flair of a magician he turned the curled fist palm up. "I have captured here your a-a-anger toward me."

"My anger?"

There was a moment of clarity for Nell, as he stood there, pretending to hold emotion captive. His pale blue eyes no longer evidenced admiration for her, only a sad and wistful longing. There was something so tragic in the loss of his admiration that she was jarred from her fruitless course to recognize a truth that startled her. She was as guilty of pretense as the duke!

She was pretending that she no longer cared for him, pretending, too, that she meant to go away and forget about him, when in truth her heart ached with denial and deception. Did she mean to deceive herself as well as him? She realized just how well she had played out her charade of indifference. He believed she had no feeling for him, and in believing, seemed prepared to abandon his pursuit of her!

Such acquiescence was not at all what she really wanted.

She had good reason to be put out with his prevarication and masquerading, but did she mean to pay back such deception with more fruitless lies? Did she mean to push him away entirely for his transgressions?

She did not despise this man. She loved him, and yet pretended not to. What did she gain in such a lie?

Nell reached out to gently touch upon his curled fingers. "Perhaps we had best let it die," she said softly.

Pale blue eyes regarded her with wary reserve. "Will this anger fade, do you think? It has been tenaciously strong until now."

She smiled at him, bashfully, unsure now of how to behave, and dropped her hand.

Slowly he opened his fingers. Hesitantly he peered into his palm. "It is vanished."

She blushed. "We must take care to see it has no reason to return."

He laughed, as though a great weight had been lifted from his heart. "I could not agree with you more."

They walked on again, in a pregnant silence, until sunlight began to filter through the trees again as they came to the end of the wood.

"I think perhaps we should make u-use of the umbrella, my lord," she suggested softly, her voice very low. "Do you mind putting it up? The sun does tend to brown my nose most odiously." Her heart began to pound rather furiously. She could not look at him, could not believe what she suggested.

Up the umbrella fluted, throwing them both into the cool gray of its shadow. His features flattened for an instant, but then he held the silver handle out to her, squinting against the sun. He meant her to have the umbrella to herself. That was not what Fanella had intended.

With only a fraction of a second's hesitation, she reached out, as if to take it from him, and clasped her hand over his on the handle. He was not going to escape so easily.

Her touch stopped him. Pale blue eyes focused on her with bewildered uncertainty.

She blushed but she did not pull her hand away. It remained, gloved fingers warm against glove. The warmth in his eyes, and in the curve of his lips, seemed to increase exponentially with the heat of their hands.

He stepped beneath the shading canopy of the umbrella, the dark pools in his eyes swelling. "In this light, you look . . ." he began, unable to find the words. The admiration she had been missing peeped out at her.

She smiled. "I have always liked the way I look as reflected in your eyes, my lord."

He froze, staring at her, searching her face. Hopeful, and yet not convinced he had reason to hope.

She tucked her hand firmly into the crook of his arm.

"You spoke earlier of the need for a companion."

"Yes?" He seemed to hold his breath as he waited for her to go on.

Her voice fell to an uncertain whisper. "Do you think I might fill the position? I am, you know, quite desperately in love with you—duke or dustman, coachman or king."

His eyes widened, and for several frozen seconds, he did not blink. At last his eyes shut, and remained shut, as though closing out pain. "Dear God, Miss Quinby," the words slid out of him like a sigh. "I began to think you did hate me."

Nell felt a moment of panic. How foolish she had been. How close to complete disaster had she led her life?

"No, no," she exclaimed. "It was not that I hated you so much that my faith in you, in all men, was dreadfully wounded. I was so very vulnerable when you reached out to me in the midst of my pain over the loss of my father." She paused to steady her voice. "It was an awful blow to discover I trusted in an illusion. I found it almost impossible to forgive you."

He winced. "I deserved that. Do you f-f-forgive me now? Can you not begin to trust in me a-again?"

She searched the depths of his pale blue eyes. "Yes, you are forgiven. Your letters most eloquently presented your case. They . . . touched me." She could not pull her gaze away from his. The look in his eyes touched her too, in ways words never could.

He sighed, and gave her hand a squeeze. "I am relieved to hear you say as much. Inordinately relieved."

As he spoke, a dangerously seductive sparkle lit the pale blue depths of his eyes, and he leaned down, dodging the pole of the umbrella, to a point where their lips hovered no more than a breath's width apart.

She thought he meant to kiss her. Her eyes shut, in anticipation of just that pleasure, but he hesitated, in order that he might ask, "Will you have me then, Fanella Quinby?" His breath swept shakily over her lips, the words like impending rain, hot and moist.

He resisted kissing her for such an interminable length of time that Nell closed the gap between them herself, lightly touching her lips to his.

With a groan, his mouth sought hers with the hunger of a starving man who tasted of something he had never hoped to taste again. She responded with no less hunger.

The gentle urgency of his mouth drew her closer, as if once returned to him, he had no intention of allowing anything to come between them. Her hair, her eyelids, the tip of her nose and ear, the tender curve of her neck, he kissed them all before proceeding to her mouth, which he explored with equal thoroughness. And when Nell thought she could be kissed no more, when her lips felt hot and full, and completely sated with kissing, she pulled away and gazed deep into the portals of his soul, those incredibly pale blue eyes. The happiness she witnessed there so filled her own heart with joy that she was forced to look away, for fear of weeping with its power.

"My dear Miss Quinby—"

Fanella blushed. "I think you must call me Nell, if we are to go on in such a manner."

He smiled, and so sweet, so loving was his smile, that her gaze dropped yet again, this time to examine the remains of the flowers drooping sadly from his coat. "I have crushed your posy once again, my lord," she said, sadly fingering the crushed blooms.

"Brampton," he said with gentle insistence. "I would hear my given name fall from these lips with whom I have been so free."

"I have smashed your pinks, Brampton," she obliged, his name strange and wonderful on her tongue.

"Not flat enough by far, to my way of thinking, Nell. You have yet to tell me you will marry me, my love."

"I will marry you, Brampton," she promised, her voice

light with her joy. "It has become quite clear to me that I love you—duke or dustman, coachman or king."

He pulled her close again, and the two of them set cheerfully to work flattening the pinks.

Epilogue

L ord Beauford paused in the grand entryway that graced
the beautiful old house known as Thorne, and looked
about him at the headless walls with satisfaction. The old
duke's hunting trophies were packed away in the attic, the
areas they once adorned refurbished with fresh wallcover-
ings and a tasteful collection of paintings, tapestry, and
etchings. The new Duchess of Heste would find nothing to
object to in her home.

"Your grace?"

It was Gates who stood in the doorway to the library, a
large parcel in his hands.

"Yes, Gates." Beau smiled at his valet. Everything made
him smile today.

"This just came, your grace, by way of courier."

"What is it, Gates? More wedding plunder? Put it with
the rest of the gifts in the little drawing room. I'm due at
the church within the half hour."

"Begging your pardon, sir, but the messenger indicated
that it comes from Mr. Tyrrwhit. He said it was to be
opened before you left for the ceremony, if you please."

Eyebrows raised, Beauford tore into the parcel. In it he
found a spotless pair of gloves, an ivory-handled umbrella, and
an exquisite hat, all in matching dove gray, along with a card
from the haberdasher where the articles had been purchased.

"I am of the opinion that the Duke of Heste requires a
new hat today. Tell me, what does a husband hat look like?
Best I could do. Regards, Chaz."

Smiling broadly, Lord Beauford slipped his fingers into
the butter-soft gloves and hooked the umbrella over his
arm. The hat, he found to be a perfect fit.